THE FOUR LIVES OF J. S. FREEMAN

Book One

STILLWATERS

Yvonne Anderson

Gannah's Gate

THE FOUR LIVES OF J. S. FREEMAN

BOOK ONE

STILLWATERS

Yvonne Anderson

Stillwaters (The Four Lives of J. S. Freeman, #1)
ISBN 978-1-946985-11-8

This novel is a work of fiction. Characters, plot, and incidents are products of the author's imagination, and any similarity to people living or dead, whether on Earth or Umban, is coincidental.

Cover design by Ken Raney
Clash Creative

TABLE OF CONTENTS

BOOK 1 – STILLWATERS

Table of Contents (continued)

Umban
NaHora
Sorona
Walpin
Tresseiital
Saltcreek Point
Ellerja
Steefren
Indopso
Arkentak
Watland
Omaseen
Fivepetals
Centre City
Cararre
Nion
Freemansland

Here's a rough diagram of the island Freemansland, nicknamed The Land of Many Mysteries:

It's a strange place. If you want to see just how strange, keep reading.

Some of this story takes place in a region of Umban called Arkentak. This might help you visualize it:

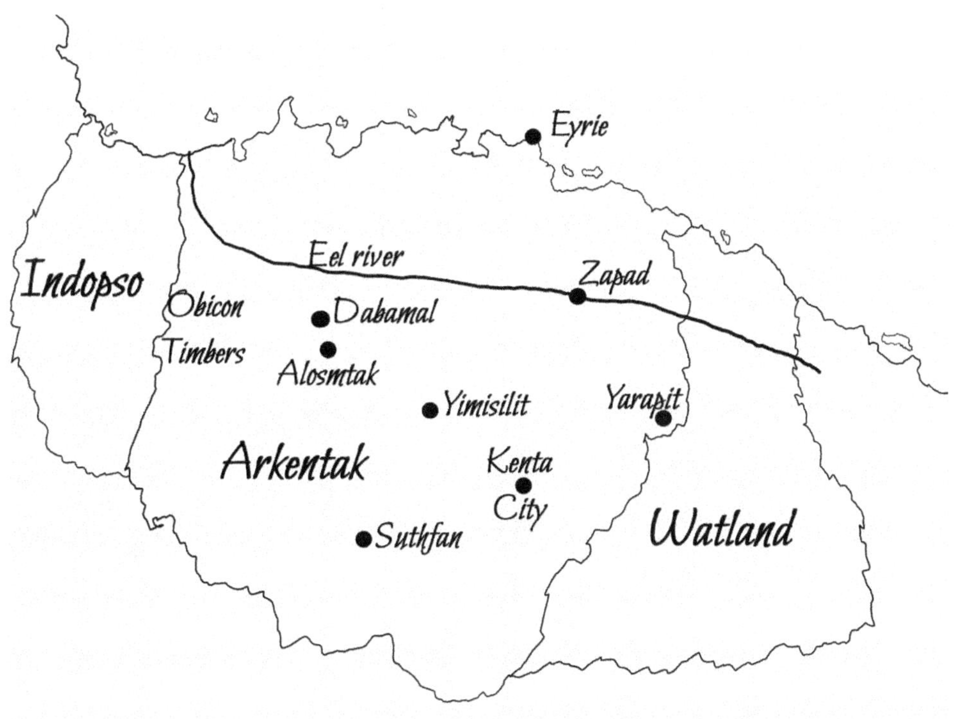

Chapter 1

MY FIRST LIFE

I SHALL NEVER forget the day my first life ended.

Not that my next life began right away after that. For a fuzzy while, I hovered between them, not certain where to land.

But for now, let me tell you about that first last day.

JERIAH AND I were about eleven, best as we can figure. Gran didn't remember when we were born, and Pa never talked about it. But we were about the same age as our friend Mayne, and he was almost twelve.

He and Jeriah found me near the cave that morning. You see, my grown brother Ibro was at the house. He didn't live there, but he hung around sometimes, like he was hiding from something. And when he was there, it wasn't wise for a girl to be anywhere nearby. That's why I'd spent the night in the cave.

When Riah and Mayne canoed around the bend, I was high up a tallpole tree picking papes for breakfast.

Riah and I had found the cave one time when Pa sent him out with two baskets to fill with papefruits. Pa didn't send *me*, of course. As far as he was concerned, *I* didn't exist. But he didn't care if I helped.

Everybody knows papevines climb the trees that grow along the lower part of the sharpfall. Sometimes you'll find them elsewhere, but they like the water best. So we'd canoed along the water's edge, searching out the rounded, green-and-white foliage that wrapped around the tree trunks, looking for pods of pink fruit high in the branches. We only found a few here and there, and it took all day to fill those two baskets. But we also found the cave hidden behind a place where water cascaded down from above.

On the morning in question, Riah couldn't see me up in the tree's umbrella, but he always called whenever he approached, so I'd know who was coming. "Jem!"

I'd seen them a mile off. "What ya want?"

Riah didn't answer. Just steered the canoe toward my voice. When they reached the bank, Mayne grabbed a rope and stepped off the bow seat onto a rock. While he tied the canoe to a scrawny tree, Riah climbed out and shaded his eyes with his hand, scanning the slope. "Pa's off dragoning."

I didn't move. "So?"

"So we have to get the skinning shed cleared out and the soaking pots ready before he gets home."

The pain in my gut, always there those days, twisted and tightened till I thought I'd fall out of the tree. "I ain't goin' home." I'd stay up there for a week if it kept me from Ibro.

Riah's gaze had been searching all that time, but it zeroed in on me now. "Ibro ain't there. Gran had him go with her to get a load of salt."

I relaxed a little, though my gut still cramped. "What do you need me for?" I knew the answer, but had to ask.

"Takes two." His tone implied I was stupid for asking.

"Only 'cause you're a gel eel."

Mayne climbed the steep slope. "I'd help, but Ma likes me to be there when she gets home from work."

Holding a pod of papes in my teeth, I shinned down the tree, trying not to wonder what it would be like to have a ma. Especially one who wanted you around. "Riah don't need your help anyway. Or he wouldn't, if he weren't such a sliming gel eel."

Riah snorted. "If I am, so are you, 'cause we're twins, y'know."

"Wish I could forget."

I handed Riah the papes. He and Mayne plucked them from the stems and ate them as we picked our way along the steep slope through brush and over rocks. After pulling off the last pink fruit, Mayne tossed the pod's gnarled skeleton into the water below, where it floated on its back like a big dead spider.

I DON'T FIGURE you've ever been to Freemansland, and probably most of what you've heard about it is wrong. So let me tell you what it's really like.

It's true that it's an island, and not a natural one. In the distant past, some unknown people built it for a purpose long since forgotten. The land itself was long forgotten after the last great war centuries ago that just about wiped out everyone. It took the rest of the world a long time to find us again—and we wished they never had.

Freemansland is an uneven oval shape, built in six levels. At the base, it's about 400 kilometers across and 350 wide. The highest level, the smallest, is flat on top like a table, with sheer rocky sides all around. This steep, almost-vertical wall, called a sharpfall, plunges about 1700 meters and ends at a moat of sorts. The stillwater, so called because there's no current and it's not much affected by tides, wraps around the whole tabletop in a watery band about a kilometer and a half wide and up to fifteen meters deep.

A high rock rim around the outside edge holds in the stillwater, except for overflow areas where it pours down to the next level. Each level is the same—a sharpfall going up to the level above, with a wide stillwater at the foot. Except that the lowest sharpfall ends at the ocean.

On the day I'm telling you about, Freemansland was all I knew, and all I wanted to know. As far as I was concerned, Freemansland was all there was.

Though most of the things you hear about the place aren't true, it does live up to its nickname, The Land of Many Mysteries. But I was learning its secrets. If I wished for anything back then, it was to learn more of them.

Well, okay, there were other things I'd have liked. To not be scared anymore, for instance, or in pain. I didn't know why I hurt all the time, but it seemed to be getting worse. Sometimes I'd be too sick to eat. Sometimes my vision blurred. And a couple of times—I never told Riah, but I'm telling you now—sometimes everything would go dark, and silent, and I wouldn't know a thing until it all came back a while later, with me wondering what had happened.

If I knew more of Freemansland's secrets, then I'd know what was wrong with me and how to fix it. Just like I'd learned what I could eat and what was poisonous. How to smear my body with a mixture of mud, rufflemint, and burrowrat dung so the dragons couldn't smell me. How to make a paste of barbweed and charcoal to soothe the yellow rash. How to move so I wouldn't be seen or heard by predator or prey, and how to enter and leave a place without leaving a sign I'd been there. Those were the secrets I knew.

I hoped if I learned more of Freemansland's secrets, maybe I'd know how to kill whatever was inside me, killing me, before there was nothing left to save.

THE BOYS AND I didn't speak as we scrambled across the rocks, because the water made so much noise rushing from above and pouring into the stillwater below. With that constant roar and the smoky mist swirling, it was like having a dragon that never slept guarding my cave. If I wanted a fire, though, I had to provide it, because the water dragon couldn't produce a flame.

Bare toes clinging to the stony sharpfall, we edged along until we came to an opening in the rock, kind of like a doorway. We passed through, down a short, dark passage, and into the indentation in the wall that was my cave. There was a big opening where you could see the water falling from above, but a tumble of rocks made a sort of barricade where you weren't likely to roll off the ledge in your sleep. I had space to lie down, and a little niche where I could keep a few things. Not that I owned much.

In the center, a fire still smoldered. I didn't need it for heat, because it never gets cold on that level. In fact, people in other parts of the world think it unbearably hot.

I didn't need it for cooking, because when I was hungry, I simply ate whatever I found, however I found it.

No, sometimes I just wanted a fire for company. It wasn't much, but it was better than nobody.

Mayne spied the whisky bottle against the wall. "Whatcha got there?"

"Just something Riah got for me." I was glad he didn't pick it up, or I'd have had to punch him. I didn't want him to think I was a drunk like Pa, or worse yet, like Ibro. But I needed the whisky now and then when the pain got real bad. That "now and then" had gotten pretty often lately, and there wasn't much left in the bottle. I'd have to steal another one soon, if I couldn't get Riah to do it for me.

To distract Mayne from the whisky, I turned to my brother. "You wouldn't'a found me if I'd kept quiet. You'd never'a' seen me in that tree."

Riah snorted. "I can always find you."

"When I let you. If I wanted to hide from you, I could."

"You smell like a rotting fish. I could find you by scent."

That might have been close to the truth, and my blood boiled. "Oh, yeah? Well, when you go through the woods, you leave a trail like a herd of rock sheep. A blind man could track you."

Mayne stood by chuckling as we argued. But when we were about to come to blows, he raised his hand. "Let's prove it."

We turned on him as one. "Prove what?"

"How good we all are at Stealth."

I could see Riah liked the idea as much as I did. The fact was, we'd played the game before, just the two of us, but it would be fun to pit our skills against Mayne's. We knew we were better than him in both hiding and seeking.

So we worked out the rules: first Riah and Mayne would take off in different directions. They couldn't use the canoe, and they couldn't stay in the water the whole time—at one point, they had to walk on dry ground. I'd give them about a quarter-hour head start, and then I'd track them. If I hadn't found them both by the time the sun was directly over the water, we'd meet back at the canoe. Then I'd take off, and they'd try to find me.

As I said, Jeriah and I had played this before, and I pretty much knew where he'd go. So when it was time for me to track them, I went looking for Mayne first.

Funny thing, though, I didn't find him until I decided I was running out of time and had better look for Jeriah instead. That's when I spied Mayne wedged between two boulders and behind a tall stand of hammergrass. Something about the shape of that clump didn't seem right. I stared more intently and could just make out the outline of his head and left shoulder as he crouched with his back toward me. I'd been moving quietly and didn't think he'd heard me.

I crept around one of the boulders and came at him from the front. I couldn't see through the grass, but I knew he was there, so I reached in and grabbed whatever I could. Which turned out to be his ear. And at the same time I whispered, "Shh!"

He didn't say anything. Just reached up and took my hand off his ear—and held my hand.

Hmm. That was weird. For some reason I liked it. Instead of pulling away, I leaned a little closer and whispered, "Let's find Riah together."

He gave my hand a squeeze then let go. I stepped back so he could crawl out of the grass. Then he stood beside me and lifted his eyebrows as if asking a question.

I pointed up the sharpfall, and he nodded, letting me lead the way in tracking Jeriah. Or, I guess that's what you call it. It wasn't so much tracking him as it was knowing him. Knowing how he thought, how he'd swerve to avoid the soft ground here where it would leave footprints, and climb the steeper way there, because a pursuer would expect him to choose the easier path. By anticipating his movements, I followed him, until after a few minutes I spotted him on a rock at the water's edge, just ready to jump in.

"Gotcha!" I yelled, with Mayne echoing the call behind me.

Riah paused and turned toward our voices. He was far enough away that I couldn't hear his expletive, but his body language was clear. He was not happy to have been caught.

He waited on the rock while we clambered down toward him, not speaking until we were in hearing range. "You Cityslime, Mayne. Slotting, slimy, sotter. Why'd you turn against me?"

"Didn't." Mayne chuckled. "She found me first. I just followed for somethin' to do." Squinting, he shaded his eyes and glanced at the sun. "But we'll get her back. It's highsun, so it's her turn to hide now."

Without answering, Riah watched something in a tree as we neared it. "Grab that lizard, Jem."

I glanced left, and the corner of my eye caught a varana, barely visible against the rough tree bark. Quick as lightning, I spun and pinned the lizard's head to the tree with one hand, then grabbed its body with the other and tossed it down to Riah. "Catch!"

It flew spread-eagle, not even wriggling. I wanted him to miss it so I could laugh at him, but he snatched it out of the air and smashed its head on a rock before it knew what was happening.

He held it up by the tail in triumph. "Who wants lunch?"

Mayne laughed as he skidded the down the slope to Riah's rock. "Slithering City, that was a good catch! There's some doglettuce over here. I'll get some."

While Mayne picked the doglettuce and Jeriah skinned and cut up the varana, I clambered up and down the sharpfall picking pebbleberries. The plants rooted to the muddy undersides of rocks, and the little fruits were plentiful, if you knew where to look. I picked as many as I could carry and brought them back to the boys.

Before eating, Mayne knelt at the edge of the water and rinsed his hands and head. Then, still on his knees, he spread his arms wide, bowed his head, and quietly muttered, "Thanks be to thee, O Good Giver, for thy generous provision."

After feasting on lizard, lettuce and berries, my stomach cramped so violently I couldn't sit upright. To disguise my pain, I leaned forward, scowling at Mayne. "Y'know you've got blickweed on your head?"

He combed his fingers through his short brown hair. "Where?"

"Everywhere." Another cramp made me catch my breath, and the light seemed to fade. I took a deep breath and blinked, then scowled deeper. "Why do you always do that, anyway?"

His fingers found a bit of blickweed and pulled it out of the hair at his temple. "Do what?"

"Wash your head and pray before you eat." I wanted to say more, but the pain stole my voice.

Mayne shrugged. "Ma always does it. She says something bad'll happen to us if we don't."

Jeriah tossed a lizard bone into the water. "Gran does it too. But Pa don't, and she don't make me do it."

"I don't do it either," I said. "And nothin' bad happens to us." The pain in my gut and the cloud across my vision called me a liar.

But the cloud wasn't only across my vision. Oncoming rain roared through the trees on the sharpfall, then reached us where we sat. We squinted against it, but rain was such a common occurrence, that was our only response.

Except I had to raise my voice to speak above the torrent as I stood. "So I'm gonna go now. Gimme a quarter hour, then try to find me."

Mayne picked his teeth with a lizard rib. "Oh, I will. I'll find you."

"Not likely," my brother and I said together. Then Riah added, "You won't, but I will."

I snorted. "Ha. So where you gonna be so you don't see what direction I go in?"

Riah pointed up the sharpfall. "There behind that yellow boulder with the tremy tree beside it. We won't see if you go left, right, or into the water."

"We won't peek, we promise." Mayne wiped the rain from his eyes with his hand. "Cityslime, we couldn't see you if we wanted to." He turned and scrambled up the sharpfall, Riah following. "But if we hain't found you by the time the sun's at three-quarter-point, meet us at the canoe. I have to head for home then."

As much as possible with my blurring vision, I watched them climb until the driving rain swallowed them. Then I slipped into the stillwater.

⁂

I SWAM NORTH awhile, not so they couldn't track me, but because it was easier than trying to scale the sharpfall in the rain. About the time the downpour eased to a steady shower, I found a little inlet and climbed out onto a rock. The pain in my stomach had spread to my chest. I gasped for breath, and my arms and legs felt like weights. The rain gave me an advantage, but I couldn't rejoice in it. I just wanted the misery of this illness to end.

I rolled off the rock onto the ground where I'd be less visible and lay there a few minutes. The rain continued to taper off, and my weakness lifted a bit. I rose to a crouch, watched and listened for signs of pursuit, then began my climb.

I'd rather go up the sharpfall than down, and the knowledge that sooner or later I'd have to come down to meet the boys at the canoe compelled me to move in an ascending angle rather than straight up. I made pretty good time at first, but then I slowed and moved more carefully. With the rain stopping, I couldn't rely on it to cover my tracks.

At one point I heard something and crouched low. It was a herd of sheep bounding past, not the boys. But after a rock they'd dislodged bounced down the sharpfall, a thin human voice came from far below. That convinced me to stay high awhile longer and not head down quite yet.

I longed for the water. Its warm embrace soothed my pain. It was easier to stay concealed there than on the land, and easier to navigate. Panting, and with my bare skin wet from sweat as well as rain, I paused again to rest. What was wrong with me?

I pushed on, angling downward now, making sure not to break a twig, loosen a stone, or leave a trace to mark my passing.

Eventually I could see the water below, and through a break in the trees, I discerned the sun's position. Still about an hour to go.

I had to travel the edge of the water before I found a place where I could slide in, barely disturbing the skim coat of blickweed, rather than jumping in and making a splash. Once I eased into the welcoming waters, some of my tension ebbed. I slipped beneath the surface and swam deep enough that my passing would make barely a ripple in the weeds. Jeriah's sharp eyes could see it if he looked, but I didn't think he was anywhere near.

From time to time I surfaced to breathe, and to scan and listen to my surroundings. But I made my way mostly underwater to within view of the canoe tethered to the shore in the distance. I paused beside a massive boulder that had rolled down from the sharpfall above. There were smaller rocks, too, that had probably slid down at the same time as the boulder. In fact, I stood on one, submerged from my mouth down, and studied the shore. A glance at the sun told me I'd soon win the game. I might as well head for the canoe and wait for the boys.

But a ripple in the water made me freeze in alarm. Was that Jeriah? Where had he come from? But no, it was too long for a boy. And a horny ridge projected from its back. My heart nearly stopped. A dragon. Coming this way.

I held still, not wanting to attract its attention. But what if it already knew I was there? Wasn't that why it was heading my direction? I was a good swimmer, but nobody could outrace a dragon.

I had to know if he was after me or something else. After a deep breath, I lowered myself slowly beneath the surface. I couldn't see much in the murk, but fish scattered, and I thought I could make out... was that a mudhog? Yes. With a shadow paddling toward it.

The dragon lashed out and snatched the big rodent. I started and stood upright, blinking the water out of my eyes. The stillwater reddened with blood a few meters away, and the dragon wriggled off with its lunch.

My knees trembled. The water seemed less comforting than before. Once the dragon was out of sight, I swam about half the distance with all the speed my remaining strength could produce. Then I slowed so as to make less noise, in case one of the boys was nearby.

I found nothing out of the ordinary as I approached the canoe, and I grinned. They hadn't found me. A few minutes from now, when they came back in defeat, I'd be here waiting for them.

I swam to the rock Mayne had stepped out onto that morning. I'd pulled myself halfway out of the water when a voice behind me said, "Gotcha."

It startled me so much I fell back with a splash then turned around. "Mayne!"

He lay in the canoe with only his head visible over the side. His laughing head. Laughing at me.

It filled me with rage. "What are you doing? That ain't fair!"

"I found you, didn't I?" He ducked to avoid the wavelet of green slime I splashed his direction. It slapped against the canoe.

"Cityslime! How can you say you found me when you didn't even look?" I swam toward him. "You waited here for me, you slotting cheater!" I grabbed the side of the canoe and tried to capsize it. "You're supposed to look for me."

Throwing himself back against the opposite side to counterbalance, he grabbed a paddle and raised it. "Let go. I don't want to have to explain to Jeriah why his sister has a lump on her head."

I knew he wouldn't make good his threat, but I let go. "He'd kill you if you hit me."

"He'd probably thank me." Mayne lowered the paddle. "I did look for you. But I knew I'd never be able to track you in that rain, so after a few minutes, I came back. Figured you'd get here sooner or later."

"Well, I still won. You didn't find me, I found you."

He tossed his hair from his eyes. "Ha! You never saw me 'till I said gotcha. It was me who found you."

WE LAY IN the canoe head-to-head, hashing it out in a lazy argument. My head hurt, my stomach hurt, and all I wanted to do was sleep. I think Mayne had been napping, because he seemed almost as groggy as I.

At the sound of dislodged stones skittering down the sharpfall, we sat up at the same time to see Jeriah clamber toward us. I pointed. "There he is."

Mayne yawned. "Good thing, too. I was about ready to leave without him. I gotta get home."

Seeing us both already there, Riah scowled. "Cityslimes. Both of you." He untied the canoe and climbed in. "Slithering cheaters, too." He grabbed a paddle and plunged it into the water. "Couple of dripping slotters is all you are."

Mayne sat on the stern seat and helped maneuver the canoe away from the rocks. I stayed where I was in the center, arms wrapped around my bent legs. "You're a sliming sore loser, Riah."

"Shut up," was all he said, and I closed my eyes, rested my forehead on my knees, and dozed while the boys paddled. He was a sore loser, that was for sure. He could never find me, so why did he keep trying? If I didn't want to be seen, nobody could find me. Nobody. Not even him.

Mayne nudged me with his bare foot. "Outta my canoe. I gotta get goin'."

I lifted my head. We were at the island.

I forgot to mention when I described the sharpfalls and the stillwaters that sometimes rockslides made a build-up of soil and rock in the water. In some places, there was enough rubble to form an island, and Pa lived on one of those, him and Gran. They'd been there since forever, almost. Gran grew up there, raised her family on that same lump of muddy rock, and after being away for a while, Pa had come back to it. Jeriah called it home, too, but I couldn't. My home was all of Freemansland.

The one-room shack hung out over the water in front, supported by stilts. A rope ladder dangled from a hole in the floor. A dock extended under the building, so a person could tie a canoe and climb up the ladder. If you were carrying a load, you could haul it along the dock onto the land and then carry it up the path to the shack's door. Or to one of the sheds on the island, if that's where you wanted to put it.

Gran kept swamp chickens in one of those sheds, when she remembered to feed them and keep their trough flooded in the dry season. If they couldn't wade in water, they'd dry up and die. They could find enough insects and rodents and things to stay alive for a few days on their own, but they couldn't live without water for more than half a day.

Pa had a shed for dragon skinning, one for tanning the hides, and another for storing them until he took them to the buyer. There was a second storage shed where he kept other stuff, including the whisky he made. I'd have to swipe a bottle before I left.

Mayne steered to the dock, waited for Riah and me to disembark, then took off for home.

Sore-Loser Riah was still grumpy. But I was in a hurry to help him get his work done so I could be gone before Ibro got back. My nap had refreshed me a bit, and I trotted along the dock, then followed the path to the skinning shed. I opened the wide double doors to let out some of the fishy smell before Riah and his scowl got there.

I could scarcely blame him for being upset, though. It was bad enough he could never seem to win at Stealth. Worse yet, it was no fun getting things ready for Pa when he came home with a catch of dragons. We didn't know how many he'd bring, but we scrubbed all three boards just in case. We checked that the salt bin was full and had a scoop in it. We fetched a couple buckets of water and set them beside the skinning table. Then we sharpened the knives, lined them up on the supply shelf, and made sure there was a good stack of towels.

That was the easy part. Getting the soaking pots ready for the tanning process was where the hard work came in. "You go get started," I told Riah. "I'll run and get a bottle for Pa, so he'll have one handy when he skins."

Jeriah grunted and trudged off. I ran to the storage shed and grabbed a whisky from the shelf. The dwindling supply worried me a little. It wouldn't be good for either Jeriah or me if Pa found out we'd been taking it. Until he made more, I'd have to find someone else to steal it from.

I worked off the stopper and downed a swig. It snatched my breath away and made my eyes water, but as soon as the burn eased a little, I took another. Then I closed the bottle securely before grabbing another and tucking it under my arm. I carried the first bottle to the skinning shed and set it on the shelf with the other supplies. The other, I hid in the swamp chicken pen, which currently had no residents.

The quick nip did make me feel a little better—or maybe it was the promise of more to come from the fresh bottle later. Something, at least, gave me the energy to hurry to the tanning shed, where I picked up two buckets and headed down the path to the water.

Riah was already kneeling on the dock and dipping in a bucket while a full one stood nearby. His posture told me he was still put out that I'd beat him at Stealth. A cold wave of panic swept over me. I couldn't stand having him mad at me. He was the only person in the world who cared if I lived or died. In fact, most people seemed to wish I *would* die.

A vision of Mayne's grin flashed through my mind, but I tossed it aside. He might not hate me all the time, like some people did—Pa, for instance—but he could never love me like Riah.

Well, Gran was nice to me, if her mind was working. But all too often she took off for someplace else, leaving her body behind. Those times, she'd just stare through you like you weren't there, and only time could bring her back.

Riah lugged the full buckets toward me, and I stepped in front of him. "Sorry you didn't find me."

He scowled deeper. "Get out of my way."

I stepped aside. "It's the rain's fault. Neither of us could help that."

He snorted without turning as he trudged toward the tanning shed. "You gonna carry water for the kettles, or do you plan to let me do it all?"

I scampered with my buckets toward the dock. "It was you Pa told to do it, y'know."

We each made a couple of trips, passing one another on the way. Then, after my third load, I needed a rest. I had a stitch in my side, my arms ached, my heart pounded, and I could hardly catch my breath.

Maybe I'd begin making the brine. There probably wouldn't be enough salt, since Gran had to get more. But at least I could get started.

I went to the bin and opened it. Sure enough, it was low. I leaned in to pick up the scoop, when something—or rather, someone—pushed my head down from behind, and the rest of my body tumbled into the bin after it.

The force of the shove and the surprise of it all knocked what little wind I still had out of me. Salt in my mouth choked me and salt in my eyes made them burn.

But the sound of Ibro's laugh made my stomach spin like a waterspout. "Haven't seen you lately, little sister."

My mind went numb with terror. I think I threw up, because I remember my throat burning almost as bad as my eyes. But what I knew most was panic as he snarled something like, "You can't hide from me in there" and yanked me out of the bin by one arm and my hair. My head cracked against the bin, but it didn't knock me out—and I remember wishing it had.

With my face full of salt, I couldn't see, could hardly breathe, and couldn't yell. But I fought with every part of my body I could use. He rewarded me with a hearty slap.

Ibro tore off my shorts and I fought some more, wondering how hard you have to wish before you can die. Surely all the power of my wishes at that moment should have done the trick, but no. Ibro went to work on me, and I still fought and wished, but stayed alive.

I guess Jeriah ran in then because he screamed, "No! Get off her!" He must have thrown a bucket of water, because in the same moment, Ibro and I were both drenched.

Ibro withdrew and spun around with a roar while I tried to crawl away. There was a crash, Ibro grabbed my ankle and dragged me, and the rest is a nauseating blur of salt and pain and noise and darkness.

Though I don't remember the rest, one thing is clear: that was the day my first life ended.

Chapter 2

INTERMISSION

THE BRIGHTNESS BEYOND my closed eyelids couldn't be from the sun, for it held no heat.

Whatever covered my body and restricted my movement was nothing like Ibro's rough, groping hands.

A stench permeated the air. Also not Ibro. Not the skinning shed, either. It was nothing I'd ever smelled before.

A steady pulsing sound worked its way into my consciousness. What in all Umban was that?

I opened my eyes a slit, then slammed them closed again. Cityslime! The light hurt, and the unfamiliar sight sent my heart to racing as if a wood ghoul was after me. The pulsating beep matched its speed.

Wherever I was, I had to get out. Now. Back to the dark safety of my cave, the comforting curtain of falling water. Light a fire. Drain my bottle.

I couldn't move, couldn't sit up. I fought to escape, but something held me with a relentless grip. A shriek rose from my chest, rasped through my dry throat, and came out in a croaking roar like a wounded dragon's.

"Jem! Keep still."

Jeriah's voice. His hand on my shoulder.

I froze.

"It's okay, Jem. Relax. It's okay." He took my hand.

I turned my head—the only part of me that was mobile—and peered toward the sound.

My narrowed gaze met one of Jeriah's blue eyes. The other was lost in a puffy mass of black, blue, and green. Some sort of tape crisscrossed scattered wounds. His head, now shaved, was lumpy and bruised.

My eyes widened. "Cityslime!" I squinted again at the brightness. "What's—" Too many sensations assailed me to put any of it into words. "City!" I didn't recognize my own hoarse voice.

Another weak effort to sit up was thwarted by a strap across my chest. "Slithering slots! Dripping, slotting Cityslime!" My hands were tied down, too, and so were my feet.

Jeriah grabbed my shoulder. "If you'd quit floppin' around and promise to be still, they'll undo those ties."

"What the City's goin' on?" I started to cry—and I *never* cried, no matter what. "Let me go! Get these things off me!"

"He is right, Jemima."

The voice and accent were foreign.

I struggled harder. "City! You slime! Let me go, slotter! Riah, help me!"

The stranger who'd spoken came near, and Jeriah bent and spoke softly in my ear. "It's okay, Jem, really. They saved our lives. No one's going to hurt you."

None of this made sense, but my struggling accomplished nothing. A new tactic was needed. "I didn't want my life saved."

Riah's voice seemed to choke. "But I did."

I remembered then. His boyish roar in my defense, Ibro pulling away.

I opened my eyes to study his battered face. Had Ibro done that?

I wanted to ask, but didn't want to hear the answers. I lifted my gaze and forced myself to look at the filthy Cityslime who stood nearby.

I'd never seen a citizen before. This one, though unnaturally clean and neat, was manly enough, not prissy. And he offered a hesitant smile.

A smile that did nothing to calm me. A trapped animal should never trust its captors.

No point letting them know I was onto them, though. I forced myself to relax onto what I now know was a bed.

I'd never seem one of those before, either. In Freemansland, we slept on mats or in hammocks. Me, I slept wherever I found a safe place. But a piece of furniture up off the ground? I'd never heard of such a thing.

It was comfortable, though, once I quit pushing against the restraints. Soft and firm at the same time, with no lumps or prickles.

The citizen spoke again. "Your brother is right, Jemima." He made a face. "What a strange name. I think I shall call you Jemma, if you don't mind."

I narrowed my eyes. What if I did mind?

He kept talking. "Your brother is right, Jemma. You are safe here. No one will hurt you."

"I can take care of myself."

He nodded. "Your brother tells us you have been doing a good job of that."

Riah spoke up. "You gonna take those strap things off? Her mind's back, she don't need 'em no more."

The citizen's sandy-colored brows lifted as he studied me. "Is that true?"

He doubted my brother's word? I scowled. "If Riah says somethin', it's true." The realization I'd just promised not to run came too late.

"Very well, then." The man worked on the strap across my chest. It tightened a little before it loosened, and he tossed it to the side so that it hung from the bed. "You may sit. But I must ask that you not disconnect anything."

Disconnect? What— That's when I realized things were sticking into me. Poking into one hand, stuck to my forehead, and another down there where Ibro had been.

Only Jeriah's hand on my shoulder kept me from flying into another rage. "Take it easy, Jem. They're helping us."

How the slot-slime did he figure that? But I wanted those straps off me, and the slime wouldn't take them off if I kept fighting it. I lay still.

The man removed the restraints from my left hand then moved down to my feet. "I hardly blame you for being alarmed to wake up and find yourself in this condition." His voice was strange and nasally, his words clipped. "But you can believe your brother when he says we are helping you." He released the last of the straps then smiled. "Did you not tell me if Jeriah says something, it is true?"

I pushed myself up to a sitting position, refusing the citizen's help when he offered his hand. I didn't appreciate the way he threw my own words back at me like that, slippery and smooth as a flickfish. I refused to look at him.

Instead, I studied Jeriah's mangled face, hoping I could speak without tears. "Ibro do that?"

Riah licked his swollen lip and nodded. "And he— But don't worry, he—he won't be around no more." He plopped into a chair beside the bed. I wanted to ask what he meant. But I didn't want to talk with the Cityslime hanging around.

The man turned to the beeping and flashing machines, studying them as if they meant something, and doodled on some sort of flat, shiny thing. Was he ever going to leave?

He pulled up a chair on the other side of my bed, where he sat back and crossed his legs. "We all have many questions. First, let us answer yours, as well as we are able."

He glanced at Riah, who didn't seem inclined to say anything. I'd rather have heard it from him, but the man filled me in while Riah and I sat with our eyes locked, listening and processing it together. Of course Riah had a head start on the processing part, but I could see he still had a hard time with it.

Turns out Ibro hadn't gone with Gran to get salt. He was, as I'd surmised, hanging around because he was in hiding. The City marshals were looking for him because of what he'd done to a citizen's daughter on Coldclime, which is what we call the Fourth Level, because it's cooler there. I've heard some people—not native Freemanslanders, but outsiders—say it's a nice climate, but normal people find it uncomfortably cold. The level above that is Thinair, and the top, the flat level, is Harsh. There are lots of stories about Harsh and how it got its name.

But none of that mattered at the moment. The citizen—his name, I learned, was Dr. Pigeon—explained that Ibro hurt a girl on Coldclime. The marshals went after him, and he took off for home. *Home* being Gran and Pa's island, where Ibro had grown up and where he didn't figure the Cityslime marshals would be able to find him.

He'd done this before. Broke some law, hid out for a while until they gave up looking. But this time, they put a little more effort into it. I guess that citizen whose daughter he hurt was important.

So when Pa told Gran to get more salt, and she asked Ibro to go with her to help, he wouldn't go. Said somebody might see him.

But Jeriah hadn't known that when he and Mayne went off to find me. As far as he knew, Gran and Ibro would both be gone all day.

Gran took off in the skiff, and he grabbed a bottle from the shed and started in on it. She got to the merchant stacks—stacks are the clusters of buildings going up the sharpfalls. They're like buildings stacked on top of each other, not like a City street where everything sprawls along flat ground. Because in Freemansland, the only flat thing is the stillwater.

When Gran tied up at the dock at the bottom of the merchant stacks, she couldn't remember what she was there for. You know how I said she was getting a bit off in the head? Well, she tied up and then sat there in the skiff for a while, staring into space.

That's where Pa found her. He'd had some trouble with his motor and had to get it fixed. He went to the mechanical supply stack, got the part he needed, and fixed the motor. He was about to leave when he saw Gran sitting there. I guess it took him a while to rouse her. There's not much a person can to do bring someone out of a trance like that. You just have to wait till it runs its course.

When she came out of it, she told him how Ibro wouldn't come with her, and I guess he got pretty mad. But it was too late for him to go dragoning by then anyway, so he figured he'd get the salt himself, take it back home, and then go out hunting in the morning.

Meanwhile, Riah came back to the skinning shed with a couple more buckets of water, and he was mad. First, because he hadn't been able to beat me at Stealth, and he thought Mayne had won. Losing to the two of us is what had him all steamy to begin with. But then, when he didn't see me come past him on my way to get more water, he thought I was being lazy, and he was mad about that too.

So he comes into the shed feeling twice mad. But when he sees Ibro on top of me, he was madder than mad. He threw a bucket at

Ibro and then clunked him with a skin-stretching pole. But it didn't hurt him bad enough. Ibro grabbed the pole and gave him a few with it. Riah snatched up another and did what he could to defend himself, until he was able to pick up a skinning knife and throw it at Ibro.

It stuck him, but drunk as he was, it just made Ibro mad. Triple mad. And he lit into Riah like to kill him right there. But about then, Pa came in. He and Gran had come home with the salt, and as soon as he heard all the crashing around in the shed, he came running to see if a marsh bear had gotten in there or something. He sees Ibro holding Riah by the hair and ready to gut him, and he gets into the fray.

All the while I'm lying there not really seeing or hearing anything, almost like Gran, I guess. And somehow, no one's really sure how, with all the hammering and stabbing and everything going on, Ibro kills Pa just as the marshals got there. They must have been pretty good at Stealth, because they'd followed Pa home without him knowing it. And when they saw him kill Pa, they killed Ibro. Blasted him with their guns, while Jeriah lay there all beat up and watching the whole thing.

That's more or less the way I heard the story. Of course Dr. Pigeon didn't word it that way, but I kept watching Jeriah's one good eye the whole time the man told the story, and somehow I saw it the way Jeriah saw it, and heard it the way he'd have said it.

The marshals took Jeriah and me—and Gran too, because she couldn't do anything but sit and cry—in their skiff to one of those big floating docks they built where they can come and go in a helicopter. They put us in the helicopter and took us to the big building where we were now, the hospital. It's built on the sharpfall between the fourth and fifth levels. It wasn't one of our buildings that the City took over, they built it from scratch.

It sprawls all up and down an acre or two of the sharpfall. Like our buildings, it's mostly underground, built into the hillside, and part of it hangs out over the roads that zigzag back and forth among the stacks. Our buildings are all separate, and you have to go outside to get from one to another. But this is one big structure, all connected with hallways and elevators and moving stairways.

Dr. Pigeon told the story and then paused. I could feel him watching me, but I didn't want to look at him. He was genuine Cityslime—not just the cuss word, but the real thing. Even though he didn't look all that awful, I hated that he was in the room with us, hated his voice droning on. Hated that I'd promised to not jump up and run.

Not that I could, with needles and tubes in me here and there. The more the man talked, the more my mind engaged, and the more aware I grew of my surroundings—altogether foreign, though I was supposedly still in Freemansland—and of my discomfort. The alien objects attached to my body were growing more intolerable by the minute.

I knew how Freemansland must have felt, if a manmade island can have feelings, when the City soldiers blew a hole in it eighty years before. They just blasted in, knocked out part of Seaview level and invaded with soldiers and machinery and declared it all theirs. Just as they'd done to me—blasted onto Pa's island and took us as theirs, without us having a chance to fight back.

His grating voice started up again. "Now that you are awake, we can disconnect some of these machines. We have already been able to remove the endotracheal tube. It may have left your throat a little sore, but that is temporary. As are all these things. Uncomfortable as they are, they are necessary to restore you to health."

He re-crossed his legs in the other direction. "I would appreciate it, Jemma, if you would look at me."

Not wanting to give him the satisfaction, I looked down at the blanket that covered me. I'd never had a blanket before, but I was glad of it, because the room was chilly. My nose was so cold I could hardly feel it.

"Do you have any questions?" Something in his tone made me give him my attention. It sounded like he was working toward something, and I wanted to see if I could figure out what was on his mind from his expression. But it told me nothing.

All I could tell was that he was waiting for a response from me. I had lots of questions, but I wasn't ready to ask them, so I shook my head. A citizen would never give me a straight answer anyway.

"Well, then. We have some questions for you." He referred to that note-taking thing in his hand. "Your name is Jemima Freeman. Your mother was Heelo Freeman, formerly Heelo Jae, is that correct?"

That was my name, but I knew nothing about my mother. So I said nothing.

He made a notation. "And your father? Jeo Freeman? Does that sound familiar?"

I didn't like his condescending attitude. "I knew my pa. Never had a ma."

"Of course you had a mother. You were born, were you not? The person who gave birth to you is your mother."

This unnatural place, all these things stuck in me, the Cityslime treating *me* like slime—it was suddenly more than I could bear. I tore off the thing from my head and threw it at the Pigeon. "I was borned, not hatched from an egg like a—"

He jumped up and grabbed my hands.

"Like a slotting *pigeon*." I spat at him. "Let go of me, you—"

Riah's cry cut me off. "Jem, you promised!"

I tried to shake off the man's grip. "I said I wouldn't run, I never promised to keep this stuff stuck all over me."

Pigeon wouldn't let go. "This is why you were in restraints. If you keep this up, we shall be forced to put them back on."

The combination of Riah's imploring and Pigeon's logic made me pause.

Riah sat on the edge of the bed. "I'll lie here with you."

The Cityslime relaxed his grip. "You may, if you think it will help."

"It helped before." Riah lay beside me. "I'll stay here with you, Jem. Nobody's going to hurt you."

Pigeon picked up the thing I'd thrown, a metallic-looking crown with wires attached. The way the beeping had changed to a steady whine told me the crown had something to do with the noises in the room, though the sounds didn't come from it directly.

Beside me, Riah spoke to the Cityslime. "Maybe if you tell her what all that stuff's for, she won't mind it so much."

The man's expression was dubious. "I doubt she would understand. But what could it hurt?" He showed me the head ring. "This is called a cranial monitor. When placed on your head, it picks up electrical impulses and records your brain activity on this machine here."

I couldn't see what machine he was talking about, but I didn't get the impression he cared if I could see it or not.

With Riah beside me, and not acting like any of this was bad, I did feel calmer. I asked him, "Were you lying beside me earlier?"

He nodded. "For a while, it was the only way you didn't go crazy, even strapped down. They couldn't do nothin' to help you if I wasn't here. Here, see this?" He lifted my hand and pointed to the needle sticking into it, taped in place, with a little tube connected. "This is taking medicine from up there," he gestured toward something behind us. "And putting it right into your vein, so it goes all through your body."

That sounded as bad as it looked. "What kind of medicine?"

"I'm not sure what all. Mostly stuff to kill the bad bugs and worms and stuff."

The Cityslime chuckled. "It sounds a bit odd, but he is correct. I will replace these electrodes, if you do not mind."

He'd have done it if I did mind, so I didn't waste my breath.

"Your body has been host to a number of parasites for quite some time, it would appear. Some of the medications your brother speaks of will kill those parasites and allow you to heal. For instance, I imagine you have been experiencing some stomach pain?"

I shrugged, irritated he would know that.

"Your gut is full of little things called montenstiprings. You have a whole city of them in there. Some of the medication is ridding them from your body. Your blood serves as a highway for a number of other parasites that cause symptoms like lung problems, muscle pain, and loss of hair and nails."

I refused to talk to the citizen, so I spoke to my brother beside me as I examined my hands. "I don't see no parasites, do you?"

The doctor answered in a scornful tone. "Do you even know what a parasite is?"

"We know," Riah said.

I addressed my brother, not the Pigeon directly. "Like the treeburst that grows in the tops of the fedars. It shoots seeds through the air to stick to another tree, where it grows into the bark of that tree and lives off o' it. Or the nineball fungus that eats into a clump of ferretgrass root and kills the grass. Or—"

The slimy citizen's brows rose. "Very good, yes. You have the idea. But these parasites are too small to see. You pick them up in the food you eat, the water you drink, or the ground you walk on, without knowing it. Sometimes even from the saliva of an insect that bites you."

How could anything be that small?

"Your body is full of them. We cannot treat them all at once because it would kill you along with the parasites. Bit by bit, however, the medications are ridding you of them."

I gave Riah a nudge. "So how come it's just me that needs all that? Don't you have no parasites or nothing?"

The doctor spoke before Riah could answer. "Perhaps because he has had better parental care, his problems are not as involved. We have not had to be quite so aggressive in his treatment."

He'd been fiddling with some of the gadgets, and now he made notes on the flat thing he held. "We keep a record of everything here in this tablet. Test results, treatments, how you respond to medications—"

One of those words was familiar. "Test?" I said to Riah. "Does he mean like in school?"

The doctor gave me a sharp look then referred to what he called the tablet, pushing things around on its surface to look at different things. "We have no record of your ever being enrolled in school. In fact, we have no record of your ever being born."

I turned to him with all the vehemence I could muster. Which was quite a lot. "Then maybe you're wrong. Maybe I was never born after all. Maybe I come up between the floorboards in a school, like a fungus. That'd explain a lot, wouldn't it?"

He emitted a sound almost like a laugh. "I am beginning to wonder, Miss Freeman, if there is any explanation for you."

❧ Chapter 3 ❧

A CUP OF GLAFFCRIM

WITH BOTH PARENTS dead, and Gran judged incompetent, we went to live with Aunt Lanie and her family.

We didn't even know we had an aunt, but the City did. And once they deemed me well enough to leave the hospital, they took it upon themselves to assign us to her care, whether we, or she, liked it or not.

Aunt Lanie lived on Glaffit—that's the third level. It's one level above where Jeriah and I lived, which was called Freedom. Until Ibro ruined everything, Freedom was all we'd ever known. Now, as wards of the City, Freedom was only a memory.

We were still in the hospital when a woman with a nervous-looking smile approached us in the hallway. We'd been evicted from our room, a crew had come in to clean and sterilize, and now we sat in the hall on the duffels that held everything we owned in the world.

Ignoring me—I was used to that, and didn't mind in the least—the woman extended her hand to my brother, who rose as she approached. "Jeriah? I'm Miss Orange, with City Children's Services."

He shook her hand. Standing straight, with his new haircut, clean clothes, and sober expression on his mostly-healed face, he almost looked like a man. "Yes, ma'am." Though common courtesy said he should introduce me, he was uncommonly courteous enough to know I didn't want him to. "Pleased to meet you."

"I expect Dr. Pigeon told you I was coming?"

Riah nodded. "Yes, ma'am."

"I apologize for the delay. I should have been here earlier, but something came up. And now we have to hurry." She sliced a glance my direction but didn't pause. "Ready?"

I rose, too, and picked up my duffle. No need to speak, with Jeriah there to do it for me.

He grabbed his bag and slung it over his shoulder. "We've been ready." That's for sure. We'd sat there more than an hour.

"Well, then, let's go." She turned and clacked down the hall, her shoes announcing her presence to the whole world. She'd be terrible at Stealth—a deaf flumotute with ear mange could have heard her. Not only that, but a weird aroma hovered about her and trailed behind. It even overpowered the reek of the cleaning solution these people slathered all over everything.

Jeriah and I followed. I held my breath so as not to gag on her stench.

We wore shoes, too—a torture neither Riah's nor my feet had experienced before. At least our shoes were softer, and likely less uncomfortable, than what Miss Orange wore. Her heels were so high I wondered how she could walk.

We followed her through a tangle of passages. And moving stairways, which I only braved because Riah did. Those things were terrifying.

As we walked, I tried to discover how to move without making a sound but hadn't found the trick by the time we burst into a broad, bustling room. The sudden expanse around me made me forget stealth and study this new thing.

Before us spread a whole wall of windows, from the gleaming floor to the far-distant ceiling. At ground level, glass doors. Exit doors. With lovely rain and fresh Freemansland air on the other side.

I wanted to run, to throw open those doors and fly through them, then kick off my shoes, strip off my clothes, and be me again, be free again. I can't tell you how much I wanted that. But, clenching my fists, I followed Riah's example and Miss Orange's disruptive footsteps across that hard, shining floor without breaking stride.

As we neared the exit, my anticipation rose until I almost quivered. The portal opened by itself, and we passed through into the outdoors. I felt the damp air on my face and breathed it in deeply.

Or maybe it was the shock that made me suck in the breath. Shock at the cool temperature. I'd been expecting it to be comfortingly hot, like Freedom was, but it felt colder than the chill in the building. And the landscape was nothing like the Freemansland I knew, with alien-looking buildings and paved streets. All the plant life was tamed, confined to pots or standing alone and afraid in a bare expanse of gravel. Trees stood here and there, tall and sad, bereft of their forest. And where was that familiar, dank smell of the stillwater?

Everything was wrong.

I took Riah's hand and fervently hoped Glaffit would be more home-like. He didn't say anything, but I knew he hoped the same.

I considered the weather, and for the first time in memory, I didn't want to be rained on. I was on the edge of shivering as it was, and the very thought of getting wet was almost enough to make my teeth chatter.

Apparently the City architects who designed this scar upon Coldclime understood that, because all the walkways were covered. Glad of the shelter as we clattered down the steps to the water's edge, I chafed to see how those sliming citizens were transforming Freemansland into a place of their own. A bit of breeze chased a puff of mist onto me, and I shuddered.

My duffel banged against my thigh as we hurried through the wet, gray air toward a ferryboat at the dock 400 meters away. The rain dotted the stillwater below with living dimples and drummed the roof above us. It felt good to walk, but it would have been better if I didn't have to carry the bag. Or wear shoes.

A sturdy wood-rail fence separated me from the water. Its shimmering languor tempted me to drop my bag and dive in. But how could I swim with clothes on?

And how could I leave my brother?

We strode on, Miss Orange clacking and Riah and me thudding softly. I'd nearly perfected silence of movement. Or maybe my footsteps were masked by the sounds of Miss Orange's heels, the rain on the roof, the slap of the duffel against my leg, the piercing call of a niserbird in search of a mate.

And the sound of my breath, unlabored, without pain. I hated to admit it, but I hadn't felt this good for as long as I could remember.

I silently cursed the Cityslimes who saved me. Better to die young in Freedom than be captive of the City.

UNCLE RHE AND Aunt Lanie lived on a glaffcrim plantation.

You're familiar with glaffcrim, the ubiquitous beverage enjoyed by people of all classes across the world. All genuine crim comes from Freemansland, but you can buy imitations from other countries, most of them sweetened and artificially flavored, like the popular brand made by LaffCrim.

Real glaffcrim is made from the fruit of the glaffit tree, which grows on the lower sharpfalls and bears fruit twice a year. The premium crims are made from the first crop. Other types, like Late Berry and Autumn Mild, come from the second picking. Any variety with *double* in its name, like Double Ewe or Double Dragon, comes from a combination of the first and second crops.

The fruits are oblong, about an inch long, with a tough, scaly skin of bright orange. They're processed through a series of steps, including a ten-day fermentation, until they've become a sort of a putty. This is pressed into bars or cubes and wrapped in paper made from the skins of the fruit, or sometimes fibers from the bark of the glaffit tree softened by soaking in a slurry of water and hair pine ash. It's packed into hair pine crates and then shipped all over the world.

Once it reaches its destination, the putty is hydrated. The liquid used for this varies, but your typical crims are softened in mineral water, then rolled flat and cut into the discs you slide into your brewer.

That's the process for ordinary glaffcrim. But several acres of Uncle Rhe's plantation were devoted to production of the specialty crim called Gracious Hen. Unless you're very wealthy, you've probably never tasted it. I have. And it's heavenly.

Uncle Rhe kept a flock of about a hundred three-foot-tall gracious fowl, so called because the birds' behavior seems oddly polite. The males bow, the females curtsey. They don't jostle one another when fed, but will step back and gesture for others to move up before them. Despite their size, they coo demurely. But, like a lot of people, their manners are only superficial. Those birds are cutthroats beneath the veneer.

Gracious fowl love glaffit fruit, but they can't digest it. They'll swallow it whole, and it sits in their stomach for two days while enzymes change the composition of the fruit and give it a richer, more nuanced flavor. Finally, it passes through.

Once it's removed from the bird's droppings and cleaned, it requires no fermentation and only minimal processing to turn it into a useable paste. Each bird can handle eating only one fruit a day, though, so production is slow. That's why the price of the Gracious Hen discs is beyond the reach of most crim drinkers.

When Jeriah and I arrived at the plantation, we didn't know any of that. But we were about to learn.

THE THREE OF us were the only passengers on the ferry that took us across the stillwater to the cadamara. That's where you can go from one level to another.

Each level is connected to the next by three cadamaras equally spaced around the circumference of the island. At each cadamara there's a sharpfall scaler—that is, a car on rails that takes you up or down—and a stairway, in case someone can't afford the scaler fare. The sharpfalls are about 1700 meters high, though, and that's a lot of steps.

Though the City invaders had improved and upgraded the scalers in recent years, they didn't invent them. A hundred years ago, Freemanslanders scaled the sharpfalls with cars hauled by ropes and pulleys and powered by roxen. It was slow going. Sometimes the roxen would balk and refuse to turn the wheel anymore, leaving the passengers stranded. Sometimes a rope would break, sending the car crashing to the bottom and killing everyone in it. There wasn't a lot of coming and going between the levels in the old days.

I should mention that no cadamara went to Harsh, the sixth level. The only way to get up there is by air, and no way to get down except the same way. Or by climbing down the sharpfall. And since it never gets warmer than about negative thirty degrees at that elevation, the sharpfall's nothing but ice and rock, and you're not likely to get very far without falling.

People have done it, though, according to legend. Specifically, my ancestors. The story goes that a previous civilization used the top level as a place to dispose of the worst kind of criminals. There were no guards to maintain order, no bars or fences or anything else to keep them there. They had a big building for shelter, some sort of fuel for heat, and greenhouses for growing food. Prisoners were dumped there and left to freeze, starve, kill one another, or survive however they could. At one point, the story goes, a group of them somehow managed to climb down, down, and down, until they stopped at the second level from the bottom. It was warm there and provided plenty of food, all kinds of food, all year round. That's why the second level is called Freedom, and the descendants of the people who settled there carry the name Freeman.

And why I deeply resented having my freedom taken away.

The ferry chugged slowly through the stillwater. Before we'd gotten halfway across, we could see we'd have to wait before we could disembark. Towers of wooden crates filled the pier, and a bevy of men loaded them onto a massive barge. It was a shipment of glaffcrim from my uncle's plantation, according to Miss Orange. I watched with interest. That was a lot of glaffcrim.

The men didn't seem to mind the rain. The three of us on the ferry, however, stayed under the roof. I wrapped myself in my arms to keep warm.

Miss Orange glanced at me then looked away. "Jeriah, do you and your sister have a sweater or a jacket in your duffel? This rain makes it a little chilly."

He shrugged. "We're okay."

I wasn't exactly okay, but I appreciated his answer. It was best not to show weakness.

Our ferry chugged toward the pier and drifted to a stop a distance away. The engine rumbled down to idle, and we waited while the men finished their loading. None of us spoke.

The rain tapered off. With the last crate stowed, some of the men got on board, and others traipsed down the pier to the building at the far end. The sign across the top said "Sharpfall Scaler 14." From where we sat, I could see two entrances. The opening on the left was marked "Freight," and the other, "Passengers."

One man who remained with the barge loosed the hawser and then hopped on deck while the enormous craft eased away from the pier, engines groaning. I jumped when a deep, throaty horn sounded. Our ferry tooted in reply and began moving forward.

"It's about time we got moving," Miss Orange said.

I only half agreed. It would be good to move to a lower level where the temperature was more reasonable, but I wasn't eager to live with other people. Any people. Especially strangers.

I stiffened at the thought that one of them might be like Ibro. If he was, I'd leave. Even if the City sent me up to Harsh for doing it, I wouldn't stay.

If Harsh was still used as a prison. Rumor was that the descendants of those who hadn't escaped still lived there, and the City continued to fly more in all the time. I did sometimes hear and see planes in our skies, but where they were going, I didn't know.

The ferry putted toward the pier, and I stared at Jeriah until he turned toward me.

His wide eyes told me he was as anxious as I.

Duffels in hand, we left the boat and clomped down the pier. The air was still cold, but the sun warmed me a little. I hated to leave it when we entered the station.

People were everywhere inside. Hurrying through, sitting on benches, talking on telecom devices, standing in line. We became part of that last category after making our way to the far end of the station, where we joined a group of six men standing in front of a sign that said, "Next car loads in 6.3 minutes." As we arrived, the flashing number changed to 6.2.

The men in front of us were the ones who'd loaded the barge. I'd never seen so many people at one time before. If Riah hadn't been with me, I'd have hidden in a corner somewhere.

When the countdown reached 5.0, a gate opened beneath the sign, and a voice intoned from a speaker somewhere above. "Passenger car for Glaffit now loading at Gate One. Departure in five minutes. Please have your tickets ready."

The line stirred to life, and we shuffled forward until we reached the doorway. A woman stood on the other side, taking tickets from everyone as they passed through. She wore a uniform, but not that of a City soldier. Hers had a tag that said Freemansland Transit Authority.

Miss Orange handed the lady three tickets. The woman smiled and nodded, then counted the three of us as we passed by her, lightly tapping Riah and me on the shoulders. I shuddered at the touch, and Riah brushed off his shoulder as soon as we entered the car.

Scalers glide on one big, wide rail. You might think they'd be tilted at a crazy angle, since they go up and down the steep sharpfalls. But they're much like an ordinary rail car, with bench seats and windows. What makes them different is the big wedge underneath. That's the angled part, the portion that attaches to the rail that climbs the sharpfall, and the car is mounted to the wedge.

I didn't like being in the confined space with a bunch of smelly men. Actually, the men didn't smell as bad as Miss Orange. At least they had a natural scent, like glaffcrim, and the outdoors, and a little bit of sweat. But they were men. And that made me uncomfortable.

Every minute, on the minute, the loudspeaker let everyone in the station know that the car was loading. Then the message changed to, "Passenger car for Glaffit is now departing. Next car will load in fifteen minutes at Gate Two." The door closed, a recorded voice warned us to remain seated, and the descent began.

I know now that scalers travel at only ten kilometers an hour, but at the time, it seemed we moved pretty fast. Having climbed around on the sharpfall my whole life, I knew how high and how steep it was. In all my rambling, I'd seldom gotten more than halfway up. But now we were traveling from the very top to the stillwater below in just a few easy minutes.

Though foreign and generally unwelcome, City technology was impressive.

At the bottom, the men motioned for the three of us to exit first, so Jeriah and I gathered our bags, Miss Orange her briefcase, and we stepped out onto a platform. A uniformed woman welcomed us to Glaffit as we moved past her into a station much like the one at the top.

More people. Why were there so many of them? Through a window, I caught a glimpse of the stillwater sparkling in the sun. And it was warmer here. Once we escaped the walls of the station, it would be delightful.

I again contemplated jumping into the water at my first opportunity. I could hold my breath a long time, and I was good at Stealth. No, I was the best at Stealth. I could dive deep, swim away under water where no one could see me, and be out of sight before I surfaced. Once I was gone, they'd never be able to find me.

And I'd never see my brother again.

I gritted my teeth, gripped my bag, and followed Miss Orange out of the station.

WE SAT ON A bench at the end of the pier to wait for the ferry and bask in the sun. The men who had ridden the scaler with us took off on a boat of their own. Several bloomfish cruised about, looking for handouts. The sun sparkled on the water's surface like laughter. Koolos cut graceful arcs through the air, feasting on insects and freedom.

Though Miss Orange hadn't said much the whole time, something seemed to come over her as the fishy breeze made her prim coif relax. Leaning against the bench back, she stretched out her legs. "I grew up on Glaffit, you know."

I wouldn't have acknowledged such an outlandish statement, but Jeriah was apparently more curious than I. "You're not from the City?"

She shook her head. "No. I went to school in Center City, but I'm Freemansland born. After I got my certification, here's where I asked to serve. And they were glad enough to let me. Not many people request a posting here."

Riah said, "I don't know why anyone would want to live anywhere else."

But my thoughts ran more toward, *Good. We don't need anyone else here.*

Now that her words were loosed, they poured out like the stillwater's overflow after a storm. "In fact, I grew up on your uncle's plantation. In the workers' stacks. My father was one of his employees."

That got the complete attention of both of us.

"I wasn't much older than you two when he was attacked by gracious fowl. By the time they got the birds off him, there wasn't much left."

Riah spoke my thoughts. "I thought they were supposed to be polite."

"Birds are never polite. People just misinterpret their habits, seeing their actions in terms of human behavior."

Riah grunted. I guess he couldn't think of anything to say. I knew I couldn't.

"Your uncle made some changes after that. He keeps them in individual pens now, so they can't gang up on a person." Her accent slipped into a Freemansland cadence. "And he killed the birds that killed my pa. That must have cost him plenty, too. Those gracious fowl are worth a ton of money. And he didn't ask the City for permission, he just did it, then reported it afterward."

She bent and pulled off her shoes. "Your uncle is a good man. And your aunt is kind. They'll do right by you."

It sounded reassuring, but she'd probably made the whole thing up. "We supposed to believe that slotting lie?"

She turned her blue gaze on me for the first time. "You frighten me, Jemma." But she didn't look scared.

"No, I don't."

"Yes, you do. Because you remind me of another girl I tried to help once, not too long ago."

More lies, no doubt. "Did she try to kill you or something? You scared I might succeed?"

She shook her head and looked down at her feet, which she flexed as if they pained her. "I should have said I'm afraid *for* you, not *of* you."

That made no sense. Even if it did, I wouldn't have believed a word she said. I just glared at her.

"Like you, she was a stellasede."

In the hospital, when they explained about all the parasites, they told me about the stellas worm. It lives in the stillwater and comes in through one of the holes we all have in our heads. You know, the eyes, nose, ears. Then it'll slowly work its way into your brain. Before it embeds itself, the proper medication can kill it. But once it's buried in the brain tissue, there's no getting rid of it. As was the case with me.

"Yeah, so what?"

Miss Orange pursed her lips before answering. "She was brilliant. Had more potential than a sunny day. I worked with her closely, wanting to help her realize that potential. But a couple years later, after she went to the Academy—"

A small boat came into view then, and she sat up straighter. "I want you to succeed in life, Jemma." She put her shoes back on. "But I won't get in your way. Won't get close to you, as I did her. Nothing personal, but I can't go through that again."

Jeriah squinted in the sun. "Did she die?"

"Everybody dies." Miss Orange set her bag in her lap, all business once again. "And stelli can lie dormant for years, even decades."

Riah frowned. "But did *she* die. The girl you were talking about."

The cuddy drew near, and Miss Orange stood. "Oh, look, here's your aunt."

Chapter 4

THE PLANTATION

ONE THING MISS Orange said was true for sure: Aunt Lanie was kind.

Not that I needed Cityslime to tell me that, for it was apparent from the moment I met her.

Okay, so Miss Orange wasn't exactly Cityslime, but she'd been slimed by the City, and she didn't seem ashamed of it.

Aunt Lanie, though, was pure Freemansland. Lean and energetic, with tanned skin, sun-reddened hair, an honest, un-made-up face, and eyes that took in everything.

She stepped off the cuddy boat onto the pier with practiced agility and greeted Miss Orange with genuine warmth. Riah and I stood watching, clutching our duffels. When she turned to us, her smile softened with sympathy, but—to my relief, at least, and I'm sure his as well—she didn't embrace us, as she had Miss Orange. She just shook her head sadly. "Kids, I'm so sorry about what happened. It's a terrible thing."

She shaded her eyes with her hand. "Sun's at an uncomfortable angle. Why don't we get in under the roof so we can talk without being blinded."

Miss Orange shook her head. "I must get back, I'm afraid. My part is to deliver the children and then return."

Aunt Lanie started to object, but Miss Orange interrupted. "I do need to get your signature on a few things, though."

Lanie waved toward the boat. "Then come aboard."

The vessel was small, but clean and new looking. We stepped down into the cabin, where Miss Orange set her briefcase on the table and pulled out a tablet.

Jeriah and I weren't sure what to do until Aunt Lanie gestured for us to sit. "I'll bet you could use a drink."

"Yes, ma'am. Thank you," said Jeriah, and I silently agreed, remembering that bottle I'd hidden in the swamp chicken shed. But when she reached into a refrigerated cabinet and pulled out small two bottles of some sort of dark beverage, I hesitated.

She smiled. "Do you like Allock? My kids love it."

I'd never heard of Allock, but what sent an icy rod of fear through me was that phrase "my kids." Miss Orange had neglected to mention that detail.

Jeriah took one of the bottles, and I copied his action. She had kids? How old were they? Were we expected to live in the same house with them?

I resisted the urge to dive into the water and swim away to freedom and instead turned my attention to the cold bottle in my hands. In Riah's and my experience, bottles were sealed with corks. We each studied the Allocks a moment then at the same time saw the words, "Twist-off cap." Sure enough, that's how it worked. I opened the bottle and gave the contents a hesitant sniff.

Aunt Lanie had already turned to Miss Orange for her explanation of the documents that needed to be signed. Something about agreeing to abide by the City's policies, complying with their regulations concerning health, safety, education, and so forth. Agreeing to periodic inspections, and certifying that the monthly stipend would be used only for the care and benefit of the children. Listening with trepidation, I sipped the Allock.

The drink was syrup-sweet with an interesting bubbly quality. I'd have liked it better with a good splash of whisky in it, but it wasn't bad.

The thought of that whisky gave me a longing that took me a little by surprise. The Cityslimes in the hospital used the word *alcoholism* like it was a disease or something. But what could be wrong with taking a drink to ease life's pains?

Then another thought surprised me, but in a different way: I didn't have any pain. Not physically, that is. Apparently there was no cure for the deep void, the ache I couldn't pinpoint but which stabbed me when I was alone, or when I wondered what it must be like to be loved.

Jeriah burped then expelled a long, "Ahhh."

I smiled. Maybe with time, that inner pain would go away too.

ONCE MISS ORANGE had taken care of business, she packed up, gave Riah a handshake and me a searching look, and stepped carefully out of the boat. Then she clack-clacked down the pier without looking back.

Aunt Lanie opened a bin and pulled out a bright yellow object, padded and flapping with straps. "If you're under age thirteen, you're supposed to wear a life jacket when you're on the water." She dropped it back in the bin and closed the lid. "But no one knows your exact age, so I'm not going to worry about it. If you want one, feel free to grab it."

Riah asked, "What's it for?"

She sat at the control and started the motor. "Keep you afloat if you fall in."

Riah and I both chuckled.

"Yeah, that's what I thought. The people who make these laws don't understand that in Freemansland, kids swim before they walk. One of you want to untie me?"

Riah hopped up and undid the rope from the cleat, then pushed off from the pier. The boat moved out into the stillwater and immediately picked up speed.

Between the wind taking our breaths away and the motor drowning out all other sound, we didn't try to converse. I'd never moved so fast in my life. A glimpse at Riah's face told me he enjoyed this new sensation.

He turned to me, and we both grinned.

Then my smile faded. Was it dangerous to feel happiness? Dare I be hopeful?

I narrowed my eyes against the wind and watched our aunt at the wheel, hair blowing like hurricane. Unlike the people in the hospital, with their sober faces and distant demeanor, she was a Freemanslander, born, bred and forever. And our uncle, if Miss Orange was to be believed, was as kind as our aunt.

But hope was an alien feeling, and I wasn't quite sure what to do with it.

※

ENCOMPASSING SOME FIVE thousand acres, Uncle Rhe's plantation was located on the southern face of Glaffit.

When I say *plantation*, you probably envision sprawling fields with rows of plants marching with military precision across a broad expanse. But this is Freemansland. That means Uncle Rhe's troops don't march across a plain, but cling to the sheer cliffs of the sharpfall. This makes a far different picture from the usual image of a plantation. It also makes for a lot of steps to climb.

We reached the pier in late afternoon. An arch overtop the entrance announced we had arrived at Moll. That was Uncle Rhe's family name, and it was the name of the plantation. Not Moll Acres or Moll Glaffcrim Company or anything like that. Just Moll. Just as it had been for generations.

It was a large pier, and probably a dozen watercraft were docked there. There was a second pier as well, for freight vessels. Barges went from one plantation to another around the stillwater picking up glaffcrim, which was then carried up to Coldclime, where the City kept a couple of massive ships called transport pads.

They were more like islands than ships. Though they floated in the water, they never went anywhere. Their function was to accept cargo from the barges, which was loaded onto planes, which took off from the pads' enormous flat decks and carried the product to City glaffcrim processors. Supplies from the City came in the same way, to be distributed on Freemansland.

These transport pads contained living quarters for the workers and their families as well as shops, medical facilities, and anything else the people could need. Most of the outside supplies brought in were for their use, or for the other foreigners living in our land. We natives had little desire for anything the City shipped in, as we got along just fine on what our own country produced.

There were four transport pads, and all of them floated in the stillwater on Coldclime. The City had built their government and administration offices on that level, as well as the hospital and the government schools. Matter of fact, the City had pretty much taken over all of Coldclime. They chose it as their base of operations because they liked its climate best. The lower levels were too hot and muggy, the upper levels, too cold. Like the juvenile dragon in the old children's tale "Little Goldenscale and the Three Marsh Bears," they considered Coldclime's temperatures just right.

Interesting as the plantation was, I yearned for Freedom, where you seldom saw any sign of the City. Though Glaffit wasn't as tainted as Coldclime, the busy docks and bustling commerce on the stillwater spoke of the invaders' presence.

Once our boat was secured in the slip, Riah and I grabbed our duffels and followed Aunt Lanie down the pier and under the arch. "Welcome to the land of Moll," she said. "I know this is a tough time for you, but I hope you'll both be happy here."

I let Jeriah answer for the both of us. "Thank you, ma'am."

Just past the arch, a stairway cut from the rock climbed the sharpfall. Not your ordinary stairway randomly hacked into the wall, but a nice one. Deliberately designed with broad, even steps, and even a sturdy handrail. A rock wall separated the stairs from the scaler track. The open-sided car at the bottom near the other pier indicated that it was used for cargo. Though the car was flat and big enough to drive a truck onto, it had a row of bench seats as well. I suppose we could have asked to ride instead of walking, but I was glad Lanie chose to go on foot. I'd been cooped up for too long and relished the exercise.

We took a flight two steps at a time, turned at a landing and went up another flight, back and forth up the steep side. Before long, Aunt Lanie quit skipping steps and climbed at a more leisurely pace. "You two can run on ahead if you'd like, but I have to slow down."

We took her advice and strode past her. I don't know about Jeriah, but I enjoyed the exertion. Three landings later, I'd worked up a good sweat and was out of breath, but nothing hurt. Nothing! We paused to lean on the rail and take in the view while our aunt caught up with us.

The stairs we'd just followed zigzagged below us like a kinked chain. Below that, the two piers extended, arm-like, across the gleaming stillwater. In the distance, a barge lumbered toward the lowering sun. The fronds of a cluster of tailfluke fern exploring the edge of the landing tickled our toes that hung over the side. Our feet were unconfined at last, for we'd removed our shoes and stuffed them into our duffels soon after boarding the cuddy.

A little red-faced, Aunt Lanie rounded the turn to the landing where we stood. "If you want to go through the main entrance, keep climbing the stairs. Personally, I prefer the back door. If you'd like to go that way, follow the path." She gestured toward a well-worn track from the landing into forested gloom.

A path to the unknown was usually my choice of routes, and Riah's too, so we opted for the shady way. As we followed Aunt Lanie through a break in the railing and into the trees, our feet welcomed the cool earth beneath them.

The trail angled steeply upward for maybe a hundred meters, then made a tight bend and continued up in the other direction. The fun part was the way it was carved out of the mountain, like half a tunnel, with a wall curving over our heads on one side but open on the other. The trail was wide enough for all three of us to walk abreast, though it narrowed when it turned, and we had to go single file.

Eventually, a break in the trees ahead hinted that we were near our destination. Sure enough, we soon emerged, huffing and puffing, into a clearing and our first sight of our new home.

~ **Chapter 5** ~

THE LAND OF MOLL

I SAW SO MANY new things that day I had no brain to spare to consider this observation, until later. But that night when I went to bed—on a mat on the floor rather than an elevated bed—I found my mind going back to what had been, until then, the best day of my life.

THAT FIRST BEST day had been the time I helped Pa with his dragoning.

He usually went alone, because that's the kind of guy he was. The loner-type. And also, he didn't like to split the profits.

But this time he needed help, because he'd slipped on the sharpfall earlier and broken his leg. A bad break, the kind where the bone pokes through. And those don't heal up none too quick.

He hated sitting around doing nothing, staring out at the stillwater. And then, while he was still laid up but on the mend, two days in a row he saw a couple dragons floating by. How could he not go after them?

Besides that, he was out of money, thanks to having to go to the doctor to set his leg. So of course he had to go dragoning. But he couldn't do it alone.

Jeriah couldn't help, because he was puking-his-guts-up-and-squirting-out-the-other-end sick, thanks to eating sickle pods.

Well, first he picked a cherub horn and popped it into his mouth, thinking it was an ordinary finian mushroom. Soon as I saw what he did, I yelled at him, but it was too late, he'd already swallowed it. He panicked and asked what he could do, and I told him only thing I knew was to eat a sickle pod, and quick. That would make him puke up the cherub horn, hopefully before the poison got into his system. Death by cherub horn is pretty awful, by all accounts.

By all the accounts he'd heard, too, and he kind of overdid it with the sickle pods. Because it took us a little while to find some, and all the while he was sure he was dying. So when we finally found a sickle bush, he ate a handful of the pods when all he needed was one.

Between those, and the cherub horn he ate first, he was in a pretty bad way. And because I was worried about him, I hung around the house. Outside, so I watched over Riah without being seen.

By the time Pa decided to go dragoning, it was obvious Riah was going to live, but he was in no shape to help with the hunt. Pa was carrying on something awful about how stupid Riah was to go make himself sick like that, didn't he know better than to eat a sickle pod? (Riah never told him about the cherub horn, or he'd have been *really* mad.) Pa had been drinking, of course, and the more he thought about those dragons out there just waiting to be caught, how he needed the money but more than that, he needed help catching them, the madder he got.

He worked up a big noisy fit, and I was afraid he was going to hurt my brother, so I came up the rope ladder into the room where Pa was slamming stuff around, and said, "I'll help you."

You'd have thought I was a ghost or something the way he spun around and stared at me, his bloodshot eyes wide as he stood all hunched with his crutches. "Who the slotting Cityslime are you?"

Your daughter! I wanted to say. But I'd learned long ago his reaction to that statement. Not being one to ask for trouble, I just said, "I can help with the dragoning."

I knew I could, too, because I'd watched him doing it and knew how it was done. More or less, anyway.

"You? Help?" Pa's laugh held no mirth. "I'm poling, not trapping, so I don't need no slotting bait. Which is all you'd be good for."

I stared him straight in the bleary eye. "I'm as good a help as Jeriah."

Riah had never been dragoning with him, so there would be no comparing my skills with his. But I was as good or better than Jeriah at everything else, so why not this?

Pa cussed a good bit and hollered at Riah a little more for being stupid. Then he dragged his broken-legged self out through the door—the walk-through door, not the trapdoor I slipped back through—and crutched down the path to the dock, where I waited by the flatboat.

It wasn't easy for him to get in, but he finally did, and then he started yelling that this was missing, and that, and why hadn't I the sense to bring it down from the shed? I ran and fetched everything he asked for, and he cussed the whole time about how I was holding him up, he should have been out at daybreak. But eventually we got underway.

And I proved my worth. I could spot a den in the bank, an island, or a rock pile in the stillwater, and I could tell if it had a dragon in it. I could climb up on top of the den, and when Pa, in the boat just outside the opening, probed the den with his pole, I didn't get scared when the dragon got mad at being poked. When it stuck its angry head out, I was right there behind it and rammed that pike clear through its skull, though I had to throw my whole weight on it to poke it through.

The one time, the dragon came out too quick and its head was past me before I could react. So I jumped on its neck and wrapped my legs around it to hold myself on while I hacked at its head. It writhed something fierce, and even rolled me under the water a couple times, but I hung on tight, jabbing away, until I finally hit the right spot and the pike went through.

Pa hooted. "Did ya see that! City, but you're a crazy slotter!"

Right then, he didn't hate me. In fact, for just a little while, he was proud of me, I could tell.

Yes, that was the best day of my life—of my first life, that is.

But I was in my second life now, and this day—the day I entered the land of Moll—was the best in this life by far.

≈⊻⊱

BUT I'VE GOTTEN ahead of myself.

Remember how I said buildings in Freemansland are piled on top of each other up the face of the sharpfall? That's why we call them stacks, not towns. Well, there were a number of stacks on the plantation, and the first one I saw was the home place.

When we emerged from that delightful half-tunnel of a path through the trees, we walked onto a flat in front of the entrance. The rest of the world would call it a porch. The first stack hung out over it, supported by pillars. Flagstones paved the floor, shake shingles clad the face of the structure. Very civilized, but in a comfortably Freemansland way.

I'd never been in such a huge dwelling. From my present perspective I realize it wasn't large at all, but it seemed excessive at the time. There was a first stack, what you might call a front room, another for food preparation, and yet another for eating in. Imagine, a special place just for eating! Not only that, but there were *three* sections for sleeping. My aunt and uncle slept in one, their children in another, and the third, which Aunt Lanie called the guest place, was for Riah and me. "At least for now," she said. "After you've gotten more comfortable here, we hope you'll want to sleep with the other kids."

None of this made any sense to me, but if that's the way things were done in Moll, I might be able to get used to it.

As long as I was never left alone with boys. If there were any, I'd be watching out for them, and that was for sure. But when we first arrived, none of the cousins were anywhere in sight.

Aunt Lanie showed us around. Above the home place, the offices for the business were stacked. Those were quite busy, with several people at work doing I had no idea what. One of the sections housed the company store, where Uncle Rhe's employees could buy necessary items at a reasonable price. There were other structures related to the business as well, places that Lanie called quality control, the lab, and R&D, though I had no idea what those terms meant.

Above that, climbing to what must have been nearly the top rim of Glaffit, was a combination processing and warehouse area. It was bigger than the hospital we'd just come from, but it didn't have many windows in it.

There were roads all over the place, going from one building to another with steep slopes and tight switchbacks. The widest one, and most traveled, ran between the scaler and the warehouse. Some of the smaller roads, cut into the sharpfall, jabbed east and west to other parts of the plantation, which Lanie said was so big it extended from the top of the sharpfall to the stillwater below, and twice that distance on either side. Glaffit groves grew everywhere between the buildings and the far boundaries, where the workers' residence stacks were.

As she showed us around, Jeriah acted nonchalant, but I could tell he felt the same as I. Fascinated, but overwhelmed by the newness, the bigness, the businesslike bustle. It was so far removed from our former lives I found it hard to comprehend that Aunt Lanie and our mother came from the same parents. From what we could see, they didn't seem to come from the same world.

Not that either of us had ever met our mother. But if she was born to something like this, why live with Pa and Gran in a one-room shack on an island of fallen rock? Why live with a man who was drunk all the time?

The last place we visited was the warehouse—a towering place of story after story climbing the sharpfall, smelling of glaffcrim and sweet hairpine wood and machine oil, and echoing with chugging motors and busy voices. It was like a separate world of its own.

As we made our way back down to the house, Lanie told us the rest of the family would be coming home for dinner soon.

Jeriah and I exchanged glances. I'm not sure what was going through his mind, but I was thinking two things. First, *Do they have to?* I'd have been happier to never meet my uncle and my cousins. And secondly, *What's dinner?*

I think I told you that in my first life, I ate when I got hungry. That was typical on Freedom. Food was everywhere, free for the taking. Gran used to cook sometimes, but when she did, she just left the pot or the meat or the bread sitting there for people to eat whenever they wanted it. Of course flies and things would go after it too, so if people smelled it cooking, they tended to come get it before it was ruined. But there was no such thing as mealtime on Freedom.

That may have been what Riah was thinking. But what he said was, "Where are they coming home from?"

"Working," was her answer. "When the kids aren't in school, they go out with their pa and work on the plantation. That way they learn the business from the ground up, so when we're gone, they'll be able to take over. Your Uncle Rhe got his training that way, and so did his father."

"Oh," Jeriah said. Not sounding very excited.

"You both will have the opportunity to work, too," she continued. "But not right away. At first, we need to make sure you'll be ready to start school next month with the others."

I had let Jeriah do all the talking, having discovered long ago that you learn more if you keep your eyes and ears open and your mouth shut. But at that news, a word escaped me. "School?"

Aunt Lane chuckled. "You sound like that's a bad thing."

When neither of us answered, she continued. "Now, Jeriah, I know you've been to school. You attended the floating school, and you were in the sixth rank."

"Yes, ma'am, that's the way it was."

She turned to me. "And I'm told you have some education, too, though there's no record of your ever being enrolled in school."

I wished she wouldn't look at me. "I ain't got nothin' like education."

"Or so you'd like us to think." She chuckled. "But you can read, can't you?" She lifted her brows and cocked her head in a silent demand for an answer.

I shrugged. I'd whiled away many long hours with books Riah had brought me, but I didn't want to get him in trouble for taking them.

"And you know how to do arithmetic." This was almost as bad as being back in the hospital where everyone was always interrogating me.

"I don't even know what 'rithmetic is."

Riah gave an exasperated grunt. "She's been to school."

I gasped and balled up my fists, ready to punch him, but he went on. "We might as well tell her, Jem. It don't matter no more. We're startin' over here, remember?"

Maneuvering between us, Aunt Lanie put a hand on each of our shoulders. "That's right. You're starting over here. And I'm not accusing anyone of anything. I just want to know what point you'll be starting from."

About the time I'd had enough of being touched, she removed her hand. "So tell me about going to school. Why the big secret?"

Pa's ranting echoed in my ears. *You're dead, you hear me?* I never understood why, but that's what he always said.

When he spoke to me at all. Most of the time he ignored me.

Aunt Lanie asked again. "Jeriah? Can you tell me?"

He gave me a sideways glance, and I glared at him. I knew he was going to tell her.

He did. "I used to teach her sometimes. I'd show her what I was learning. I taught her to read and stuff. But then she started coming herself sometimes."

Aunt Lanie seemed surprised, but to my relief, she never looked my way. "They let her come as... your guest?"

"No, she just showed up one day. Swam out to the school boat and sneaked around at first. Then one time the teacher saw her—"

My face flamed with embarrassment at the memory of being discovered. "She made me wear clothes."

Aunt Lanie made a choking sound. I think she started to laugh but tried not to. If I could have taken off and hidden right then, I'd have done it. But where could I go? I didn't know this place. And there were people everywhere...

Lanie put a gentle hand on my arm. "It's okay, hon. You're safe here."

Hon? My breath caught. No one had ever called me that before.

"I snuck into the class when her back was turned—" I hadn't intended to explain, but that was my voice speaking. "And slipped into the corner where I'd hid before. Except there was a can there. You know, the kind people throw stuff in that they don't want?"

"A waste can, yes." Aunt Lanie's tone was relaxed. Accepting.

"And I bumped into it. And she turned around and saw me." It had been an awful moment. But as I confessed it to Aunt Lanie, the agony seemed to lose its intensity.

Aunt Lanie spoke gently. "And she let you stay?"

"Only if I put clothes on. I didn't have none, so she gave me a dress."

Aunt Lanie nodded. "That was nice of her."

"She showed me where she kept it in a cabinet in a storeroom. Said next time I came, I should put it on before I came to class."

"She sounds like an understanding person."

"I guess so."

We rounded the last bend before the house, where Uncle Rhe sat outside the door on a tube bench, chewing an occabot stick. He spat out a wad of the green goo, then looked up at us and smiled.

Aunt Lanie beamed. "Oh, good, they're home. Time to meet the rest of the family."

❧ Chapter 6 ❧

WE HAVE COUSINS

WHEN UNCLE RHE stood up, he wasn't much taller than Riah and me. And that was before that growth spurt we had after we got to Aunt Lanie's house.

It wasn't just me who'd had parasites—Riah did too. We both had enough to keep us from growing to, as Dr. Pigeon said, our full potential. Once those were killed off, we made up for lost time.

I doubt Uncle Rhe had parasites, but he wasn't very big despite being almost forty years old. His clear blue eyes, barely higher with ours, crinkled in the corners when he smiled. His hands were hard and dry, and his grip was firm when he shook our hands. He even shook mine, though I didn't much like it.

His voice was deep for such a small man. "Welcome to Moll. What do you think of your new home?"

I wasn't ready to call it home yet. Doubted I ever would be. Maybe I could persuade Riah to go with me back to my cave. The two of us would be fine there.

That must not have been what Riah was thinking, though, because his answer to Uncle Rhe sounded sincere. "We like it fine, sir. Never seen anything like it."

Uncle Rhe grinned. "There *is* nothing like it. Oh, there are other glaffcrim plantations, but none so modern. We're the most productive in the world, and we have the happiest workers. It's a fact, young man. I'm rather proud of the place, and it's a pleasure to welcome the two of you. I hope you'll enjoy your time here, and maybe learn a thing or two that will help you on your way, wherever you go from here."

He turned his gaze to me as if offering me the chance to say something. When I didn't, he showed no offense. Merely hollered over his shoulder, "Kids! Come meet your cousins!"

I'd been hearing them, and I could tell Jeriah had too, from the way he looked toward an opening in the wall behind our uncle. Children's voices, laughter, and splashing told us the kids were getting cleaned up.

City people think Freemanslanders are uncouth because our customs are different from theirs. But at least we have more sense than to have bathrooms in our living quarters. What City people call a bathroom, we call an ablution, and ours is outside where it belongs.

In our old house on Freedom, the ablution wasn't actually a structure. More like a hole in the ground a ways off from the house where we'd take care of business, hidden from view by piles of rock. Sometimes, if it was storming and we didn't want to go out, we'd use the hole in the middle of the floor. Everything went onto the dock beneath, but the rain just washed it off, so it didn't matter.

Here at Aunt Lanie's, the ablution was a separate building on the far side of the patio.

"Coming, Pa!" a girl's voice said, and a moment later, three kids skittered out through the doorway.

Aunt Lanie stretched an arm toward them. "Kids, come meet your cousins, Jeriah and Jemima." She gestured in our direction. "They're twins, about a year older than you, Daree."

When the children approached, Aunt Lanie put her hands on the girl's shoulders. "This is our oldest, Daree. She's ten."

The girl's, "How do you do? I'm very pleased to meet you," was well rehearsed and unconvincing.

"Hi," grunted Jeriah.

Lanie moved one of her hands to the boy beside her. "This is Arn, who's nine. And this little guy—" she ruffled the hair of the youngest—"is Kane. He's not quite six."

The boys regarded us with curiosity. Arn repeated the phrase Daree had chanted, and Riah gave him another grunting response. But Kane bounced around like a kyukur cub in front of Jeriah and me. "I'm taller than you, when I'm on stilts. Can you walk on stilts? I'm really good on them, I hardly ever fall off, they make you really tall, I'm even taller than Pa when I'm on stilts."

Uncle Rhe grabbed his shirt and pulled him back. "Down, boy. Let the kids breathe."

Aunt Lanie shook her head, her expression amused. "You can show them the stilts later. Right now, we'll let them get washed up, then we'll all go in for dinner."

Riah and I exchanged glances. Dinner—was that a meal? And were we expected to wash our hands and heads and pray, like Gran did, and Mayne? No, the kids didn't have wet hair, so maybe we were just supposed to wash our hands.

Riah nodded. "Thank you, ma'am." He headed for the ablution, and I followed. We'd find out exactly what *dinner* meant when we went into the house. For now, I'd wash my hands, but nobody could make me pray.

I'D NEVER SAT to eat with other people around a table before, nor had I ever heard of what Aunt Lanie called *table manners*. It was all very odd. And embarrassing for Riah and me, as we had no idea what we did that our cousins found so amusing.

Our aunt and uncle didn't allow them to laugh at us, and their instruction was gentle and clear. Nevertheless, it was humiliating to think the way we'd been eating our whole lives wasn't good enough for the high-and-mighty people of Moll.

Actually, we did *everything* wrong, not just eat. But our lack of training was most apparent at the dinner table. How are you expected to chew your food if you can't open your mouth? If your nose is running, why can't you wipe off the drip on your hand? And speaking of hands, why can't you touch your food with them? Whoever came up with the idea of eating with utensils should be weighted down with a sack of rocks and thrown into the stillwater. What's the point of washing your hands before eating if you aren't going to use them?

If not for all these new constraints, I might have enjoyed the food. An employee named Brin had prepared it all, and once we'd assembled in the dining room and sat in the seats Aunt Lanie directed us to, Brin carried in a procession of bowls and platters containing an amazing variety of things. I thought it must be a feast for some special occasion, but I later learned they always ate that way.

One platter contained pieces of fish. Though they were cooked, it had a good flavor. There were also two kinds of vegetables, as well as fruit and bread.

The adults had wine, but us kids had some nasty white stuff to drink. Uncle Rhe encouraged Riah and me to try it. "Sheep's milk is good for growing kids. Scrawny as you two are, it looks like you could use some."

We exchanged glances. We knew what milk was. It's what mother animals fed their babies. And human mothers, too, if they could. When we envisioned where milk came from, and especially the vessels from which those baby animals drank, it struck us both as enormously funny. But apparently it wasn't polite to laugh at the table, so we stifled our amusement behind our hands.

Until Aunt Lanie said gently, "If you must wipe your mouth, use your napery, remember?"

Best way to keep from laughing is to think about something awful, so I thought of Ibro. That sobered me up right quick. And the knowledge that the other kids were drinking milk and didn't seem to mind it made it possible to pick up the glass and take a sip.

I almost spit it out. As it was, I choked and dropped the glass, spilling that nasty stuff all over the table, the cloth that covered it, and everything in the vicinity.

Who covers a table with a cloth, anyway? In my limited experience, the only thing cloth did was get wet, dirty, and smelly. Houses were cleaner without it.

By the time dinner was over, I was ready to crawl away and hide, but Aunt Lanie kept us busy. First, all us kids cleared the table and helped Brin clean up. It would have been a lot of work for one person, but it wasn't so much that Brin needed five to help her. So mostly, Riah and I did what we were told, Arn pitched in too, Kane made a pest of himself, and Daree stayed off to the side, watching. Every time I looked her way, she was staring at me with contempt.

Or maybe I misinterpreted her expression. I never could figure that girl out. She wasn't exactly cruel, but neither was she friendly. When she spoke to me at all, it was with careful civility, strained and formal. Even though we shared the same living space for a few years, I've always considered her a stranger.

Once the kitchen was clean, Brin went home for the evening, and our cousins entertained us outdoors. Kane brought out those stilts and insisted Riah and I both try them. Arn produced a ball, and he and Daree played a game that involved throwing and catching, bouncing the ball on the ground or against the wall, and jumping over it on the bounce. While waiting for the boys to take their turn on the stilts, I watched the game and figured out how it was played, but they never asked me to join them.

I wandered around the patio, admiring the view, wondering where all the roads and paths led, and mostly, how I might have the opportunity to explore on my own. And maybe never come back. Because, as much as Aunt Lanie tried to make me feel welcome, I didn't. Between her and Uncle Rhe, though, there was always at least one careful eye on me, so I didn't make an effort to slip away. But their vigilance didn't keep me from thinking about it.

When dusk fell, Aunt Lanie had us all get ready for bed. This involved more cleaning up, including brushing our teeth, a chore we'd been taught in the hospital. We also changed into clean clothes—nightclothes, they called them. They didn't look much different from what we wore during the day, but they were only for sleeping in, a precaution that kept us from getting what Aunt Lanie called our "daily dirt" in our beds. Then, in the light of electrical fixtures similar to what we'd seen in the hospital, we were allowed to sit on our mats and read for a while before it was time to sleep.

All the constant to-do about keeping clean seemed pointless, but I liked the reading part. Uncle Rhe took Kane in another room and read aloud to him, and the rest of us each chose a book for ourselves. There were bookcases in all three bedrooms as well as one in the living room, and all of them were filled. The prospect of working my way through those books one by one was almost enough to make me reconsider leaving.

It had been a long day, and I had a hard time keeping my eyes open. So I wasn't disappointed when Uncle Rhe came upstairs carrying a sleeping Kane, laid him on his mat, and told the rest of us it was time to close our books and go to sleep too.

The three cousins each had a corner of their stack, and Riah and I lay close to one another in ours. Though the stack had no window, a lamp at the top of the stairway kept it from being as dark as a cave. The mat was thick enough that the hard floor beneath didn't dig into my bones, but it was firmer comfortable than the off-the-floor bed in the hospital had been.

And there were no bars, no straps. Nothing keeping me there.

I thought of the wine rack in the area where we'd eaten.

Uncle Rhe and Aunt Lanie were still up downstairs. In a conversation between themselves earlier, they'd said something about doing some paperwork for the business that evening. But sooner or later they'd be finished and would go to bed too. I'd wait until they came upstairs and settled in. Once they were asleep, I'd slip down the steps and take a sip or two of that wine. Not enough that they'd notice any was gone, but enough to satisfy my craving.

Then I'd come back and wake Riah. We'd sneak away together. We were both good at Stealth, and we'd have all the rest of the night to travel before anyone looked for us. I was sure, once I woke him up and got him downstairs to talk, I could persuade him to go.

Maybe I'd steal a couple bottles from the wine rack. And books. Not too much to carry, just a few. I envisioned Riah and me on Freedom, living in my cave behind the waterfall. We'd let Mayne find us, but nobody else would know we were there.

We'd hunt and forage for food. Steal wine or whisky or books when we wanted them. And no one would tell us we couldn't eat with our hands, or make us drink milk, or glare at us like we were creeping slime molds.

And then Aunt Lanie turned on the light. "Good morning darlings!"

❦ Chapter 7 ❧

JUMPING AHEAD

OUR THIRD YEAR with aunt Lanie, she sent us to the government school on Coldclime. It was nothing against us, because she and Uncle Rhe sent the other kids there too, when they were old enough. They wanted us all to get the best education, gain the knowledge that would enable us to succeed in life.

In other words, to be indoctrinated in the City way of thinking.

So, toward that end, she bought us new, bigger duffels, new uniforms—and for the first time in our lives, cold-weather jackets—and took us to the scaler station. Uncle Rhe wasn't there to send us off, but Aunt Lanie had tears in her eyes when she said goodbye. She hugged us. Even me.

And though I still hated to be touched, I hugged her back.

This wasn't the first time we'd been up to Coldclime since coming to Moll. We went for medical check-ups, or to see one City official or another at Children's Services. However, this was the first time we went unaccompanied. Aunt Lanie took us only as far as the entrance to the scaler. Once we boarded it, we were on our own.

After almost three years off Freedom, I still dreamed about going back. Nowadays, though, I seldom seriously considered it. My thoughts were mostly fantasies.

We drew no attention to ourselves. Those of our fellow scaler passengers who noticed us nodded pleasantly or smiled. We wore school uniforms, clean shoes, and neatly trimmed hair, and our manners were perfect. People thought we were good, respectable kids.

As the car slowed to a stop at the station, I leaned toward Riah and muttered, "We should have gone down one level, not up."

When he didn't answer, I added, "We still can, you know."

Without looking at me, he bent and pulled his book satchel from its rack under his seat. "Shut up and move."

I shrugged and did as he said. I didn't want Freedom badly enough to go alone.

We exited the scaler with the crowd and allowed ourselves to be swept toward the station doors, where a cold wind fired volleys of rain.

Joining the other travelers under the porch roof, we rummaged in our bags for jackets and umbrellas. These we respectively donned and unfurled, then re-zipped and shouldered our bags and followed the herd onto the wharf.

I peered ahead at the signs over the individual docks. "Aunt Lanie said we need one that says east."

"Ya Cityslime. I ain't deaf, y'know."

A chuckle bubbled out of me. We hadn't been allowed to cuss in Moll, and Riah's casual step back into our old ways reassured me.

"I'm glad you're still Riah."

"Who else would I be, ya slotter?" Squinting against the rain, he pointed to a sign toward the end of the wharf that read, *Destination East.* "There's where we'll catch the boat that goes to the landing on the East side, where the school's at."

"Ya Cityslime. I ain't stupid, y'know."

His laugh warmed me despite the chill air. By the time we reached the dock, we were both laughing. As long as we were together, this new school might not be too bad.

IT TURNED OUT to be better than I expected, and also worse.

We boarded the ferry and paid our fare. After entering the passenger cabin to get out of the cold, we never budged until we reached the East dock. From there, we had no trouble finding the school stacks, because we'd been there before, when Aunt Lanie registered us.

Once on campus, we entered the Administration building in the lowest part of the center stack. We closed our umbrellas and dripped across the already-wet floor as we followed the signs to the room marked, "New Student Sign-In."

At the desk, we handed a woman our registration cards to scan. After nodding at the information on her computer screen, she handed us each an electronic tablet. "You'll find your class schedules already loaded, along with some instructions and important information."

We'd learned the basics of computers and personal tablets on Moll, so that didn't worry us.

Then she fastened each of our cards into a little holder that hung at the end of a lanyard. "Wear this at all times." She handed me mine then went to work on Riah's. "You'll need it for everything. To get into your dorm, sign in for each class, get food from the dining hall, even to do your laundry. If you lose it, we can reissue it, but it will create a lot of trouble for everyone. So hang onto this like your life depends on it."

Riah took the lanyard from her and put it around his neck. Aunt Lanie had already impressed upon us the necessity of keeping track of our card, so that didn't alarm us either.

It wasn't until the lady gave us our dormitory assignments that a cold wave of fear sucked the wind right out of me.

"Boys' dorm is on the south side, girls' on the north." She gestured as she spoke. "Go out the doors you came in. Then Jeriah, you'll head to the left. Follow the main road, and it will take you up to the boys' dormitory. If you don't want to walk all the way on the zigzag, you can take the steps to the top of the stack. It's a long climb, but it's quicker than taking the road the whole way."

She turned to me, smiling. If my expression revealed how stricken I felt, she didn't seem to notice. "Jemima, you'll turn right after you leave the Admin building. The girls' dorm is at the top on the north side."

I visualized the distance between the two, and my mouth went dry with terror. I nudged Riah, willing him to speak.

He got the message. "Excuse me, ma'am, but we thought, um, that we'd be together."

She glanced back and forth between us, her smile widening. "Why, of course! As first-year students, I'm sure you'll have several classes together, and you can see each other at meals and free time as well. But boys and girls are never housed together." I guess her pat to his arm was supposed to be reassuring. "Your sister will still be able to look after you, if that's your concern."

She winked at me. "Did your mother ask you to make sure he behaves himself?"

Obviously, she hadn't been apprised of our situation. When she went to touch my arm as she had Riah's, I jerked away.

And stepped on the toes of the girl behind me, who let out a yelp. "Hey, watch it!"

I didn't turn, didn't apologize. Just glared at the woman until that pasted-on smile melted into a look of alarm, and she flushed.

"Well, you each know the way—" She paused when her voice broke, then cleared her throat and pulled the smile back into service. "We hope you'll both have a profitable time here at Freemansland City Academy East."

She waved us away from the table. "If you have any questions after reading the provided information, your dorm master's door is always open." Turning to the girl whose foot I'd stepped on, she perked up. "Thank you for waiting, young lady. Do you have your registration card?"

I wasn't ready to give up, but Jeriah grabbed me and pulled me toward the doors. "She can't help it."

She can't help what? I wanted to scream, but there were people around.

"She's just doing her job."

I wanted to throw down that shiny new tablet and smash it. I wanted to punch Jeriah in the face for dragging me away from the person I *really* wanted to hit. I wanted to plant my feet and say, *No! I'm not going anywhere!* And plop myself down right there in the middle of the lobby and not move until someone—whoever made these stupid decisions—said Riah and I could have *all* the same classes, and sleep in the same room, and do everything together.

But everyone would look at me if I did it here. I'd have to wait until we were alone somewhere before I threw a fit. But throw one I would, because this was intolerable. I'd put up with Cityslime nonsense for the past three years, but this was going too far.

He let go of my arm but continued for the entrance with determined steps. Knowing I'd follow. That I wouldn't make a scene.

I tagged behind, hating that he was right.

I'd made up my mind to throw my tablet, duffel, and everything over the wall into the stillwater as soon as we got outside, just to make a statement, when Mayne strode through the door.

Riah couldn't have stopped more suddenly if he'd run into a tree. I took a step or two more, trying to figure out if what I saw was real or a vision.

It was real. It truly was Mayne, with merry blue eyes framed in long, dark lashes. The eyes were the same, but they no longer belonged to the same gangly kid, bare and brown from the sun. This Mayne looked more like a man than a boy, despite the school uniform and matching duffel.

A mammoth grin lit his face like a sunrise, and I swear his eyes turned a brighter shade of blue. When he spoke, it was with a new voice, manly and deep. "What the slime—"

The next moment he and Riah were hugging, and before I knew it, they'd brought me into the embrace.

And I didn't pull away.

So much for not making a scene.

AFTER MAYNE CHECKED in, the three of us exited Administration together. It was still pouring, but most of the walkway was under a canopy, so we didn't use our umbrellas.

Mayne gazed southward through the torrent. "I'm on the top floor of Residence B. Lady said it's this way. Is that where you are, too?"

I snorted. "Cityslime, no. You know what that 'B' stands for, don't you?"

His brows rose. "The letter after A and before C, I figure."

"No. It means Boys. I'm in the top floor of Residence G. That stands for Girls, in case you couldn't figure that out."

Mayne gaped. "You're not together?"

Riah shook his head. "They do things a little different here."

We'd come to the end of the walk where our ways diverged. "Our aunt was not entirely forthcoming with us on that part of the plan," I said.

Mayne chuckled. "Since when do you talk like that?"

"Since I been reading a lot, you slotter. While you been slimin' around the past couple years swimmin' an' fishin', I been improving my mind."

"Don't listen to her," Riah said. "She can't put words together like that herself, she's just quoting a movie. *Smooth Man Muek.* Ever seen it?"

I was embarrassed for Mayne because I didn't figure he'd ever seen any movie. At least, Riah and I hadn't before we went to Moll. "I'll have you know, I'm pretty good at putting words together when I want to. But even though Aunt Lanie didn't warn us about the sleeping arrangements, I don't blame her."

Riah and Mayne answered together. "You don't?"

"Slime, no. I'd have refused to come here if I'd known, and she'd have had a fight on her hands."

Riah nodded. "True enough."

"Now that I think about it, though, I'm glad boys and girls are separate."

"You *are?*"

Their expressions were so comical I had a hard time not laughing. "Yes," I lied. "Because, well... you know..." That bit about being good at putting words together? I'd lied about that too.

But with Riah, I didn't need to speak. "I know," he said.

Mayne nodded. Either because he understood I was thinking of Ibro, or just had the sense not to ask what I meant.

I adjusted my bag on my shoulder. "Well, you slimy slotters. I guess we'd better go." I silently screamed, *I can't go alone!*

Riah's gaze caressed my face. "You're okay?"

"Why wouldn't I be?" *No! Of course I'm not okay!*

Mayne glanced back and forth between us, his eye lingering longer on me. "Want us to walk up with you?"

I scowled. "I ain't no slithering baby, y'know."

"No." Mayne's expression turned... I don't know. I couldn't figure out what he was thinking. "No, you're not."

He and Riah both hesitated. But someone had to take the initiative, so I turned and started down the road to the right. "See ya around, slotters."

Mayne's strange new voice had an odd edge to it. "I ain't no slotter, y'know."

I replied with a rude gesture, without turning. If I had to be alone, then I'd better start getting used to it.

I took the stairway that climbed straight up the sharpfall instead of walking the road that zigzagged the long way. Being in peak condition from clambering around the glaffcrim plantation, I was only a little winded by the time I'd reached the top, 516 steps later.

Only a little winded, but a lot wet. Not cold, thanks to the exertion. But I didn't like the way my clothes clung to me and wished I could take them off. I should have used my umbrella.

I mentioned our school uniforms before, but I didn't describe them. They were the usual City school outfits without alterations to accommodate Freemansland tastes. That meant boys and girls dressed much the same, with vests over blousy shirts, cravats, and pants for boys, culottes for girls. Every fiber of which was drenched when I stepped under the covered approach to the four-storied Residence G embedded in the hillside.

At the door, I pulled my lanyard out from under my blouse. I wasn't worried about it being wet, because when the lady said we should wear it at all times, she'd added, "Even in the shower." I ran the card under the scanner, and the door unlatched with a loud click. After a deep, fortifying breath, I entered.

Just inside the door, two girls sitting at a table looked up. One did, anyway. "Welcome to City Academy East."

The other girl giggled at a message on her tablet. "She says sure. Don't be late." She lifted her head and turned to me. "Yeah, welcome. Firstie?"

Of course I was a Firstie, what did she think? I nodded.

The friendlier girl, whose nametag identified her as Ixa Mun, smiled. "You'll be on the top floor, then. You can take the stairs, over there, or the elevator, which is through those doors and to your right."

The giggly one's nametag read Ajis Smoo. "Miss Pripp, the first-year advisor, is up there already. She'll tell you everything you need to know." She went back to her tablet.

"You're soaked," Ixa said. "Don't you have an umbrella? You should have received one with your uniforms. It's part of the kit."

Jeriah wasn't there to answer for me, and I couldn't find the words on my own. What would Aunt Lanie want me to say?

The stairway was closer than the elevator, so I spun and headed that way. "Got one, thanks." I almost ran to the stairway, then scampered up the first flight as if a dragon were after me, heart pounding more from the encounter than from the climb.

I'd only survived in Moll because Jeriah was there. How could I make it at this Cityslime school? All these people, all these buildings. Freedom two whole levels below. And with every step, I moved farther away.

As I climbed the remaining flights, I tried to pretend Riah was beside me. But he wasn't. And with every step, every dripping piece of me throbbed with the awareness that I was alone.

Riah had Mayne with him. But I was alone.

I was alone.

❧ Chapter 8 ❧

TOP FLOOR, RESIDENCE G

THE FIRST THING I heard when I exited the stairwell was happy girlish chatter.

The sound filled me with such terror I would have turned around and fled back down the stairs, if Miss Pripp hadn't spotted me and given a holler. "Ahoy, we have another passenger on deck!"

I turned around to see if she meant someone else. Even though she looked directly at me, and I knew there was no one behind me.

She laughed as she rolled in my direction—it appeared they fed the help well at this school—and extended her hand. "You're a natural comedian. I love it! Welcome aboard."

I clutched my duffle and backpack with both hands and tried to shrink within myself. She'd probably hoped I'd shake her hand, but when I failed to live up to expectations, she didn't seem to care.

"I'm Miss Pripp." She chuckled and put her hammy hand to her headband, from which sprouted a tall, narrow sign, like a feather, sporting her name. "But unless you're blind or illiterate, you've already figured that out. I'm the First-Year Advisor for you girls."

I nodded.

"I'll bet you have a name too."

I showed her my ID card.

She lifted her brows as she read, then pulled a tablet from a pocket in her voluminous sweater. "Freeman. Je-mi-ma. Yes, here you are. You'll be in Room 22." She slipped the tablet back in her pocket. "Let me show you." She started down the well-lit hall, and after a half-second hesitation, I followed. What else could I do?

"We have a bargeload of Freemans around here, but Jemima's unusual. Do you have a nickname?"

When I didn't answer, Miss Pripp turned, eyebrows raised. "Dragon got your tongue?"

That would be painful. "A dragon would eat my whole head."

She resumed walking as she threw back her head and laughed. "You got me there. So, do you have a nickname, honey?"

I shrugged. "My brother calls me Jem."

"Brother. He here too?" She stopped to consult her tablet again. "I thought I saw something about that... Yes. Jeriah. You're twins?" She peered at me over top of the device.

I nodded.

"And you're used to letting him do the talking, I'll bet."

She was hard to not like. I shrugged, making an effort to not smile.

She laughed again as she lumbered down the hall. "I'm glad you're here, Jem. You're a lot of fun. Anyone ever tell you that?"

I couldn't even dignify that with a shake of my head.

But she didn't wait for an answer. "Here we are, dragonfly. The lily pad whereon you'll rest."

And she thought *I* was strange?

We'd come to a good-sized room with beds along two of the walls. Off-the-floor beds, like City people use, not normal floor mats. Two double-decker ones, actually, which I later learned were called bunks.

Beside each bed was a dresser with four drawers. Four chairs were equally spaced along a wall-to-wall counter on the far side of the room. A computer sat before each chair, and above, a bookshelf ran the length of the wall.

In the midst of all that, two girls organizing their things looked up as we came in.

Miss Pripp addressed them. "Girls, this is Jem Freeman. She comes here from Glaffit."

I cleared my throat. "Freedom."

Someone in a nearby room called, "Miss Pripp!"

The Advisor hollered over her shoulder. "Just a minny, hon!" Then she glanced to her tablet before lifting her eyebrows at me. "Says here Glaffit."

I felt the other girls' stares, and my heart pounded. But facts were facts. "I'm from Freedom."

Miss Pripp shook her head. "*Born* on Freedom, maybe. But you've been living in Moll on Glaffit for the past three years. Don't deny it, I can smell the glaffcrim on you, and it's making me want a cup." Her face softened. "None of that's anything to be ashamed of."

Two girls giggled outside the door behind us. "Miss Pripp?"

She turned her head. "I told you, I'll be there in a minute." Then she directed her attention to my roommates, waving her tablet toward the tall girl with three braids sprouting from the top of her head. "This fine lady is Tosa Pape. She's always lived here on Coldclime, most recently in the town of Not. And this cutie—" She gestured toward the smaller one with the short boyish haircut— "is

Seena Freeman. From Freedom. Like I said, we've got a bargeload of Freemans on this floor, so you'll have lots of friends."

Miss Pripp lifted my ID tag still dangling outside my uniform and pointed to the number below my name. "As you can see, you've been assigned number RG-T22-C. In case you don't know, RG is Residence G—that's the building you live in. T means top floor, 22's the room number, and C means you get the furniture and computer marked C. All those are yours and nobody else's as long as you're here. So take care of them."

She patted the top mattress on one of the bunks. "All right then. This one's yours, hon. As you can see, the bedding's here in a stack, and you'll have to make the bed yourself. You might want to change into dry clothes before you do anything else, though. Take some time to get to know one another, settle in. Then we'll all get together for a Floor meeting in the common room at sixteen hundred."

She turned toward the girls in the hall. "All right ladies, what do you need?"

"My bed's short a blanket." The girl's voice was whiny and shrill as a scrimbird's. "And Exxie can't get into her computer."

"You only get one blanket." Miss Pripp waddled around the corner with her two twittering ducklings. "If you want another, you'll have to buy it."

Still clutching my book bag and duffel, I looked at my mattress and wondered if I'd be allowed to lay it on the floor.

Tall-with-braids spoke. "So you gonna just stand there in my way and drip on the floor? Or are you going to move, so I can finish unpacking?"

I looked her in the eye. Beyond that, I had no idea what to do.

"My suitcase is on the bed, and you're blocking it."

Sure enough, a bag lay open on the bottom bunk, half unpacked.

"You're still dripping."

I looked at the floor, but didn't see much water on it.

"And you're still in the way."

It seemed some response was necessary, so I said the first thing that came to mind. "And you still have a fruity name."

Tosa's eyes widened.

"Did you fall out of a tree?"

I almost thought she was going to hit me. But then the shorter girl spoke up. "Hey, Jem, why don't you put your bags over there on the dresser?"

My feet must have thought that was a good idea, because without engaging my brain, they took me to the dresser with two drawers marked C.

At the other dresser, Seena laid a pair of uniform culottes in a drawer.

Behind me, Tosa Pape made a hissing sound. "Slots. The girl's a certified crazy."

I set my bags on the dresser. Where was Riah? What was he doing right now?

Probably putting his clothes away in a room that looked much like this. He'd have roommates, like I did.

And he wouldn't be scared. He'd be making the best of it.

Somehow, I'd get through this. But only because I knew Riah was nearby.

THE LAST OF my dorm room's foursome arrived a short time later. Serep Stonn, who was from Seaview. I'd never met anyone from the first level before, but she didn't impress me. It took about a minny to realize she was like most of the others around here. Giddy, loud, and too wrapped up in herself to be aware anyone else existed.

That last didn't bother me, though. In fact, I'd have preferred it if *no one* was aware I existed.

A bell sounded at sixteen hundred, prompting all us first-years to make our way to the common room, a wide space filled with sofas, chairs and small tables. Miss Pripp stood behind the podium at one end. It looked like she was checking off our names on her tablet as we arrived, all the while maintaining conversations with several of the girls. How could she follow all those disparate threads of thought? The very idea made me dizzy.

Overhead, a skylight bulged upward like a gigantic bubble. The rain beat upon it and ran off in defeat, unable to pass through. The ash gray sky behind the dome matched my mood.

I found an empty wingback chair and sat in it cross-legged, careful to look at no one directly. I'd learned long ago that people are more likely to overlook you if you ignore them.

After this stupid floor meeting, we'd go to dinner. That's all I cared about. It's not that I was hungry, but I could hardly wait to find Jeriah. *So let's get this thing rolling and be done with it.*

After a few minutes, Miss Pripp called a couple of names. "Dove Freeman? Are you here? How about Droplet Plink?" She scanned the room. "Oh, there you are, Droplet, I didn't see you come in. Dove? Dove Freeman?"

"Here!" A girl hurried in from the hall. "I had to use the restroom."

"That's fine, that's fine. Okay, Firsties, looks like we're all here. Let's get started."

Yes, let's. I nestled deeper into the chair.

Miss Pripp went over the basics, everything we'd already been told at registration, what she'd told each of us when we arrived, and the information loaded on our tablets. Got it. Don't need it repeated a third time.

She asked if anyone had any questions, and there were several. All of which would have been answered if the slotting fools had been paying attention. I couldn't figure why Miss Pripp was so patient with them.

Only one question interested me, asked by Dove Freeman. "Do we have to use those high beds? I mean, um, can't we just, you know, put our mattress on the floor?"

Miss Pripp pursed her lips and shook her head. "No. Your parents are sending you here to get a complete education, and that means an education in the City way of life. We want you to be fully acclimated, so when you go into the world, you'll be ready to take on new challenges without having to learn the basics. That means wearing clothes. Wearing shoes. Having regular mealtimes, knowing the finer points of how to comport yourself at table. And sleeping in a bed, not on the floor."

Great. I already knew how to use a knife and fork. And I had no intention of going out into the world. Once I was of age and no longer a ward of the City, I was out of here. Me and Jeriah both. Back to Freedom, where we could shed all the City ways they were force-feeding us.

The longer I sat listening to all that sliming nonsense, the more determined I grew. Soon as the meeting was over, I was finding Jeriah and seeing if I could persuade him to ditch these uniforms, all the City rules and courtesies, and head for home two levels down. Even if we had no money for ferry and scaler fares, we could swim the stillwaters and climb down the stairways...

And freeze to death in the rain, which still pelted the skylight with more determination than I felt, suddenly, as I contemplated the cold, hungry distance that stood between us and Freedom.

With no further questions from the bubble-headed girls, Miss Pripp moved on. "There are fifty-nine of you on the Firstie floor this term, and you come from all over Freemansland. You'll get to know one another quite well before we're through, and many of you will end up being lifelong friends. So to start off, I'd like each of you to introduce yourself. One at a time, stand up, state your name and what level you're from, and give us one fun fact about yourself. I'll go first, just to give you an example. Then we'll start in the back corner over there, with Exxie, and work our way through the room as quickly as possible so we can all go to dinner. Okay?"

Most people murmured, "Okay," or "Sure," or "Do we have to?" But she ignored the rumbling and raised her hand. "I'm already standing, but let's pretend I just stood up." She swiveled her rotund self back and forth and waved to the room. "My name is Pippa Pripp, from Coldclime, and I like to do needlepoint."

Though no one clapped, she took a bow. "Now, it's your turn." She pointed to the back corner. "Exxie?"

One of the girls rose, giggling. "Okay. My name is Exxie. But you all know that already. Um, Exxie Aras. From Glaffit. And... I... like... to... um..." She put her hands to her cheeks. "What do I like? I like to, um, spend time with my friends."

She tugged the hand of the girl beside her. "Your turn. Stand up, Bee."

The girl beside her rose, Exxie sat, and Bee gave the required information—giggling all the while, like Exxie.

One by one, the other girls did the same. Stammering, laughing, acting like perfect imbeciles, all of them. I'd seen mud with more sense than most of them. But at least they all kept it brief, and before I knew it, Miss Pripp was looking at me. "Jem? You're up next."

From the first introduction, an undercurrent of silliness had begun to ripple around the room like the wake of a diving otter. By this time, the giggles came from everywhere, and it was hard to hear some of the girls when they spoke. I stood, but most of the others chattered amongst themselves and paid me little mind. I planned to speak quickly and quietly and get it over with, but before I could get started, Miss Pripp raised a hand.

"Girls! Shush, now. We're almost through. Pipe down so we can hear these last few." She turned to me. "Okay, sorry to interrupt. You were saying?"

The din simmered down, and most eyes turned to me. My mouth went dry. The power of speech fled. My head buzzed.

Miss Pripp winked. "Go ahead, hon."

I thought of Jeriah at the dining hall, looking for me. I needed to do this so I could get out of here. If I didn't get to him soon, I'd fall apart.

I took a breath. "My name is Jemima Freeman. I was born on Freedom but I been livin' on Glaffit. And I'm a stellasede."

Why had I said that? I'd meant to say, "I'm a twin," but that's not what came out of my mouth. Face flaming, I sat.

No one moved. No one giggled. They all stared like they were expecting me to transform in to a frothing lunatic or something.

Because that's what a stellasede did, right? Went crazy? Usually it was a slow slide off the edge, but sometimes it was sudden, wasn't it? I could be sane one day and a monster the next?

Miss Pripp's jolliness was absent as she consulted her tablet. Then she looked up at me, gave a slight nod, and addressed the group. "Jem has a clean bill of health, girls. The stelli are dormant, and the doctors assure us they show no signs of waking for years to come. We have nothing to worry about."

She drew a fresh smile from her quiver and shot it pointedly at the girl in the next chair. "Okay, we have only three more girls to meet, and then it's dinnertime. Your turn, Cee."

Tossing a worried glance my direction but not meeting my eye, the girl rose, smoothed her culottes, and proclaimed in a too-loud voice, "I'm Cee Mehom from Coldclime. I have eight sisters and three brothers."

She plopped back into her chair amid a chorus of exclamations and questions. It sounded like everyone was eager for the chance to leave the subject of brain-worms.

As was I, even more than they.

A stellasede. I never meant to say that. But later, I was glad I had, for it made the girls avoid me. It couldn't have worked out better had I planned it.

❧ Chapter 9 ❧

SHHH… THE STELLI ARE SLEEPING

IN THE DINING hall, I found Jeriah right away, standing in the food line. Even though his back was to me, and everyone in the room was dressed alike, I could spot him blindfolded.

He must not have been looking for me, though, because he was with three others, talking and laughing, acting like boys. Like he didn't care if I was there or not.

Standing a little apart from the rest, Mayne saw me coming and gave a wave, then poked Jeriah. "Hey, you. Jem's here."

Riah turned, and his expression showed relief. He'd been worried about me after all. I tried to close the distance between us without seeming to hurry, but in my anxiety, I practically ran.

One of the boys, about Riah's height but heavier, eyed me up. "What's this, you got a girlfriend, Freeman?"

"I got a sister." His gaze probed my face, checking to make sure I was okay. My mouth spasmed in a quick almost-smile to let him know I was surviving. "And she's spoken for."

My eyebrows flew up. What…

He clapped Mayne on the back. "You meet Mayne Dabo yet?"

A bolt of surprise flashed across Mayne's face, but only for an instant, and then he nodded. "That's right. She's spoken for."

I felt hot and cold at the same time. What in the world was going on here?

One of the other boys shook his head. "I ain't ready to be tied down yet." He nudged the boy next to him. "I want to taste a lot of samples before I buy."

The boy he'd poked was the one who'd given me the eye when I first approached. Still ogling, he grinned. "Yeah, I could sample that."

I was trying to decide which I should deliver to the slotter's vitals, my knee or my foot, when Mayne stepped in and blocked his view. "Spoken for, remember?" Then he took my arm. "What are you doing over there? Come get in line."

That started some grumbling behind us. "Hey, no cutting in."

Jeriah faced them down. "She's with us. We were just holding her place."

I shrugged off Mayne's hand out of habit—I never did like to be touched. But I wasn't annoyed. I'd finally figured out what was going on. He and Jeriah were protecting me.

Though no longer commonplace, it wasn't unheard-of for parents to contract marriages for their children in infancy, and the arrangements were as binding as an actual marriage. No, more so. Once the contract was made, the parents had no legal right to terminate it, and the children couldn't because they were minors. In adulthood, only rarely did the young couples go through the convoluted court procedure of dissolving the arrangement.

Modern Freemanslanders—the sort who sent their kids to City schools—were less inclined to follow the old ways, but the tradition was widely respected everywhere on the island. Jeriah's off-the-cuff lie was a stroke of brilliance, and I silently applauded Mayne for immediately understanding and going along with it.

But, grateful as I was, I didn't thank either of them. Just got in the food line with my "husband" as commanded, and if the kids behind us didn't like it, too bad.

Things were looking up for me. The girls, being afraid the bomb in my brain might explode any minute, would steer clear of me. And as far as the boys were concerned, I had "Do Not Touch" written all over me.

This might not be quite as bad as I'd feared.

NOT THAT I wasn't miserable. Because I was. Pretty much every waking minute during those years, I looked forward to being freed from the place, released from the City's control and allowed to make my own choices in life. But I did acknowledge that it could have been worse.

The worms in my brain provided more benefits than merely enabling me to keep my distance from people. Those little critters—the doctors said there were two of them embedded in my brain tissue, not just one, lucky me—secreted minute amounts of an enzyme called trioxydiosmicoline stellase. Among biochemists and doctors who study these things, the substance is affectionately called stella juice.

Once they start to stir, they'll produce more juice, which has fatal consequences for the brain that hosts them. Always. Fatal. But in the meantime, while they sleep, they snore out the faintest amounts of the stuff. And in such miniscule doses, the brain thrives on it.

Despite all the studies and tests and scans and probes, no one's been able to figure out the mechanics of what, exactly, stella juice does. But however it works, it enables the brain to perform quite remarkably in a few areas.

Like memory, for instance. Observation. Sensory perception. I always scored off the charts in those areas, and they said it was the stella juice ramping things up.

Which, of course, was beneficial where schoolwork was concerned. I say school*work*, but none of it was laborious. *Work* is climbing a steep sharpfall in the rain. Lugging buckets of water from the stillwater to fill curing vats. Hanging onto a writhing dragon while stabbing it between the eyes. Holding frustration in check when I wanted to lash out at the people around me.

Schoolwork, on the other hand, was entertaining, like puzzles and games. I doubt I'd have worked hard at it if it had been difficult, but since it came easily, I excelled.

What I hated was simply being there. I chafed at the cold climate, the indoor environment, the close and constant proximity to people. I hated being subjected to a barrage of Cityslime indoctrination from every direction, from the furnishings in my room to the clothes I wore, the food I ate, and the teaching in the classroom. Though geographically I was in Freemansland, I was immersed in City.

Hardly a day went by that I didn't contemplate taking off. So why didn't I? I wouldn't have admitted it, but the truth was, I was scared. Leaving school meant leaving Jeriah, which would have been like leaving half my body behind.

And he, apparently, was more adaptable.

I called him a sell-out to the City, but even as I threw the insult, I knew he remained as much a Freeman as I. To me, being a Freeman meant isolation from everything City. To him, it meant getting as much out of the City as he could.

"It's like eggs," he said one day when we were arguing about it.

It was the holiday after our first quarter-term, when we were back in Moll for two weeks. All us kids were in the glaffit groves with Uncle Rhe, pruning off sucker shoots. Riah worked on one terrace, I was on the next one up, when he found a bird nest that had blown from one of the trees. It lay on the ground, the eggs still intact, but the mother was nowhere around.

I'd clambered down to his terrace to see what he was talking about. When he said that, I snorted. "How's going to a City school like finding eggs?"

"Say you're hungry. You're feeling wobbly-legged. You know of someone who keeps swamp hens nearby, but you don't like the guy. Are you going to refuse to take his eggs because you want nothing to do with him? Or are you going to help yourself to them?"

I picked one of the eggs out of the nest. There was a time when I'd have eaten it without a qualm, then done the same with the rest. Now, though, I held it up to the sun. "That's a stupid comparison. If I were on Freedom, I could always find food." The tiny embryo was visible inside, and something in me ached at the thought that the little motherless thing would never hatch. "I wouldn't need that guy's eggs."

Riah rolled his eyes. "It's you that's stupid. The City's giving us everything we need. Why shouldn't we get all we can, since it's free for the taking?"

I set the egg back in the nest. Maybe the mother would come back when Riah and I were out of sight. "Because I hate the City and everything about it." I climbed back up to my terrace. "I want to go back to Freedom. I want everything to be like it was. I wish the City had never come to Freemansland."

Riah went to the next tree in his row. "Well, it's here, whether we like it or not. But look at this." He waved his arm in a gesture that encompassed the grove, with our cousins several terraces lower and some employees working above us. "Uncle Rhe and Aunt Lanie went to school and learned about the City. They do a lot of things the City way, but they're still Freemanslanders, and they have a great life here. I have the chance to do the same thing, and I'm not going to waste it."

I couldn't put my objections into words, so I said nothing. He knew I disagreed with him, though, and a few minutes later resumed the discussion.

"That's why Mayne's there, you know."

Of course I knew, but I didn't want him to think I considered the subject worth dwelling on. "What's why Mayne's where? What're ya talkin' about?"

"At school. He's there so he can get ahead, not have to live like the rest of his family. I mean, his mother works all the time, doing everything she can to send him to school. She doesn't want him to have to live the way she does, to die like—"

He bit off his words. Because Mayne's father, a stellasede, had died horribly.

"Yeah, and it's a little late for me to think about avoiding that fate. I was born on Freedom, and that's where I want to die."

Jeriah's face darkened like a whole sky full of storm clouds. "Well, then, go back. But I'm gonna let the City give me every slotting advantage they're willing to give. I want to— Well, I don't know what I want to do. But, what the slime, there's nothing wrong with having options."

What he didn't say echoed in my ears. That is, that I didn't have any options. Unlike him, I had a time bomb in my head, and it was ticking.

❧ Chapter 10 ❧

FROM FIRSTIE TO QUIRTSIE

AT FREEMANSLAND CITY Academy East, first-year students were called Firsties for obvious reasons. But the other classes had nicknames too.

Second-years, the Quirtsies, were named after Jico and Essa Quirt, the husband and wife who were Second Year Advisors during the first two decades of the school's existence. Legend had it that both were eager to wield said implement at the slightest infraction. Ever since, second-year students bore the name, if not the welts, of the quirt.

The third-year students were known as Worsties. This might have had something to do with their attitude toward the younger students, whom tradition dictated they treat as inferiors. Their arrogance made them the worst class in the school.

Fourth-years took the name Thirsties. Officially, this suggested their thirst for the brave new world that beckoned from beyond the portal of graduation. Unofficially, it had more to do with the fact that they'd reached the legal drinking age.

Not that anyone cared about legal. Nobody but City people, anyway. As long as we weren't disruptive, school officials looked the other way, for on Freemansland, alcohol was an ordinary part of life.

ONE DAY DURING our Quirtsie year, Aunt Lanie came to take Jeriah and me out to lunch. This was unprecedented. Unexpected. And therefore, suspicious.

We'd seen her often enough since being enrolled at the Academy, between the scheduled breaks as well as programs and events that families could attend. But she'd never visited us like this in the middle of the day, and I could think of no good reason why she would.

As arranged, we met her in the lobby of the admin building at noon. Jeriah and I had come from the same class, so we arrived together to find her chatting with Dr. Fish, the sciences instructor who also coached the swim team. He took off right away, but seeing him answered my questions as to the reason for Aunt Lanie's visit.

She smiled a greeting and embraced my brother, but refrained from hugging me. Perhaps my expression told her I wasn't in the mood.

She looked up at Riah, who'd grown noticeably taller in the two months since we'd last seen her. "How much time do we have?"

"My next class is in an hour and a half." Seeing I wasn't about to answer, he gave me a pointed glance.

I shifted the bag on my back. "Yeah, me too." It wasn't true, but I had time for lunch, and that's all she needed to know.

"Oh, good." She glanced at the big clock on the far wall. "Time enough to go to Tenney's, if that's okay with you?"

"Sure," Riah said, and the three of us headed out.

Tenney's was a trendy café just off campus, built on the sharpfall but with seating on a pier extending over the stillwater. Today, the crowd consisted mostly of business people and government officials. There were also two tables of Thirsties, the only class allowed to leave the school for lunch without an adult.

All three of us ordered the same thing—a fish sandwich with a side of deep fried bicio blossoms. We took our trays outside and found seats on the pier, with Aunt Lanie and Jeriah making small talk the whole time.

It disgusted me how comfortable he was with this new life. He could converse with anyone. All the school instructors seemed to like him. He had no trouble making friends. And even though he was only a Quirtsie, he'd secured himself a spot as alternate launcher on the grappleball First Team.

Though he still looked out for me as much as he could, I sometimes felt abandoned.

Once we got settled, Aunt Lanie turned her attention to me. "So how have you been doing, Jem? You and Riah have both passed me by, height-wise."

I shrugged and took a big bite of sandwich to avoid having to answer.

She popped a crispy bicio into her mouth. "Mmm, these are good today. Sometimes they're a little strong, but these are perfect."

"Ever have them stuffed with cheese?" Though Riah spoke with his mouth full, Aunt Lanie didn't correct him.

"No. I didn't see them on the menu. Do they have that here?"

He shook his head and finished chewing. "A friend's mother made some and sent them to her, and she gave me one to try. She says they're even better when they're fresh, but they were pretty good just as they were."

She. Of course. If you asked me, he spent too much time with the girls.

"I'll have to try that some time." Aunt Lanie turned to me again. "So, Jem, you're quite the star of the swim team."

Sure enough, that's what this was all about. "Yeah." I took another big bite. It's not polite to talk with your mouth full, after all.

Jeriah answered for me. "She wins every meet. Last time, she finished one heat so far ahead, she almost had time to get out and dry off before the others finished."

Aunt Lanie chuckled. "That's what I hear. We wanted to see you compete at West the other day, but things were crazy at the plantation and we simply couldn't get away."

"Doesn't matter." I shrugged.

"Oh, but we love to watch! I'm sure you'll impress everyone at Ellerja."

I stopped eating.

But perhaps all this requires a little explanation.

Because of the City's view that sports are vital to society, they required all the students to participate in a team sport. Learning the games in athletics class wasn't enough. We must also be involved in inter-scholastic competition. But with Freemansland being in the middle of the ocean with no land within nine thousand kilometers, travel to other schools was a challenge.

I was convinced that's why, about a dozen years earlier, they'd established another school in Freemansland—City Academy West. Not merely so they could indoctrinate greater numbers of Freemansland's youth, but also to provide us at East someone to compete with in sports, which we did several times every season. We also played against informal adult and youth teams throughout the island. But the highlight of the academic year was the annual pilgrimage to Ellerja, where East and West both assembled with dozens of other schools for a two-week orgy of athletic tournaments.

I knew that's what she'd been talking about with Dr. Fish. About how the coach had asked me to go and represent them at

Ellerja, but I had refused. At the very thought of leaving Freemansland, panic froze me solid.

I pushed my tray and sort-of inadvertently whammed it into hers, but she merely slid hers back into position and continued, smiling. "Your uncle and I have arranged to take some time off so we can leave the plantation and go to the games. We're so excited you've both been invited to participate even though you're only second-years. What an honor for the two of you! We wouldn't miss it for all the urexi in Umban."

I picked up my bag. "Then I hope you enjoy it, and I'm sure Riah'll make you proud. But I ain't goin'." I rose from my chair. "As you well know." Holding my bag aloft so as to not hit other customers in the head when I passed, I exited as quickly as possible.

Neither of them went after me. They didn't even call for me to stop.

But I didn't care what they did. I only knew I wasn't leaving Freemansland. Not now, not ever, not for anything. Not even to swim in an international competition, no matter how much of an honor it was. Even though I felt sure I could win it. For my life was in Freemansland, heart, body, and soul. Surely, if I ever left, I'd cease to breathe.

☀

THOSE OF US who didn't go to Ellerja remained at school, though classes were cancelled during the tournaments.

The games were broadcast live on the video screens in all the common areas. Because the time in Ellerja was seven hours later than in Freemansland, some of the events were played at odd hours. But curfews were lifted, lights-out rules didn't exist, and the dining hall remained open around the clock, enabling us to view whatever games we wanted.

Or none, if we preferred, though skipping them altogether was frowned upon, and I don't know of anyone who did. Even I watched several swimming events, and of course Riah's game. I say singular "game," because they never made it past the first round. The swimmers did better, with one of the boys and a girls' relay team bringing home medals.

It was routine for the other students to ignore me, but the cold shoulders were more pronounced than usual those two weeks. Everybody knew that if I'd been there, we'd have brought home more medals in swimming than any school at the event. No one could understand why I'd refused to go, and I wouldn't have explained if they'd asked.

After the games but before the athletes returned, we got together with Academy West for a big fancy dance to celebrate our medals. The gala had been discussed and prepared for since the beginning of the year, and at some point, I'm not sure how or when, it was decided that I would attend, escorted by Mayne.

The whole thing was preposterous. Me? At a dance?

I only agreed because—well, I guess there was more than one reason. For one, I'd refused to go to Ellerja, and after all that foot-planting and pulling back, I was running out of energy to resist. Also, I'd learned the year before that by the end of the tournaments, with no swim practice and no classes, I was bored. Going to the dance would break the awful monotony.

But the main reason was that Mayne and I were supposed to be almost married. And—by Freemansland tradition, not by City policy—I was expected to appear with him at functions like that. Although we weren't *really* promised to each other, it did seem wise to keep up the appearance.

So—and I roll my eyes as I say this—I shopped for a dress. First time ever. And shoes with heels—though not too high. Seena, my roommate of two years and the closest thing I had to a friend, showed me how to put up my hair and let me use her make-up.

I couldn't believe I was going through all that, but I did. And the result when we were finished? Well, when I looked in the full-length mirror, I almost fell over. I couldn't decide if I should grin with delight, or hide under my bed. It didn't look like me, that was for sure, and I wished Riah could see me. He never would have believed it.

When I went down to the lobby, Mayne was waiting. He must have come early, because I wasn't late.

Though he wasn't as tall as Riah, he filled out his suit nicely, and the way his blue eyes—no, not his eyes, his whole face—lit up when he saw me made me flush clear down to my toes, which were already aching from the shoes, but at that moment, I didn't care. I didn't try to understand why his look made me feel that way. I merely enjoyed the brief sensation without trying to dissect it.

We weren't alone, of course. Several other guys were there waiting for their girls, and girls waiting for their guys, and couples getting their pictures taken by various and sundry. When I came in the room, every single one of them, without exception, gaped for a moment, then averted their eyes.

Noticing their reactions, Mayne chuckled. It occurred to me then that I loved that sound, and always had. I couldn't help but grin back, and he offered me his arm, and I took it—don't tell me *that* wasn't a strange feeling—and went with him out into the night. Everyone's stares bored into my back, and Mayne must have felt it too, because as soon as we were outside and the doors closed behind us, his chuckle turned into a laugh, and my grin spilled into my voice, and the two of us strolled down the walk giggling so hard we had to hold each other up.

The dance was at Glaff Hall, just this side of the admin building and nearly at the bottom of the sharpfall. In the clear night, the lights below glittered with excitement as we made our way down the stairway, me in my idiotic shoes and Mayne slowing to accommodate my footwear disability.

Beyond the hall, a ferry blinked at the pier, delivering the students from City Academy West. As we drew closer, we saw couples approaching from the pier, and fellow East students trickled toward the hall from the other direction. A few more steps down, and we felt as well as heard the music from the hall. Yes, this was quite the party.

At the bottom of the long flight, I started toward a bench overlooking the stillwater, which sparkled with jewels of reflected light. "I gotta give my feet a break."

Mayne went with me. "We got all night."

I sat and took my shoes off. "Slot. They might look nice, but the slithery things sure are slimy." I rubbed one foot.

His chuckle, almost a giggle, danced softly through the night. "They've relaxed a lot of the rules for the event, but I don't think we're allowed to cuss like that even now."

"D'ya think I give a slotting City?"

"Same old Jem despite the new look."

I glanced at his profile—surprising how different it looked in the night, and how handsome. "You look good too."

His head swiveled my way, brows high. "Oh? Well, I didn't say you looked good. Just different."

"That's a relief." I leaned against the bench. But it was cold on my back, unprotected as it was in the low-cut dress, and I sat upright again quickly. "I'd hate to think you were complimenting me."

We sat for a while, listening to the music and watching the lights on the water. But despite my aching feet, I was restless. I wrenched my shoes back on. "I suppose we should go."

At the same instant, he said, "Let's not go."

"What?" we said together, and giggled. Yes, his chuckle could definitely be called that.

He spoke first. "I don't want to go in there any more than you do. So why do it?"

I gave a little tug at the skirt of my dress. "Because we're not exactly dressed for night fishing."

"Okay, so we won't do that either. How about a picnic?" He bent and picked up one of my feet. "Here." He removed the shoe. "Take these off. You won't need them where we're going."

I slipped out of the other and picked them both up. "Where are we going?"

"Leave 'em here. We'll come back for them." He turned and strode down the walk away from the hall.

Curious, I dropped the shoes on the bench and scampered after him.

❧ Chapter 11 ❧

QUIRTSIE TO THIRSTIE

MAYNE AND I sat on the end of the pier that connected to Tenney's dining area.

The café was closed for the night. With the moon on the other side of the island, only the stars above illuminated the black stillwater. A bucket of steamed rappu legs, bought just before the café closed, stood between us along with a bottle of wine. We didn't bother with glasses.

The bucket was nearly empty. For the past half hour we'd been leisurely cracking the legs open, plucking out the sweet meat, then tossing the empty shells into the water.

Mayne pushed the bucket toward me. "One left. It's yours."

He'd eaten more than I, so I didn't feel greedy taking it. I pulled out the leg and cracked it in half, holding it over the bucket to catch the juices. "I used to think it was weird to cook food, but I have to admit these are better than the raw ones we ate back then."

"Yeah, they are."

Mayne had given me his jacket earlier, because I was cold. I probably got rappu juice all over it, but it was too dark out there on the dock to tell.

We could still hear the music from the dance, if we listened. But we mostly blocked it out, giving our attention to the calls of the night gulls, the orchestra of insects in the sharpfall behind us, and the occasional splash as the tail of a risingfish slapped the water.

When the last shell was empty, I tossed it into the stillwater. Several fish, I couldn't see well enough to know what kind, stirred the water, investigating. I stretched out on my stomach along the edge of the pier so I could reach the water with the bucket, which I rinsed out and then filled.

"Hands sticky? Want to rinse them?" I set the bucket where it had been.

"Yeah. Good idea."

We both rinsed our hands and dried them on the remainder of the paper naperies. They always give you lots of those when you buy rappu legs, but messy as they are to eat, it's not usually enough.

When we were done, Mayne emptied the water from the bucket. He carried it to the dining area and left it on a table, and threw the used paper naperies in the trashcan. Then he came back and sat beside me—a little closer this time.

We sat in silence and watched the night gulls soaring in the starlight for a minute or two. Then he said, "I'm glad you didn't go."

"Hmm?" My mind had been wandering, and it took me a moment to realize what he was talking about. "To Ellerja? If so, you're the only one who is. Everybody else is mad at me."

"Do you care? That they're mad at you?"

I pulled up my knees and wrapped my arms around them. "No, of course not. Jeriah's not mad, because he understands. And you're not. I don't care what anyone else thinks."

He seemed to like that answer. Don't know why, but I got that impression. Then after another moment he broke the silence again. "I'm probably going next year. Coach said for sure when I'm a fourth-year, but probably next year too."

I wanted to say *I don't care what you do*, but that wasn't strictly true. So I grunted.

Then on second thought, I said, "So how come our grappleballers did so bad?" I'd watched the game, and it had been embarrassing.

"Coach said Freemanslanders are never good at grappleball." He pulled his knees up and sat as I did, with his arms around his legs. "Other places, the kids start learning it when they're little. By the time they're ten, they know the rules, the strategies, the tricks. When they develop physically enough to get the skills down, they already know all the mental stuff. But here, we aren't usually exposed to it until we come to the academy, so we're like little kids in big bodies. We're lost on the field when we're up against players who've known the game all their lives."

That made sense. "When we were in Moll, Riah used to watch it with Uncle Rhe sometimes. He knew a lot about it before we came here."

"Coach says that's why he's so good at it."

I nodded. "Next thing you know, the City'll make everybody on the island get a video screen, and kids'll be required to watch grappleball every Firstday whether they like it or not."

He picked up the bottle. "Wouldn't put it past them." He took a gulp and offered it to me.

I accepted. "So you like grappleball?"

"It's a good game. I like that it's really physical, but it's mental too. It teaches tactics and strategy, discipline and stamina, helps you develop strength and agility. As coach says, it's the best preparation there is for the military. And it's fun besides."

I almost choked on the wine. "The military?"

He nodded. "If I graduate high enough in the class, I have a chance to get into officers' school. And even if I don't get in, you get a better position in all the services if you have high marks from a City academy."

His usual slow, casual way of speaking accelerated with excitement. "I'll get career training in whatever field I want. With all the most up-to-date methods and technology. It'll all be provided by the City, I won't have to pay a nidir for it. In fact, they'll pay *me* to learn it. And if I stay in for ten years, I'll get full citizenship."

I could hardly believe what I was hearing. "You want to be a *citizen?*"

"Why wouldn't I?"

I'd have pounded on him if I wasn't too shocked to move. "Why *would* you? A slimy, slotting *citizen?* And how many countries will you have to invade and conquer during those ten years? Assuming you even make it that long without getting killed or something." He had to be teasing me. Surely he wasn't serious about this.

But he didn't sound like he was teasing. "The whole world's conquered already. Freemansland was one of the last, and we've been part of the Greater City for almost a hundred years. Now that the world's united, all that remains for the military to do is oversee it."

This whole conversation was too strange. I couldn't take it in. "You really believe all that stuff they teach us? That the City ended all wars, the whole world is at peace, and the government is wise and fair? You know what they did to us, don't you, blowing a hole in the island to get a foothold and—"

"I know what they're doing for us now. They're giving us technology and medicine, clean water, the tools to pull ourselves out of poverty and disease—"

"But they're the *City*, and—"

"And you'd be dead by now if it weren't for them. Going blind, half-starved—"

"There's plenty of food on Freedom, I never—"

"But you were too sick to eat much, and most of what you did eat, all those parasites sucked out of you. You were almost dead when they got to you, Jem. They saved your life." Emotion choked his voice. "And look at you now. You're smart—"

"I've always been smart." I didn't mean to sound surly. Well, okay, maybe I did, but he deserved it.

"At something other than Stealth, I mean." I liked the way the side of his face creased when he smiled.

I hadn't intended to brag, but the late hour must have loosened my tongue. "I'm still good at Stealth, you know. I've been all over this campus without anyone seeing me. Residence B included."

He lifted one eyebrow. "Really?"

"Really. In fact, I've been in your dorm room."

"You have not."

I proceeded to describe, in exquisite detail, the room as it was when I was there, right down to the smashed spider in the corner.

He gaped when I started listing the dirty laundry and other things kicked under his bed and interrupted me before I could finish. "Okay, so you're still good at Stealth." He shook his head. "And you *were* always smart. But the thing is, you're alive now. Which you wouldn't have been if the City hadn't been here. You'd have been dragon food five years ago."

I wanted to argue, but he was right.

"I know you resent the City for invading us, but thanks to them, you're alive. You're well-fed and healthy, you're beautiful, you're getting a good education—"

"What was that? I'm beautiful?"

He stared out across the water, and I watched his Adam's apple bob—up and down three times—before he spoke again. "You're an idiot, you know that?"

"It's you who's spouting crazy-talk, not me."

He unclasped his legs and sat cross-legged. "Okay, so we don't need to talk about that anymore. Except—"

The relief that rose at the first part of that statement thudded to the ground. "Except what?"

"What I was working toward was this. After the ten years, I plan to come back. I want to learn what I can, earn me some money, and then go back to Freedom."

"Now, that's more like it."

"'Cause I don't belong in the City any more than you do. Not for the long term, anyway. Just to learn stuff and bring that knowledge back home."

"You're not saying you want to teach at the Academy, are you? 'Cause you sound like one of the teachers."

He paused. "I'm not sure what I want to do, exactly. But I've got fourteen, fifteen years to figure that out. Whatever I end up doing, I know where I want to live."

"Freedom, of course." I pulled his jacket closer around me. "Why would anyone want to live anywhere else?"

He unfurled his legs and lay on his back, hands behind his head. "That's what I say."

I remained huddled. It was too cold to stretch out. "Freedom's a lot warmer."

When had the music stopped? I hadn't noticed when it quit, but it was quiet now, and the ferry that brought the kids from West was pulling away from the next dock down. "We must have been sitting here a while."

He lifted his head as if to listen. "Yeah. Looks like the party's over. Sorry we missed it?"

"Who, me? Slime, no."

"I love it when you talk dirty."

I laughed, more loudly than I'd expected, and covered my mouth. "Slots, you must get a drippy kick out of most of our conversations, then."

"Yeah, usually. But about Freedom. Remember that big old stone house the three of us found once when we were exploring? Way up top, almost to the next level."

I knew exactly what he was talking about. "Sure. Old Man Four Four and his wife lived there. Might be living there still for all I know."

"Whoa." He lifted a hand in a lazy *hold on there* gesture. "Old Man Four Four?"

"Yeah. Four Four Freeman. He was the forty-fourth Freeman to be born in that house. In that family, they didn't name their kids, they numbered them, and—"

"You're not going to convince me he was one of forty-four children."

I giggled. "Of course not. According to him, his great-great-grandparents or whatever built that house, and the family's been living there ever since. And every baby that's born in it gets a number instead of a name. And he was the forty-fourth. Did you know, a generation or so ago, they tapped into the stillwater above and have running water in that place? And they have a—"

Mayne sat up. "How do you know all this? We just saw it one day from a distance. You couldn't get all that from just looking at it."

"*You* just saw it one day from a distance. I already knew it was there. But I didn't tell anyone about it, 'cause they're kind of private, and I didn't think they'd like people to know about them."

"So that's why you dragged us away when we wanted to take a closer look."

I nodded. "They were nice to me. I hung around there sometimes when—well, when I needed someplace. You know, just a couple days now and then. I think they felt sorry for me or something. Or maybe they were just lonely for their own kids. 'Cause their son, Four Six, got killed by a dragon, and Four Seven fell down the sharpfall and broke her neck, and... I forget what happened to the rest of 'em. No, it was Four Eight who fell down the sharpfall. Four Seven died in infancy. And—"

"I get the picture. Why'd you leave them, then? You could have stayed with them. Or wouldn't they let you?"

I shrugged. "I'd never leave Jeriah. And I promised I'd never tell anyone about them, not even him."

"Hm." His attitude sobered, and the starlight glittered strangely in his eyes. "I guess you just broke your promise then."

I caught my breath. "I guess I just did." I took a deep breath, trying to sweep away the rush of guilt. "Well, it's okay, 'cause you're not going to go visit them or anything. You might know about them, but you'll leave them alone."

He seemed to relax. "No, they're safe. Unlike you, I'll never whisper a word to anyone."

I scowled at him.

"But that house captured my imagination. And when I say I want to come back and live on Freedom, I have that very place in mind. When we come back to Freemansland, you can go see if they're still there. If they're not—"

"When *we* come back? I ain't never leavin'."

WHEN THE WINE was gone, we walked for a while. But we weren't the only ones. Even though the dance was over, people were still out and about.

Mayne knew where all the popular make-out spots were and suggested we sneak up on a few couples and scare them. I laughed, thinking of several people I'd enjoy doing that to, but decided the repercussions wouldn't be worth it. They ignored me, so I'd ignore them, and we'd all get through school without bloodshed.

Before the sky paled into dawn, I found my shoes on the bench where I'd left them. Didn't put them on, though. Let them dangle from my fingers as I climbed the long stairway to Residence G.

"You don't have to go all the way up with me," I said.

"It's okay. Helps me stay in shape for grappleball."

I snorted. "Whatever."

The sport must have had him in good condition, because when we were almost at the top, he still had the wind to talk without gasping. "You know, if we really were betrothed—"

I giggled. Must have been tired. "I was just imagining your ma and my pa getting together to make the agreement."

He grinned. "Ain't that a picture. Yeah. If Ma ever gets wind of the rumor, she'll haul over here and transfer me to West quicker than you could say slime."

"And that's pretty quick."

We laughed all the way to the entrance. I swiped my card, and the door opened.

We stepped in. Or rather, I stepped in. He stayed outside. The guard at the night desk was watching.

"If we really *were* betrothed," he said, "it wouldn't be a bad thing."

His Adam's apple did that bobbing thing again, and I couldn't take my eyes off it for a second. "I guess it wouldn't." I glanced up into his sleepy blue eyes then looked away. "It was a fun night. Never thought I'd enjoy a dance so much." I headed into the building. "But I gotta hit the mat."

"You get a mat? I have to sleep in a bed."

I turned back and paused. "Figure of speech." My gaze slid up to meet his. "Well, good night. Or good morning. Or whatever it is.

It really was a good night. I mean, I liked it. Last night." I gave my head a shake. "I never did know what to do with words."

"You're a great dancer, though."

I turned away again, smiling, and the door closed between us.

It wasn't until I was halfway to my room that I realized I still wore his jacket. Dried rappu juice streaked the front of it and spotted both sleeves.

⁓

RIGHT ABOUT NOW, you might be thinking that night was a turning point. The moment my shell cracked, and I came crawling out of it.

If that's what you're thinking, you're wrong. Nothing changed.

I still avoided looking at people, and they at me. I had no interest in being sociable. Not with Mayne, not with anyone. About the only person I ever talked to was a teacher if I couldn't avoid it, or Jeriah. And he was too busy being popular to spend much time with me.

But I didn't need much time. I was used to being alone. I will say, though, that he made it a point to talk to me when he could. He'd often tell his friends, "Hey, I'll see ya later" in order to give some attention to me for a while.

I wish I could say I appreciated it. If I'd thought about it, I'd have realized that I was glad he didn't abandon me. But I never thought about it. I just lived one day after another, waiting to be out from under the City's guardianship. I never considered if I was lonely or grateful or happy or sad.

I also wish I could tell you I cleaned Mayne's jacket and brought it back to him all fresh and pressed (it) and sweet and smiling (me). But I didn't. I wadded it up in a bag and gave it to Jeriah to give to him.

Our conversation that night had disturbed me, and I wanted to put it all out of my mind.

As the grappleball coach had told him, Mayne did go to Ellerja with the team the next year, and so did Jeriah. They made it through two rounds our Worstie year, and to the final round as Thirsties. The school was hysterical with joy and greeted the athletes—all of them, not just the grappleballers—like returning heroes.

I kept swimming, and winning at all the local meets. But they never got me to Ellerja, no matter how they wheedled, begged, bribed, or threatened. No way was I leaving Freemansland.

As Worsties, we had smaller rooms, but only one roommate. I stuck with Seena, because she was, as I said, the closest thing I had to a friend. And she stuck with me because she had a mad crush on my brother.

Which didn't set her apart from any other girl at the school. *Everybody* had a crush on my brother, including some of the teachers. I can't say he took advantage of it, but, well, he did his share of slotting around and wasn't ashamed to admit it. To my knowledge, he didn't fool around with the teachers. But he did know how to manipulate some of them with a smile.

As Thirsties, we could have private rooms if we wanted, but I roomed with Seena again. I realized she had no friends either, and I took pity on her. Imagine that.

Jeriah and I officially came of age during our last quarter-year. Since nobody knew what our real birthday was, the City took it upon themselves to assign us one when we became their wards.

I was free! But I was also only a couple months away from graduating from the most prestigious institution on Freemansland, with honors. Academically, I was at the top of the class, but they gave credits for other things too, like participation in clubs, social service activities, going to Ellerja, and other things I didn't do.

I earned no points for personality, either.

So I had the best marks, but not the most points, and I didn't care. But I was willing to put in the rest of my time, get a diploma—for whatever use that might be in steamy, insect-infested Freedom—and get back to living my own life as my own person.

Funny thing, though. No longer a ward of the City, no longer under Aunt Lanie and Uncle Rhe's kind care, I had no idea what to do.

And then Jeriah rang my room one Seventhday—we had classes six days a week, but not the seventh—and said, "Hey, ya busy?"

I was working on a paper for school, but I had plenty of time to finish—I was never the sort who left things for the last minute. So I said, "Not really."

"Come on out, then. We're goin' somewhere."

I didn't ask where. For some reason, I didn't wonder where. Jeriah said we're going, and I trusted him.

Maybe I shouldn't have.

He was waiting when I came out. Him and Mayne. "We're going to town. Buy you some ice cream?"

I couldn't say no to ice cream. It was one City innovation of which I wholeheartedly approved. If they'd promised me ice cream if I went to Ellerja, I'd have gone.

Well, maybe not, but I'd have considered it.

As Thirsties of the age of majority, we were allowed off campus whenever we wanted. "Town" was what the City folks called the stack of buildings north of the school. It was still a stack, but City style, with covered walks and streetlights and plantings to make it look planned. The Freemanslander stacks were usually just a jumble of buildings that sprawled up a sharpfall with no logic or forethought. Their builders simply found a foothold and dug in.

Mayne ordered a bowlful the size of his head, with five flavors of ice cream, three flavors of syrup, and two kinds of berries, topped with whipped cream, nuts, and a candied papefruit at the peak of all that wonderfulness.

And three spoons.

He carried it out to the small table on the patio where I sat in the sun waiting, hoping to warm myself before I dug in. I wished I'd brought a sweater, because eating ice cream always made me cold.

We didn't talk much as we ate, but there was no need. The camaraderie was food for the soul. We'd been a trio before, and we were again. I'd never felt so whole, so content.

Nor so full, by the time we were done.

All at the same time, Jeriah wiped his mouth, Mayne burped, and I shivered.

Mayne looked across the table at me, his expression amused. "I'd let you wear my jacket if I had one. That's okay, though. You'd have just got ice cream all over it."

I was too happily full to take offense.

Jeriah leaned back in his chair. "You're not going to jump over the table and scratch his eyes out?"

I didn't bother to answer. Just wrapped my arms around myself in a vain attempt to warm up. "Maybe it would be better if I got up and moved around."

Jeriah dropped his spoon in the bowl with a clatter. "Good idea. You can clean this stuff up and take it back inside. And then we'll take a walk."

Moving around was my idea, so I didn't object to the cleanup duty. After I got back to the porch, the boys thudded down the steps to the walk.

I followed. "So where are we going?"

Mayne answered. "Next building over."

"That's a government office."

He nodded.

Jeriah said, "Um hmm."

They walked with determination, and I had to work to keep up. "So what are we doing here?"

We'd reached the place by then, and Mayne opened the door.

Riah motioned for me to go first, and I did.

And then he answered my question. "We're going to sign up."

"For what?" The ice cream must have frozen my brain, because I was seriously clueless.

Mayne led the way down the hall that took us straight into the bowels of the sharpfall. The sign on the first door on the right said, "Recruiting Center" in big, bold letters, and beneath that, "Land. Sea. Air," with the official logos of each of the major armed forces respectively.

Mayne grinned. "We're signing up."

The ice cream curdled in my stomach, and I turned to Jeriah. "*He's* signing up. What are *you* doing here?"

He grinned too. "Signing up with him. What are *you* doing here?"

I gaped. I almost wet myself. I wanted to scratch someone's eyes out, but I didn't know who to start with.

Instead of scratching, I punched Jeriah in the chest. "You are not!"

He grabbed my wrist, and then the other as I tried to hit him again.

I didn't want to scream and make a scene, but I think my low growl got the point across. "You are not! You are not–both–leaving me!" I yanked my wrists from his hands. "You are not!"

Jeriah locked his blue eyes on mine. "We're not leaving you, Jem, if you come with us."

Yes, he *was* leaving me. They both were. Leaving Freemansland. Going to join the City.

Leaving me alone.

Life without Jeriah?

My heart pounded. I couldn't catch my breath. The floor seemed to tilt beneath me.

Jeriah held my gaze, waiting. I turned to Mayne.

He lifted an eyebrow, then opened the door and went in. Jeriah entered behind him.

And I followed.

❧ Chapter 12 ❧

MY SECOND LIFE KICKS IN

WE GRADUATED.

I cannot describe how much I hated Mayne Dabo that day. I delivered my last words to him with a calm I in no way felt. "I hate you, Mayne Dabo. I shall hate you as long as I live."

Then he went home to Freedom. Jeriah and I went to Moll, until we had to ship out for Foundational Training. Each on a different day, and to a different location.

Because, despite the recruiter's smiling promises and reassuring nods as we signed our lives away in his office, Mayne was ordered to report to the Air Support Service, Jeriah to the Naval Authority, and I to the Ground Forces.

Alone.

And so it was that six days after graduation, I left Freemansland.

Alone.

When Jeriah and I parted company, he apologized with tears.

I said nothing at all.

It was too late for apologies.

WHILE STILL IN school, I'd followed the recruiter's advice to do everything possible to prepare. This involved ramping up physical workouts, changing my eating habits, and learning the fundamentals of military culture.

He also recommended establishing a different sleep schedule, but that didn't happen. The school instructors liked hands-on learning, which meant they assigned time-consuming projects that must be completed if we were to graduate. Between school assignments and preparation for Foundational, my sleep suffered.

The hardest part—until I learned Jeriah and I would be separated; *that* was the hardest part—was giving up glaffcrim. The recruiter told us we would have nothing to drink but water during Foundational, so we'd be wise to rid our systems of crim and/or alcohol if we had dependencies.

Of course we had dependencies. We lived on Freemansland, where glaffcrim is more of a staple than bread. It was fortunate we had time to ease out of the habit gradually, because even so, we had withdrawal headaches after finally cutting ourselves off completely.

I say "we," because the three of us made our plans together, prepared together, studied and worked out together, and supported one another in our resolve to do this crazy thing. Of course we knew men and women didn't do Foundational together, but we'd probably be on the same base, and the separation would be temporary. After that, we'd keep close throughout our careers.

All the while I kept thinking, *If Jeriah can do this, I can do this. He never could beat me at a game.*

Two days before graduation, we got our orders.

It was like we'd been slammed against a boulder head-first.

We talked about what we should do, and Mayne stormed into town to confront the recruiter about his lies. Which, of course, the

Cityslime denied with wide-eyed sincerity before reminding Mayne of the consequences if we failed to report as ordered.

And I, of course, considered backing out anyway, consequences be slotted. But the boys helped me see that a decade of slavery to the City was preferable to a lifetime of being hunted by them.

Besides, I'd become too citified to live wild anymore. When I contemplated hiding among the rocks and in the stillwater, foraging for food—being constantly wet—facing down dragons, marsh bears and wild hogs—dealing with poisonous plants, swarms of insects, and a variety of parasites—and doing it all under the cover of darkness because I couldn't allow myself to be seen—I reckoned the boys were right.

That was when I was still speaking to Mayne. Once the bitter, unthinkable reality of what was about to happen sank in, I declared to him my undying hatred and vowed never to speak to him again.

Jeriah fared little better. I did speak to him, if you can call wordless snarls speaking. But I didn't hate him. Angry as I was that he and Mayne had shoved me down this path, I could never hate Jeriah.

⁂

BECAUSE I'D NEVER been on a plane before, I'd never seen Freemansland from the air. I'd seen pictures, and I thought I knew what it looked like. But as I gazed down from above and saw it through the window of that big, humming City aircraft, a shocking truth drew back its hand and knocked me stupid with a stunning slap.

Freemansland was grotesque and unnatural.

It rose from the surrounding flat sea like an uneven, multi-layered cake created by a giant baker. A mad baker who worked with rock instead of flour, whose purpose was to imprison, not to feed. To isolate, not celebrate. There was nothing sweet about this monument to punishment. It was created to torture the souls who were left there to struggle and die.

The top level, aptly called Harsh, was a horrible white plain of snow and ice. I'd never seen snow, and the only ice I knew was put into beverages or packed on injuries to reduce swelling. But I knew it was painfully cold. I couldn't imagine a world in which water didn't exist because it turned to a frigid, rock-like substance. There it was below me, though, the frosting on the cake of Freemansland, oozing down the topmost sharpfall in an icing of ice. In glaciers of glaze. In a topping of terror. (This, from a person who doesn't do words? Perhaps extreme pain awakes creativity.)

I ignored the conversation going on in my brain without me and stared at my homeland in something like distaste, which hardened into a little knot in my chest that felt an awful lot like hatred.

I was a Freeman of Freemansland. How could I hate it? That would be like hating myself, wouldn't it?

I mulled the thought as the aberrant island fell out of sight.

I'd almost thought that once I was removed from my home, my namesake, I would expire. As it was gone, so I would go, whether through death or dissipation or some other means.

But there I sat, still alive. I felt the seat beneath me, the cold of the window glass beside me, heard my breath passing in and out through my nose and the rumble-hum of the flying conveyance in which I sat. In which I *still* sat, un-dissipated, though separated from Freemansland.

But... perhaps I did disappear.

The Jemima Freeman who sat in this plane was certainly not the little wild thing who'd haunted the sharpfall and stillwater of Freedom. Nor was she the Academy student who refused to leave the island to swim for glory in Ellerja.

Yes, I was gone. The wild girl was gone, the student was no more. What I would become still remained to be seen. But Freemansland was behind me, and a new life begun.

FOUNDATIONAL TRAINING IS designed to be difficult, and it achieves its objective.

I was glad I'd taken such pains to prepare. (Notice how I say *I* took such pains. There was no *we* anymore.) Every pain taken earlier meant one fewer to suffer now, and believe me, there were still plenty left.

If I'd allowed myself to think about it, I may have wondered where these people ever got the idea I wanted to be a soldier. (Maybe because I'd volunteered?)

I might also have wondered what sort of tortures they put the men through, and how Jeriah was making out. He did come to mind now and then, simply out of lifelong habit. But I didn't think long or hard on the question.

More often, I thought of Ibro. Because this Foundational experience was almost as severe a violation of body and mind as what he used to do. Nothing was mine. Nothing was private. And everything hurt.

His attacks came suddenly and were soon past, leaving me alone to quake and to heal.

This attack came suddenly, too—or at least it felt like it. But it was not soon past. And I was not alone. I was never alone, for anything. Ever. For me, that was one of the hardest things to take. If any aspect of the ordeal would have driven me mad, it would have been that.

Which brings me to an interesting point. One aspect of the treatment for a patient with a stellas worm is the avoidance of stress. At school, everyone knew that. So whenever I'd start to get riled, people would back down—and fast—to prevent me from boiling over. I suppose I took advantage of that, at least a little.

Well, okay, maybe more than a little.

In Foundational, though, everything was upside-down. If I succeeded at a task, my torturers increased the difficulty and made me do it again. If I mastered a skill, they threw a new one at me to learn, even if others were still working at the first. The pressure was not only intense and unrelenting, but clearly intentional and personal.

Obviously, the trainers didn't think the stress would awaken my stelli.

Or was that the goal? Was I an experiment? Did they want to see how hard a stellasede could be pushed?

If that was the game, then I'd play it. And I was determined to win, just as I always won. If my head exploded, it exploded, and the game would be over. Until then, I'd give it my all, and see how much "all" I could muster. And it was only for nine weeks, right?

Well, no.

I never signed on for additional training, but before I had time to blink in surprise, I was ordered to report for another six weeks. More fitness training, more weapons, hand-to-hand combat, and tactical. By the time I was finished with that, it was almost easy.

Almost.

AFTER THE MOST intense experience imaginable—except I'm pretty sure you can't imagine it—it was finally over.

And after fifteen weeks on City soil, all I'd seen was the base at Fivepetals. Which seemed bigger than all of Freemansland. And an alien planet.

You see, it was flat, and I'd never seen flat, except water. All that running we did, the obstacle courses, the long hikes and week-long wilderness excursions, were done on level ground. What the others called hills, I called lumps, and what they called a ravine I considered a wrinkle. It was flat, I tell you. And that was just weird.

But by the time I was through, I no longer found it strange that the land went on and on, farther than you could see. It seemed normal to have buildings sprawl across the face of the ground instead of burrowing into it. Though the vast flatness of the terrain at Fivepetals made me dizzy when I first arrived, after fifteen weeks, I almost wondered why I'd once thought it strange.

It hadn't changed, of course. I had.

Another graduation. Some of my fellow recruits had family there to cheer for them, parents and siblings beaming and proud.

I had a stack of e-messages, mostly from Jeriah, which I hadn't been able to access until after graduation. There were also two from Aunt Lanie.

But more urgently, I had City orders to report to the Medical Complex at Fivepetal City Center on 23rd Nonomoon at fifteen hundred hours. Which was two hours after the orders were given to me.

I didn't dare take the time to read Riah's messages before working this new puzzle.

Fivepetal City Center was not on base. I'd never been off base before. How would I get to the medical complex?

But I hadn't been through fifteen weeks of training without learning to think—and learning where to go for help when I needed it. I took a quick crash course in public transportation, packed everything I owned—with military precision, I might add—into a duffel, and stepped off a trolley in front of the Medical Complex with a quarter hour to spare.

Trying not to look bewildered.

Six others exited with me: an elderly man and a woman I presumed was his wife; a mother with a sleeping child drooling on her shoulder; a middle-aged man and woman, not together; and a woman a bit older. They seemed to know where they were going, so I followed them.

I couldn't look around much. There was too much to see, and I couldn't take it all in. I'd tried, when I first left the base, but I soon grew overwhelmed. If I hadn't blinded myself to all but what was right before me, I'd have gone mad.

A directory in the lobby provided a diagram of the facility, and after a few seconds of searching, I located the place I was looking for: Suite 1025, Building E. A shuttle around the corner could take me to the building, or I could walk.

With the diagram affixed in my mind, I readjusted my bag on my shoulder and took off on foot. I'd had enough of tight spaces crammed with people.

The walk gave me time to wonder what this appointment was all about.

I was certainly no stranger to hospitals. Since the City had taken me in almost eight years ago, my medical chart was the size of an unabridged dictionary. But I'd never before been ordered to appear without knowing to whom I was reporting and for what purpose.

Building E. Does E stand for Experiment?

I wondered that idly. When I later learned that it did, I laughed.

The E designation was really another way of saying Building 5, as the buildings were given letters rather than numbers. But that section of the facility was dedicated to research. So in a way, E did stand for Experiment.

And I was the research subject.

On the tenth floor of Building E, the door to Suite 1025 gave entrance to a small waiting area, brightly lit with simple but pleasant décor, and no people. No people? What a delight! I might have sat awhile and reveled in the luxury if not for the fact that a monitor hanging from the ceiling lit up to reveal a woman's smiling face. It looked to be computer generated rather than an actual person. "Foot Rank One Jemima Freeman?"

I hesitated half a second, for I'd forgotten I was promoted to One upon graduation. "Yes, ma'am." It felt funny speaking to a computer. Even funnier to realize I'd come to attention. At least I stopped myself from saluting.

"You're right on time," said the face. "Come in, please."

Beside the monitor, a wall panel slid back, making a doorway. I walked through into a hall with no visible doors. But since the door wasn't visible in the entry room until it opened, I expected the hallway was the same.

As no further instructions were forthcoming, I started walking—and marched the whole length of the passage without a door opening. Once I reached the end, it looked like I'd have a choice of right or left. But as I approached the cross of the T, a voice to my left said, "This way, please."

Another monitor, and the same woman's face.

"Yes, ma'am," I answered it.

This hall was shorter, but not by much. As I neared the end, the back wall opened, and I entered a room that looked much like the first waiting room. But here, the door on the far side was already open, and Dr. Pigeon filled the gap.

His welcoming smile was about as warm as the monitor's. "Well, well, Miss Freeman. Or should I say, Footrank Freeman? You look every bit the part too."

"Thank you, sir." *Did I really just say that?*

His smile broadened. He must have liked that "sir" business. "Come into my office. We need to talk." He took a step back and made a broad gesture with his arm.

As a good soldier, I obeyed.

✽ Chapter 13 ✽

BETWEEN FREEDOM AND THE CITY

THE PIGEON BROUGHT me into his spacious office—a room bigger than the average house on Freedom. Apparently, this was his *real* office. His base of operations wasn't at the hospital on Coldclime, as I'd previously thought.

The plush carpet, luxurious window treatments, original artwork, and exquisite furnishings all reeked of Pigeon pride. The room reflected the mindset of a citizen who could blow a hole in Freemansland and subjugate the populace. Cityslime practically dripped from the—

No, what was I thinking? I belonged to the City now. I was one of them.

Revise: The plush office reflected refined and discerning tastes and evidenced the quality of the man who possessed it.

Quality he made sure no one missed.

In an alcove to the left, a fireplace formed the focal point for the four princely chairs that faced it. As the Pigeon waded through the deep pile toward the grouping, a woman rose from one of the chairs and turned toward me.

A Land Forces officer. A major, from the insignia, a head shorter than the doctor though she stood tall and straight.

I dropped my duffle, came to attention, and snapped a salute. "Major Gate." I'd never seen her before, but her uniform included a nameplate.

She returned the salute. "At ease, Footrank."

The Pidge gestured toward a chair. "Yes, please, Jemma. Make yourself comfortable."

There was no getting comfortable in this setting, but I moved my duffle to a spot beside the nearest chair and sat, waiting to see what strange thing would happen next.

Major Gate took the chair beside mine. "I've been following your progress, Footrank Freeman."

Why would a major take interest in the likes of me? "Ma'am?"

"Dr. Pigeon predicted you'd do well, and he was right. Frankly, I'm surprised. I had no idea a stellasede could handle the pressure. Even most healthy women would have cracked from the stress you've been under."

The way they both looked at me, it seemed they expected me to say something. "That might be so, Major." I hoped that would do for a response.

Apparently it didn't, because they continued to stare at me. Or maybe *stare* isn't the right word. *Study* is more like it. As if I were a flatworm under a microscope. *Let's slice its head in half lengthwise and see if it grows two new ones.* I had nothing more to say, so I let them stare.

Which they did, for probably a full minute. If they thought it would rattle me, they were mistaken. I'd been half unglued before I got here, but by now I was in detached mode. More an observer than a participant.

The petite major was the first to speak. "I understand you're a good observer."

"So I've been told, ma'am."

"As have I." She almost smiled. "Let's put it to the test. Without looking around, tell me about Dr. Pigeon's art collection."

How was I supposed to describe what I'd never seen? "I'm sorry, ma'am, but I'm not familiar with that." Then it dawned on me. "Oh, do you mean what's in this room?"

"Yes, of course. What did you observe when you came in just now?"

I visualized the office. "Four large paintings in elaborate frames. I don't know the artists or styles, but the first on the left as you come in the door is in shades of brown and shows a woman sitting. She's dressed as a common woman, someone who's weary from labor. The sleeves of her white blouse are pushed above her elbows."

I paused, remembering. "No, you can only see one arm. I only assume both sleeves are pushed up. And she's wearing an olive green skirt.

"The painting beyond that is in browns and oranges. It's not clear to me what's pictured, but it might be a sunset, or perhaps a fire. On the opposite wall, one painting shows a little barefoot girl in a white dress picking up seashells on a beach. A bird, maybe a koolo, is standing nearby and four more are in the air. The fourth painting, like the second, is a little obscure. It appears to be a field of flowers that meets a sky full of white clouds, but the lines are blurred. There might be people in the field, possibly picking the flowers."

The doctor and the major said nothing, so I went on to describe the glassware in the lighted case, the three small classical nudes on pillars, the geometric metal sculpture affixed to the wall behind the desk. "And the stairway on the far side of the room has some ancient god or something standing at the foot of it."

Still no reaction from them.

"And, of course, over the fireplace, there's an arrangement of seven small sketches showing various parts of the human anatomy. But we can all see those clearly, so there's no point in my describing them."

The major finally spoke. "Since you entered this wing, how many doors did you pass on your way this office?"

That was a tough one. "Once I left the first waiting room into the hall, there were no visible doors. I expect there were some, but they were indistinguishable from the walls. However, I did notice a pattern of... I'd have to call them raised dimples. Small, round raised areas about the size of my thumbnail, with an indentation in them. They were at regular intervals along both sides of the hall, every, oh, meter and a half or so, about a meter up from the floor. But I can't say if those indicated doors. I could only identify three doors for certain. One into the waiting room, another leading to that series of hallways, and the one to this office." I reconsidered. "But I never saw that last door itself. Just the opening."

She nodded. "And what color are the roses in the vase on the table behind us?"

"The flowers are a mix of pink, white, and a sort of melon color. And I don't know what kind of flower they are, but I don't believe they're roses, ma'am."

The Pigeon's face twisted as if he were trying to contain a grin. "As you can see, Major Gate, her powers of observation are exceptional, as is her memory. What more proof do you need?"

She continued to watch me as she answered him. "You're sure she's never been here before?"

"I am positive."

"Tell me yourself, Footrank Freeman. Is this the first time you have ever been in this room?"

She'd take my word over the Pigeon's? "Yes, Major. I didn't know it existed until today."

"You've seen no photographs of it, nor seen it in a dream?"

Where did she get these questions? A dream? "No, ma'am."

She glanced at the Pigeon. "I can use this one. She might prove quite a find." She turned back to me. "They are roses, by the way, but perhaps not a variety you're familiar with. They're called Sorona roses, native to the Sorona plains."

She might be right, but they neither looked nor smelled like any rose I knew. "That's interesting. Thank you, Major."

"Have you eaten, Footrank?"

The change in topic caught me off guard. "Not since breakfast, no, ma'am."

She stood. "Feed her, doctor." And to me, "You'll receive your new orders soon. But your first assignment is to take a few days off, get some well-earned rest. I want you fresh for the next phase of your training."

When she stood, the Pigeon rose too, and I hopped up and stood at attention.

She spoke to me, ignoring the Pigeon. "Where are you staying?"

"I don't know that yet, ma'am." I'd be welcome back at Moll, but the distance and cost of travel made it out of the question. Where else could I go?

"The doctor will find a place for you." She looked up at him. "That won't be a problem, will it?"

He bent his head in what was almost a bow. "Not at all."

"Very good, then. See to it."

She left without a backward glance, leaving the Pigeon and me both at a loss for words. Which wasn't unusual in my case, but it amused me to see him in that state.

To my surprise—and from his expression, his as well—I was the first to speak. "If you hadn't called for me, I would have contacted you soon anyway. I need a refill on my prescription."

A look of confusion crossed his face for a second, then he chuckled and headed toward his desk. "Go ahead and sit down again, dear, while I book you a room at the Rosmas. Will that be satisfactory?"

I followed him and took a chair near the desk. Not so I could be close to him, but to get another view of the office. I was curious to see if I'd described everything accurately. "Yes, that would be fine." I had no idea what the Rosmas was, but I'd be happy with a bare room with a bucket for waste and a floor mat for sleeping, as long as I didn't have to share it with anyone.

He activated his computer. "And you might as well throw out what pills you have left."

"I'm sorry?"

"I had forgotten you had them. They are inert. Just a placebo." He never looked up from the screen. "You have been off your medication for the past year."

My head buzzed. "But I thought..."

"Of course you did. You were supposed to. That is why they call it a placebo." He typed and clicked as he spoke, making his words hard to follow. "It was an experiment. No one really knew how effective the medication was, and how else to find out? It's proven in cases where the worm's still on the brain's surface, sure." He paused to make a choice on the screen. "But once it's embedded, there's been no clear effect. Mere speculation, mostly. Whether or not medication of a stellasede is truly indicated."

He looked up. "So tell me, Jemma. Now that that big secret is out, how have you been feeling?" He went back to the computer. "About a year ago, when you first went on the placebo, did you notice a difference, would you say? We saw no difference in your overall health. Your grades were always good, so we saw no change in your schoolwork. But how about attitude? Mood?"

Apparently he was done booking the room, because he turned toward me with a smile and folded his hands on his desk. "Were you aware that anything was different?"

My last year of school seemed so long ago. I'd learned and changed so much since then it was almost as if another person had lived that life. But now that he mentioned it...

"I believe so, yes. It was a gradual change, but as last year went on, I grew more—more open to change, you might say. More cheerful, maybe. You're saying the medication I'd been on before had an effect on those things?"

He shrugged. "It is possible. Nobody really knows how a patient will react long-term, because—well, frankly, patients seldom take it long-term. Either the stellas is superficial and the drug causes it to wither, after which the treatment can be discontinued. Or else—"

He seemed embarrassed, so I finished the thought for him. "Or else the worm wakes up and the person dies horribly. No need to pretend otherwise. It's a common tale in my world."

He nodded, seeming relieved to speak plainly. "That is all true, yes."

"And I'm a test case. You want to see if all that expensive medication is necessary. And what a stellasede can be trained to do. How the City might put their investment in a freak like me to practical use."

"Now, Jemma." He shook his head. "Do not put it that way. It is true, you show the mental capabilities associated with stellasedes but without the usual fragility. However—"

In that instant, the accumulated stress of the past couple of months rolled over me in a sudden wave of exhaustion. I needed to escape. To be alone, for once.

I stood. "Did you get me a room? And what about food?"

That Pigeon smile widened. "Of course, my dear. It is arranged. I have ordered an autocab to take you to the hotel, and food will be provided for you there. You will find the car waiting outside the main entrance." Referencing his screen, he jotted something on a slip of paper and handed it to me.

I glanced at the numbers he'd written and grabbed my bag. "Thank you." I wasn't usually that polite to the doc, but weary as I was, I felt truly grateful for his help. "I'll find it." I left the paper on his desk, as I'd committed the numbers to memory.

"I have no doubt you will. It has been good seeing you again, Jemma."

I wasn't polite enough to reply to that one. Or maybe I was too polite to say what I really thought. Instead, I shouldered my bag without another word and left the room.

☀

I WAS A LITTLE concerned I might have trouble finding my way out of that strange doorless hall, but it turned out to be easy. As if the building had a mind of its own, it opened the portals I needed of its own volition. It struck me as a bit creepy, but so did a lot of City ways. And I was too tired to think much about it. I just walked.

Though the Pigeon's instructions had been cryptic, I was too proud and pig-headed to ask for clarifications, assuming I'd figure it out as I went along. (Had he known I'd do that? I hated it that he knew me so well.) And, just as the doors in the hall opened for me, everything else fell into place too.

Three driverless autocabs stood in a line along the edge of a paved area east of the building, and a man who'd exited the medical center in front of me headed in that direction. As I followed him, a fourth cab pulled up at the end of the line and a woman stepped out from the back seat. The sign on top of the vehicle read, "In use," until a few seconds after she exited. Then the sign changed to, "Available."

Two of the others said the same, but the one at the head of line said, "Reserved for Ft1 JF." That must be mine.

The man I followed approached the second cab, opened the back door, and got in. So when I reached the reserved car, I did the same, tossing my bag in ahead of me. Soothing music played softly within.

As I sat, a female voice greeted me. "Welcome to City Autocab Number FP0191. Please scan your pass or speak your passcode."

That was easy. I recited the code the Pigeon had given me. "28376.78W."

"Thank you, Footrank One Jemima Freeman. You wish to go to the Rosmas Inn at the Rose Petal Plaza. Is that correct?"

"Yes."

"Your fare is paid in full. You will be the only passenger on this run. I will not stop to take on others. Doors locking." A dull clicking sound accompanied that statement, and a light on the doors turned from green to red. "Estimated travel time is twenty minutes."

The car moved forward slowly. "You may change the audio by voice command at any time, or switch to video. Do you wish to make a change?"

"No. I mean, yes. Can you shut it off entirely?" The sound wasn't unpleasant, but I was experiencing sensory overload.

"I am sorry, that is not possible. However, I will turn down the volume to its lowest setting."

The music faded until it was barely perceptible.

The vehicle came to a stop at a traffic control signal similar to what I'd seen on the army base. When the light turned to green, the car entered the main road, which was divided into four parallel lanes. All the vehicles went the same direction, and across a landscaped divide, another road handled the traffic going the opposite way. Every now and then a branch allowed passage to other streets. For the next quarter hour, I stared out the windows, trying to make sense of it all.

The autocab's voice stirred me from my reverie. "Approaching Rose Petal Plaza. We will be at the Rosmas Inn in two minutes."

The narrower road the car had recently taken now spilled onto a circular area where the pavement curved and the buildings around it had graceful arcing shapes. In the center of the circle, on my left, was a well-tended park, shaded with trees and brilliant with flowers. I later learned that, when seen from the air, the design of this plaza resembled a rose, with the buildings forming the petals.

The car slowed to a stop. "We are now at the Rosmas Inn. Thank you for allowing me to drive you today." From the sound, I guessed the doors unlocked. Yes, a light on the handle turned from red to green.

At least, I assumed that was a handle. Never having been in a car before, I wasn't sure. But I pulled it, and the door opened. So I grabbed my bag and stepped out.

I closed the door and headed toward the building. Hearing the car move behind me, I turned to see the sign on top of the vehicle change from "In Use" to "Reserved" as the cab pulled away to its next destination.

With its departure, an unexpected wave of loneliness swept over me.

The messages from Jeriah seemed to make my tablet burn in the duffel. I wanted to open and read them right there on the sidewalk, but no, I should be alone for that. The hotel towered above me like a treeless sharpfall.

A man standing inside the hotel doors greeted me, glancing at my nameplate. "Welcome to the Rosmas. How may I help you, Footrank Freeman?"

I tried not to show how out of place I felt, but I doubt he was convinced. "I have—" My voice squeaked like my vocal cords were pinched. I cleared my throat and tried again. "I have a reservation."

"We're delighted to have you as our guest." Smiling, he gestured toward a long counter across the room. "Our reception agents can help you get settled in."

I thanked him and made my way to the reception desk. I hoped this wouldn't take long, because I was exhausted and near exploding from all the unfamiliar things around me.

All the agents were occupied with other guests when I reached the counter, but I listened to the conversation between the agent and the man in front of me. As a result, I was able to act like I knew what I was doing when I approached the counter.

After verifying that I did, in fact, have a reservation—and that it was already paid for—the agent scanned my left eye with a portable device. "Have you stayed with us before? Are you familiar with the new hotel security?"

"No," I answered.

"You'll be pleased to know we no longer have keys. I'll have the porter take you to your room and show you how the iris scanner works. Entry to guest rooms is now hack-proof, and there's no key card to have to keep track of."

Though I had only one bag and was plainly capable of carrying it myself, the porter insisted on taking it for me when he escorted me to the fifth floor. "You give me pleasure, ma'am, by allowing me to serve you in this way."

I didn't know how to respond to that, nor to any of his other attempts to make small talk, so we rode the elevator in silence, then walked along a curving hall and took one turnoff before arriving at a door marked 545.

He pointed to a circle on the marker. "The iris scanner is here. Put your eye directly in front of it with your brow almost touching the ridge above." He bent and demonstrated. "Then press this button to scan your iris. Make sure you don't close your eye. If it registers correctly, you'll hear the door unlatch. You have to open it within ten seconds, or it will latch again. I recommend you try it before I leave to make sure it works."

I followed his instructions. Everything worked the way it was supposed to, and the door opened easily. He remained in the hall while he handed me my bag. "Will you need anything else, ma'am?"

"No, thank you." I tried to sound pleasant but was in a hurry to close the door.

Which I did, then leaned back against it with a sigh.

The carpeted room contained a bed big enough for three to sleep in without touching. In a separate area stood a sofa, a large video screen, and a desk with an ergonomic chair. In a small kitchen area, a covered tray sat on the table. That must be the food the Pigeon had promised.

But the thought of Riah's messages overrode my hunger. I dropped the duffel on the desk, pulled out the tablet, and powered it up. As soon as it came to life, I went to my personal mail.

Two messages from Aunt Lanie appeared along with several unsolicited commercial messages. But the inbox had line after line of messages from Jeriah. I opened the most recent and read:

"Where are you? Are you okay? I knew you couldn't contact me until after Foundational, but that was weeks ago. Why aren't you answering?"

I envisioned his anxious face, heard his voice. My heart raced, as I knew his did as he'd typed the message. What if it had been me trying to reach him and I'd gotten no response? It would have killed me.

The worst part was the rest of what he said: "I'm shipping out in ten minutes on a quiet mission." I knew what "quiet" meant in the military – no outside contact. "But as soon as you get this, please reply! I'll check for your answer as soon as I can. I'm pretty mad at you for ignoring me, you know."

My legs wobbled and I sank into the chair. I couldn't stand it when he was mad at me—but I knew he wasn't, really. He was worried. And who could blame him? He knew I'd never ignore him if I had a choice.

I dashed off a response with a quick explanation, adding, "I'll read the rest of your messages and answer them too, but first I wanted to let you know I'm okay."

Why were my hands trembling? Oh, yeah, I needed to eat. I took the tablet to the table, lifted the cover from the tray, and ate everything there without tasting it as I read Riah's messages, oldest to newest.

All the while, wondering how we'd come to such a place—Riah and me, together from the womb, communicating electronically from opposite sides of the world. Him on a City naval vessel somewhere, and me in a fancy hotel room in Fivepetals.

Weak with emotion and exhaustion, I yanked a blanket from the bed and curled up on the floor in it, holding the tablet—the nearest thing to Riah, but not near enough—wrapped in my arms.

❧ Chapter 14 ❧

THE CITY ABSORBS ME

MAJOR GATE WAS a recruiter—a talent scout, you might say—for Information Acquisition. Though the division had been working quietly behind the scenes for generations, I'd never heard of it until I was invited to join its ranks.

IA, or The Division as it's often called, is made up of select personnel from the three military branches, each specially trained for gathering information. My gifts for stealth and observation made me an obvious choice for the job, but sneakiness isn't the only method the Division uses for acquiring information. Back in my day, many of our people were investigators in the good, old-fashioned detective style. Some were cybersleuths, some were skilled in the art of interrogation, and others were multi-talented.

The Division has a separate ranking system, but not its own uniforms. If you came into the IA from the Land Forces, as I did, you continued to wear the Land Forces uniform, but with IA insignia and rank. But when we worked under cover, of course, we didn't wear uniforms.

Though the physical aspect of my IA training was enough to keep me in shape, it was not as intense as what I'd just come through. Mostly, the training challenged my mind.

I hated to admit it, but I loved this new phase of my life. I got to do all the things I enjoyed and sharpen my skills to a finer hone than I'd ever thought possible. The study of dialects and culture—things I'd need if I were to blend in with my surroundings in various regions of the City's global empire—broadened my understanding of the world and opened new avenues of thought.

Despite the fact that all this made me a City tool through and through, I reveled in it.

FROM MY GRADUATION from Freemansland Academy to becoming an IA Specialist took little more than an eyeblink. Actually, it was over a year, but it seemed no time at all.

And suddenly, life was good. Jeriah and I communicated when we could, though it wasn't always possible. One or the other of us had to go "quiet" pretty often, and we couldn't tell the other what we were doing. But we each enjoyed our jobs, and just knowing the other was out there served to keep us steady.

I did miss him, though.

After I'd been with the Division for ten months or so, I was in a bar with a couple others on my team in a city called Spindletown, in Walpin. One aspect of our assignment involved hobnobbing with the locals to get a feel for the people's attitude toward the City and our policies.

Yes, I did say *our*. I was one of them.

Even so, I'd maintained my integrity and didn't cuddle up with any men. Thanks to my rude initiations by Ibro, I had no interest in exchanging bodily fluids with anyone, male or female. So, no slotting, no sliming. I left that nonsense to the rest of the world and stuck to official City business.

Which, on this occasion, involved a little dancing, drinking, and letting down of the hair, so to speak.

Naka Nutt and I had been bar hopping all night, chatting people up in the sort of environment where people tend to speak freely. Two male team members, Spen and Hook, did the same, either following or preceding us from bar to bar, so the four of us could keep an eye on one another. The plan was to get the lay of the land and then head home between two and three hundred hours, depending on how things worked out.

It was nearing three hundred, and Naka and I were at a table sharing a bowl of breaded fish fingers with a couple of guys who plainly had something else on their minds. One, a smelly thing with bad teeth and waxy hairs sticking out of his ears, was almost wild-eyed with desperation. As if he had to be with a woman or die. Though his buddy was nothing to get excited about, at least he didn't have a fermented air about him.

Naka and I were friendly, but only enough to hear what the guys had to say without giving them hope for anything other than talk.

She glanced across the room toward Spen and Hook, who must have given the *let's get out of here* signal, because she looked at her phone. "Oh, glish, I didn't realize it was so late. I've got an early appointment tomorrow." She turned to me. "You coming? I don't like to ride the tram alone this time of night."

I downed the rest of my beer, which turned out to be a little more of a gulp than I could handle and still remain ladylike. Oh, well. I wiped the dribble from the corners of my mouth with the back of my hand. "Yeah, I guess I could go now."

Smelly Man put his hand on my arm. "Ah, no, lemme buy you another."

At the same time, his friend leaned his face into Naka's. "I'll take you home, nothin' to worry about."

We each pulled away from the advances, Naka with a grimace. I disguised my shudder by taking out my pocketbook mirror and checking my makeup.

Naka waved her hand, fanning away Buddy Boy's spirited breath. "No, really, I need to get some sleep."

"Me too." I addressed Smelly from behind my mirror. "Look at these eyes." I pulled down on a lower lid. "Bloodshot. If I don't put a few drops in them and get some rest, my boss will fire me. He won't have a slotting drunk receiving clients."

"You ain't a drunk," he slurred, "but I'll bet you like a good slot, though, don'tcha?"

My stomach churned, but I remained calm. "Maybe next time. Do you come here often?"

His face distorted in a snaggle-toothed leer. "I could, pretty lady. I could come as often as you'd like."

He reached for me, but I stood up, as did Naka.

She grabbed my arm. "Let's get going. See you tomorrow, boys?"

Smelly licked the rim of his mug, perhaps afraid he'd missed a drop. "What time?"

I tossed him a smile calculated to entice as I made for the exit. "Look for us around twenty-two hundred."

Buddy Boy, who'd been gentlemanly enough to rise when we ladies did, had a difficult time keeping himself upright. "You better be I believe here—you be there better—" He smacked his lips and tried again. "You better believe I'll be here."

Naka wiggled her fingers at them. "See ya, guys."

"Hey!" Smelly called after us. "How 'bout a goodnight kiss!"

I blew him one across the room, then turned and followed Naka out the door.

The nearest tram stop wasn't far. Spen was already there. Then Hook came along, and, keeping up the pretense in case anyone was paying attention, we pretended to flirt with each other.

Though I never had any intention of going anywhere with it, I liked to flirt. The ease with which I could manipulate a man was a never-ending source of fascination for me. Did they never catch on to what we were doing? Did lust make them stupid? It sure made them pliable.

The tram pulled up, empty of passengers. All four of us sat in the back away from the attendant. With Spen and Naka sharing a bench, and Hook and I each in our own seats on opposite sides of the aisle, we spoke in low tones.

Fingers entwined, Spen stretched his arms and cracked his knuckles. "Well, that went well, don't you think?"

Naka shrugged. "We'll make our reports and let the analysts decide what's well and what's not."

Hook, across the aisle from me with legs stretched out along the seat and the back of his head resting on the window, gave me a meaningful look. "You know what would really be well?"

I yawned. "A hole in the ground with water in it?"

He chuckled. "I was thinking more along the lines of our sharing a room tonight."

It was my turn to laugh. "Don't think so, friend. You know I'm all talk."

"What's the matter, don't you like me?"

"Of course." I smiled, trying to ease his hurt expression. "But friendship only goes so far."

He glanced at Naga and Spen, sitting together in quiet conversation of their own. "No law against friends having a little fun if they want."

An edge crept into my voice. "No, but there is one against insisting a friend do something against her will." I hadn't meant to sound quite so sharp.

He expelled an exasperated sigh as the tram stopped and took on two new passengers. That ended our conversation.

NAKA AND I shared an apartment on the third floor, where the four of us got together to make our report before calling it a day.

As Spen had said, it did seem our foray had gone well. Each of us had met someone that night who had a complaint with the recent laws concerning ownership of a Walpinian weapon called a gattri.

Since long before the City took over, the men of Walpin—and even sometimes the women, though it was traditionally a man's duty—defended the family's honor through duels to the death, and the gattri was the official weapon for these face-offs. Gattris were often passed down from father to son as treasured family heirlooms, and new ones were common wedding gifts. Every Walpinian household possessed one, though the practice of honor duels had fallen out of fashion two or three generations ago.

Recently, however, a strong resurgence of the old tradition was sweeping across Walpin, and the City was alarmed at the trend. They hoped a law requiring all gattris be rendered permanently inoperable might help put an end to it. Weapons could be kept as keepsakes or display pieces, but they couldn't be fired.

Despite the fact that a functional one had no purpose other than to commit murder, the Walpinians didn't want their gattri messed with. Our investigation uncovered widespread resentment of the law, though we found no indication of any sort of organized resistance. It should be possible to defuse the tension before it became a problem.

But as Naka said, our job was merely to report our findings, and anything more was not our concern. Once our report was made, the guys left for their own place upstairs to catch some sleep. We were to leave town in the morning.

Naka made herself a cup of hedgethistle tea. Despite a notable lack of evidence to support the claim, she said it counteracted the detrimental effects of alcohol and prevented hangover.

She stood outside the bathroom door sipping her tea and watching me brush my teeth. "I don't see how you can drink so much and never get drunk. Are you immune or something?"

I shrugged, waiting to answer until after I'd spat. Then said, "It's a gift."

"Kinda like the way you can flirt with guys but never get amorous. You're like a machine, you know that? A thinking, drinking, hormone-revving robot. I'm not sure you're real."

"And I'm not sure I know what you're talking about."

She narrowed her eyes but stepped aside to let me leave the room. "That's *exactly* what I'm talking about. You do these things like you don't know you're doing them. What kind of freak are you? Some experiment the scientists concocted?"

"Something like that, yeah. I'm going to bed." I went to my room and closed the door.

Nobody understood me like Jeriah. Just knowing he was out there balanced me. Without him, I'd be a body with just one arm. And my, how I missed him that night. One way or another, we'd have to find a way to see each other.

As always, I checked my messages before going to bed. And tonight, I smiled and felt the tension ebb. Just when I needed it most, there was a message from Riah.

"Hey, Jem - checking in to see how you're doing. I'm doing great. In fact, I've got some good news. You're not going to believe it, but I got married yesterday."

My knees buckled and I plopped to the floor. You *what?*

"Remember your roommate from school, Seena Freeman? Well, guess what? She's a civilian contractor here at the base at Zaffre, working in Food Services.

"It was so nice to be with a Freemanslander again. It was like coming up for air after a long dive. She was happy to see me here too. Turns out she had a crush on me all along, did you know that? I'd never paid much attention to her at school, but now I can't believe I missed a beauty like her. The time wasn't right before, I guess. But it sure is now.

"Both of us being Freemanslanders, we had no ceremony like a lot of City people do. We just went to the marriage agent with a couple of the guys to sign as witnesses. But we're married for sure and legal.

"We really do have to meet up somewhere, the three of us. You can drink a toast to us – to your new sister!"

I put down the tablet for fear I'd throw up on it.

It was supposed to be Riah and me. *Just* Riah and me. Two arms to balance the body. Who needs a third arm? I never liked Seena anyway.

Well, okay, I guess I did. Seena was always nice to me, even before she knew I had a hunk of a brother. Nicer than anyone else in the whole school, except for Riah.

And Mayne.

The thought of him made me grit my teeth. He was responsible for this, for tearing me away from Freemansland and everyone and everything I'd ever known, for putting Seena as a wedge between Riah and me, for–.

For giving Jeriah the chance to find happiness.

I took a deep breath and wiped my eyes. Okay. I'd get over this. I'd be happy for him.

I wasn't all right with it now, but I would be. I'd be happy for him. I'd be happy for Seena, too, because she'd always been good to me.

But all that would come later. I couldn't manage it yet.

Chapter 15

I LOSE AT STEALTH

NOT LONG AFTER the assignment in Walpin, I was sent on a winter training exercise.

I was given no details, only that I was to report to a Colonel Redruff at the Land Forces base at Memtic in central NaHora.

Though NaHora is famous for its beautiful cities, architectural wonders, and rugged, wooded mountains, the climate is cold. Not the sort of place a person of Freemansland blood could enjoy visiting, particularly in winter.

Nevertheless, to Memtic I went, where a blast of icy wind sucked the breath from my lungs when I exited the airport terminal. This did nothing to improve my sour mood.

I still hadn't come to terms with Jeriah's marriage—his abandonment, as I saw it. To help quell the loneliness, I'd been out with some friends the night before. They introduced me to a drink called the sleeping bear, which they said would warm me up for my journey. Made no sense to me how a drink tonight could keep me warm tomorrow, but I gave it a try. Turned out a couple of those bears were enough to make even me feel them. They didn't make me go into hibernation, but I was greeted the next day with a hammering headache.

A hangover is miserable for anyone, but my biggest worry with a headache was that the stelli might be waking up. That thought didn't improve my mood.

By the time I found a cab to take me to Memtic, my face felt frostbitten, my teeth chattered, and I was pretty sure I was dying.

I cracked open a window to keep my nausea at bay, but that only made the heater blast hotter, which made me feel sicker. I asked the car if it could turn down the heat, but its answer was, "Interior temperature is maintained at a range of fifteen to twenty degrees in the winter months."

"I'm hot," I said. "Can you turn it down?"

"If you wish." The heat quit blasting, but the window shut as well. I hate a smart aleck car.

Yep. Pretty sure I was going to die.

I SURVIVED THE ride, but if I'd had anything in my stomach when I got in the cab, I'd have had less when I got out.

As soon as the door opened, I took a desperate gulp of cold air. Halfway down my windpipe, it froze and sent me into a coughing fit. The car intoned, "Thank you for allowing me to dri—" but I slammed the door before it finished.

Which didn't help my headache.

All Land Forces bases are arranged much the same, so I had no difficulty finding the commandant's office from the address I was given. But first, having time to spare, I found a restroom and tried to make myself look more presentable than I felt.

I splashed my face with cold water, but bending over at the sink made my head feel like it was going to fall off, so I did it quickly. I reapplied just enough make-up to keep me from looking cadaverous but not enough to be obvious.

By the time I left the restroom, my reflection looked pretty well put together. Good thing, because I sure didn't feel that way.

I hoped whatever sort of training exercise Major Redruff had in mind wasn't supposed to take place outdoors. But of course it would. If weather didn't play a factor, it wouldn't be called a "winter" exercise. Delightful. Maybe one of those stelli would eat my brain in the next ten minutes so I wouldn't have to go outdoors again.

But no, they made you go mad before they killed you.

Maybe I was already mad and didn't know it. Yes, of course I was. Mad for leaving Freemansland to join the military.

Colonel Redruff's aide greeted me in his outer office. "The colonel will be with you shortly. He invites you to wait."

"Thank you." He *invites* me to wait? Did he invite me to sit, or was I expected to stand? As the aide had turned away, I could pick up no clues from his demeanor.

I sat.

Across from me, a detailed topo map glowed from a video screen. Although it wasn't labeled, I realized it depicted the base and the surrounding mountains. Ah. That's what I was supposed to do while I waited – study the map, so when the exercises began, I'd be familiar with the terrain.

I've always been good with maps. Headache or not, I soon had a good grasp of the lay of the land.

After a short time, the aide ushered me into the colonel's office. Where I was not invited to sit.

I'd never heard of Colonel Redruff before, but he didn't impress me. His tall frame couldn't disguise the paunch pressing against his shirt like rising bread dough. His prominent brow bones were the sort I'd come to associate with the most obnoxious citizens, beginning with Dr. Pigeon. In fact, Jeriah and I called a person with a pronounced brow ridge a pigeonhead.

And I'd never met a pigeonhead I liked.

He looked me over. "So you're who they sent, are you, Specialist Freeman?"

The way he pronounced my name like a sneer came as no surprise. Pigeonheads usually felt the same way about people named Freeman as I felt about pigeonheads.

"Apparently so, Colonel."

He stared at me. "I asked for the best they had. Someone who can challenge a good tracker."

"I am the best they have, sir."

After a pause, he shook his head. "Well, he can't be as good as they say. He's Navy, for slime's sake, and they're always slotting worthless." Then he muttered something like, "...tripping over a slinking Freeman every time I turn around."

On a screen on the wall, he projected the map I'd just been looking at, but with place names marked. "Be that as it may, here's the game. For the purposes of this exercise, you are a detainee escaping from our custody. Your objective is to evade pursuit and rendezvous with a fellow conspirator here, at this shack just outside the boundary." A small square on the map flashed to indicate its location.

"There is no conspirator, of course, and you're not actually detained. But if you manage to make it that far without being captured, one of my people will meet you at the shack. If you're not there in six hours, he leaves. Game over, you lose."

I nodded. "I'll be there, Colonel."

"My orders are to equip you with suitable clothing so you don't freeze to death. I suppose the idea is that you were wearing the things when you were captured. You will put on the gear and proceed immediately for the shack. In thirty minutes, the pursuit will begin. Do you have any questions?"

If I knew what equipment was provided, I might know if I had questions. As it was, I only had one. "Am I permitted to take any equipment I need that hasn't been issued? And may I use any nonlethal means at my disposal to evade capture?"

As I'd hoped, the second question seemed to have driven the first from his mind. "Uh, yes. I suppose. Nonlethal and non-crippling. But you haven't much time. Pursuit will begin in—" he glanced at his watch. "Twenty-nine minutes and twelve seconds. You're dismissed."

I saluted and left. Outside his office, the aide handed me an armload of better outdoor clothing than what I'd arrived in, which I put on. Even the boots fit perfectly. I should have expected that, for the City knew everything about me, including my sizes.

As I laced up the boots, I spoke to the aide. "I'm going to need the passcode for an all-weather vehicle."

His expression showed surprise. "Of course. Yes, I can help you with that." He pulled up a list on his computer. "There's a Groundeater 640 available. It should be suitable for the current conditions." He grabbed a slip of paper and a pen. "I'll write the passcode for you."

"No need. I'll remember it."

He showed me the screen. "Here's the vehicle. It's in Garage 3, Bay 17. And the passcode." He pointed, and I scanned the combination of letters and numbers, committing them to memory.

"Thanks. You've been very helpful." After setting the timer on my phone for twenty-seven minutes, I slipped out.

I loved Stealth as a kid, but playing it in the military was a million times better. Now, the rush of adrenaline made me forget my hangover.

Once I went outside, I was glad of every thread that covered me. Stepping out into that kind of temperature was like getting a hard slap out of nowhere. How could anyone live in this climate?

I pulled my cowl over my face and ran through blowing snow to the motor yard and then to the third garage. I waved at the guard in the booth, but she didn't brave the cold to check my credentials. Smart girl.

A Groundeater 640 waited in Bay 17 as promised. I lifted the flap covering the keypad but had to remove a glove to punch in the code. The dull click of the doors unlocking reminded me of my first trip in a car, the ride from the medical center in Fivepetals. When I'd heard that sound that day, I wasn't sure what it was. Nowadays I knew how to operate just about any vehicle on this base.

I got in, re-entered the code on the dash panel, and pushed the On button. It started with a roar.

According to the map, I should be able to take the first road to the left out of the motor yard, make a right, and then another right would take me halfway up the mountain.

And perhaps I could have done that, if not for the snow. Never having driven in those conditions before, I hadn't taken that factor into account.

I started out okay. Long-armed rubber scrapers swiped back and forth across the front window, and all sorts of warning messages glowed on the dash.

Freezing temperatures; road may be icy.

No kidding.

Snow detected on road surface.

Figured that out, did you? What an intelligent machine.

Interior heat malfunction.

What? Well, at least I was out of the wind. Even without heat, it was warmer in here than it was out there.

The vehicle skidded on the first turn, and a new warning flashed.

Reduce speed on slippery surfaces.

My flipping stomach told me that much. I barreled on, but slowed for the next turn. And kept my speed down because the road was winding. And hilly. In places, steep. And then, about the time it straightened out, it ended.

It probably didn't end, exactly, but whoever had removed the first few layers of snow decided not to go any farther.

They called this thing a Groundeater. Could it eat snow as well? I'd find out.

When I came to the end of the plowed portion, I kept going.

A new message flashed. *Rugged terrain mode engaged: Deep snow. 1500 RPM maximum.*

The Groundeater growled, but it kept moving. I glanced at the timer. The search would begin in eighteen minutes. I glanced in the rear-view mirror. I was leaving tracks a blind man could follow with his hands tied behind his back.

I was supposed to be on foot, though, so the search wouldn't likely start at the motor yard. By the time my pursuer figured out I was driving, I'd have a good head start.

When I played Stealth as a kid with Jeriah and Mayne, we all knew how the other thought and could anticipate what our opponents might do. Here, I was pitting my wits with a stranger. The only thing I knew was he was a Navy man, someone in whom Major Gates, the IA recruiter, had seen potential and pulled out of regular duty to train for IA service.

Would a Navy man expect an escaped detainee to steal a Groundeater and drive off in a snowstorm?

Maybe he would. If he were as good as advertised, he'd expect his quarry to do whatever it took.

The timer was down to fifteen minutes.

The higher I climbed, the more the Groundeater skidded, labored and groaned. I wasn't sure where the road was anymore, but as long as I moved upward, I didn't care. My destination was on the other side of this mountain, and I was making far better time than I would on foot.

The vehicle wove crazily. Warning messages flashed like holiday lights. A sudden swerve to the left, a drunken stagger, and an alarm sounded as the Groundeater slid sideways down a snowy slope and came to rest on its side. The view out every window was the same—solid white. The clanging of the alarm woke my headache. The flashing lights didn't help either, and I think I banged my head when the vehicle tipped over.

I shut off the engine, but the clanging and flashing persisted for at least a full minute. Squinting against the clamor, I climbed up to the passenger door and tried the latch. It was unlocked. I gave it a shove upward, and it opened to admit a cascade of snow. I was about to climb out but then remembered my phone, which had been on the seat beside me before I'd rolled over. I fumbled around for it, not sure if the search was worth the wasted time. I found it after half a minute, zipped it into a jacket pocket, and clambered out.

Playing Stealth in the snow presents special challenges. If the snow is fresh, it's impossible to go anywhere without leaving obvious footprints. But when it's blowing and falling, as it was that day, if you choose wisely where to walk, and with a big enough head start, the snow can sometimes cover your tracks.

In one regard, therefore, I had an advantage. But it would take a snow tornado to erase the trail I'd just left. And the wake of my wading through the drifts as I made my escape from the vehicle would be just as bad.

I made a surprising discovery, though, as I perched on the edge of the Groundeater, surveying my location and plotting my next move. Unless my eyes deceived me, the vehicle had fallen into a tunnel of spirlbristle, a wild shrub that grows in a circular pattern. A number of the plants growing together will often take the shape of a tube, with the branches growing outward around a hollow interior formed by the flat, woody stems.

In the heavy snow, I wouldn't have noticed the Groundeater had landed in such a channel, except that an opening in the shrubby tunnel was visible near the vehicle's roof.

Another glance around, and I knew what I had to do. I dropped back into the Groundeater, pulling the door shut above me in hopes the blowing snow would cover the closed door and make the vehicle less noticeable. Then I worked at the sunroof—at this tipped-over angle, it was more like a side door—until I'd opened it enough to crawl through. I squirmed out and into an almost perfectly round tube of shrubbery wide enough in diameter for me to crawl through.

Though a little snow filtered through the branches, the passage was not blocked. Not much daylight shone through the white walls. How far would this tunnel take me? Far enough, I hoped, that when the tracker came across the abandoned vehicle, he wouldn't see foot tracks leading away from it.

I crept, crawled, and wriggled through the scratchy tube, making my way over lumps of roots and rocks and who-knew-what else, and through scattered nuggets of rodent pellets. If I were an animal, I'd live here too. I could hear things scurrying away ahead of me. The shrubbery seemed to be taking me steadily down a gentle hill.

My phone alarm sounded, signaling the start of the pursuit. But I was too cramped to get the phone out of my pocket. I'd have to let it beep until I got out of the spirlbristle.

I can't say how far I went before the tunnel ended in a brushy wall. The going was slow, so I couldn't have made much progress, but wherever I was, it had taken quite a while to get there.

I clawed an opening through the roof of curved branches above me and stood. When I was upright, the branches came to about mid-thigh. Snow came at me from all sides, and I was tempted to crawl back into the tunnel. But I had to move forward.

Which direction? Though I couldn't see the sun, I knew what direction I'd been going when I started out. The spirlbristle I'd crawled through made an elongated mound beneath the snow as far behind me as I could see. Which wasn't all that far.

On the ridge above, a flat treeless band suggested the road I'd been trying to follow before I'd slid off. But it was just a suggestion, not a statement of fact.

I pulled off a glove then pulled out my phone, finally able to silence it. Though my escape hadn't gone quite according to plan, I had a pretty good head start.

But I had a long way to go, and the going would be difficult. I zipped the phone back in my pocket, pulled my cowl up to protect my face, and continued up the valley I'd fallen into, as it seemed to take me roughly the direction I wanted to go.

I worked my way to the top of the ridge and the edge of a fir wood. If the road was there, I couldn't see it. What with the trees, the falling snow, and the fading light, I couldn't see much of anything. As the sun sank low, the wind weakened. A breeze sent wisps of fine flakes skittering across the white ground, but the powerful gusts had called it a day.

Now that it was calmer, the frigid scene had a forbidding loveliness about it. My labored respirations slowed, and I heard the quiet little taps of the snowflakes landing on the boughs above. Tree trunks stood at attention all around me, watching. Though dim, the light seemed a bit clearer, as if the clouds were thinning.

I envisioned the map, tried to figure my present location and the best route to my destination.

What was that sound? I held my breath and listened. An engine of some sort. Hard to tell where it was coming from, but it was definitely a vehicle. A small one, though. Not a Groundeater.

I listened a few more seconds, then headed for the far side of the ridge. Anyone approaching would spot me easily at the crest. I bounded through the snow across the top then descended the other side. It was rocky, but not terribly steep. Never thought I'd miss the wind, but with it gone, my tracks would be clearly visible half a kilometer away.

I went around a thicket that would hide me from a pursuer's view above and paused to listen. Moving through snow was hard work, and I had to hold my breath or I'd hear nothing else.

The engine noise drew nearer.

I plotted my course, a zigzag journey from rock to tree over the roughest ground I could find in hopes of making my footprints less noticeable. If I were lucky.

After a few minutes I realized I was wasting my time. This wouldn't fool even an idiot tracker. After that decision was made, I moved as quickly as I could and didn't worry about what marks I left. If he came across them, he'd follow them. It couldn't be helped. In this deep snow, I knew of no trick that would work.

The vehicle, whatever it was, was above me now. The dim light could work to my advantage, but if I came out from beneath the trees, my silhouette would stand out against the white snow, so I took care not to be seen.

As darkness fell, I grew numb from the cold. Now it was important that I keep moving to keep warm. Every now and then a little light from the moon would seep out from behind the clouds, but for the most part, I had to feel my way in the dark.

Night wasn't the only thing that fell. I did too. Twice. I wasn't hurt either time, and I was thankful the good clothing kept me dry.

I descended that mountain and started up the next. My objective was on the other side of a formation the map called Demon's Nose. A glow of moonlight eased out and illuminated a far cliff with the shape of a bulbous-beaked human face. That surely must be the landmark I needed. I adjusted my course to head toward it.

I thanked the moon for its gift and trudged onward. I no longer thought about foot tracks. By now it was a race, not an exercise to evade a tracker.

It was probably an hour or so by the time I reached the Demon's Nose and stood beneath it, panting. Breathing through the cowl warmed the bitter air before it entered my lungs and damaged them, but my breath turned to ice on the fabric, and the frozen nuggets rubbed my face raw.

I was chilled to the core, probably near hypothermia. The snow had stopped, the breeze still. Though the moon shone, I couldn't see more than a meter into the dark forest. How much farther was the boundary fence? According to the map in my mind, it should only be 800 meters or so. If I kept straight after passing the Nose, I couldn't miss it.

Or so I hoped.

That's when my pocket vibrated.

What the—

My phone jangled.

Jeriah's ring.

I was upset at his marriage, but not enough to ignore his call. Not even while standing under the drip of a Demon's Nose in the middle of a Stealth game on a shivering arctic night. I tore off my glove, unzipped the pocket, and pulled out the phone before the fourth ring. "Riah?"

"It *is* you I'm following, isn't it?"

My mind grappled with the question. "Huh?"

"That's you I see, standing under that face on the cliff."

I almost dropped the phone. My head swiveled and eyes darted everywhere as I stepped back against the rock. "What the slime are you talking about?"

He laughed. "Gotcha! You lose."

"What?"

"Stay where you are. I'll be there in a minute." He disconnected.

I stared at the phone in bewilderment until its mocking glow faded and left me standing alone in the cold night.

❧ Chapter 16 ❧

TOGETHER AGAIN... MAYBE

SHIVERED IN the dark, eyes and ears straining to detect any movement. If I knew which direction Jeriah was coming from, I'd have gone the other way. I was so angry I didn't want to see him, much less speak to him.

Within a few seconds of his call, a small engine started up, revved, and ran steady.

He must have driven here and waited for me, knowing I'd come this way. But what was he driving? I'd learned from experience that even a monster Groundeater was useless in these horrible conditions.

I forgot about escape. Maybe the sudden desire to see my brother for the first time in two years kept me rooted in place. More likely, I was too cold to move. I turned my head toward the sound and waited for about a minute while the vehicle drew closer. Headlight beams shone from around the side of the rock then angled my direction, blinding me.

I shielded my eyes with my frozen-gloved hand and squinted. The vehicle was a one-person conveyance on runners rather than wheels. Of course. A motorized sled. If I'd known such things existed, I'd have stolen one myself.

I remained planted beneath the Nose while Riah drove the noisy thing near and stopped in front of me. He swung off the seat, removing the helmet that engulfed his head and made him look like a space alien. His eyes lit on me, and his chiseled face grinned in the moonlight.

Next instant, the helmet was on the ground and I was in his arms, my face buried in his frosty, pine-scented coat.

AFTER A COUPLE hours' rest, Jeriah and I met with Colonel Redruff and Air Troops Colonel Hammer for debriefing. Hammer wore Division insignia on his sleeve, which made us answerable to him, not to Redruff.

I hated to lose at Stealth. But this hardly felt like a loss. I had survived the ordeal and was now out of the cold, sipping a heavenly cup of hot glaffcrim while listening to the sonorous voice of my brother, who sat near enough that my knee felt the warmth of his.

Much as when we were kids, I mostly listened while Riah answered the officers' questions. The training exercise had been set up for his benefit, after all, with my participation merely that of a tool. A rabbit for the hound to chase.

I liked that kind of role. It allowed me to go unnoticed.

But of course at one point, the topic of the Groundeater came up. *The stolen vehicle*, as Colonel Redruff put it as he turned his attention to me.

"My apologies, Colonel," I said. "I understand it will be difficult to recover from where I left it. But with all due respect, I was told I could take anything I needed."

His jaw thrust forward. "You received no such instruction. Who would have told you such a thing?"

I'm pretty sure I was successful in keeping the smirk out of my voice. "You did, sir. In our meeting yesterday afternoon, I asked if I were permitted to take any equipment in addition to what I was issued. I believe your answer was, 'Uh, yes. I suppose.' But the recording you made of our conversation will confirm the exact wording."

The commandant's face reddened. "Well, no one gave you permission to lose it out there."

"It's not lost, sir. I can tell you exactly where it is."

He snorted. "It doesn't take a bloodhound to follow the slotting trail you made with it. And it's lost for good if we can't get it out of the gully you drove it into. What were you—"

Colonel Hammer interrupted. "I'd think the Land Forces might be capable of pulling a truck out of a ditch. But if you have trouble, give us a call, and the Air Troops can help you with that."

Hammer turned his attention to Jeriah and me. "A good job, all in all, if not perfect. Both of you. Though the temperatures were fairly mild, the fresh snowfall was a complication."

Mild? Calling those temperatures mild was like putting a dragon in a bonnet and calling it a baby. Coo at it all you want, but it'll still eat your arm clean off.

The colonel went on. "You both used the conditions to your advantage. Did I understand you to say, Specialist Freeman—" He chuckled. "You both have the same name. I mean Specialist *Jeriah* Freeman. Did I understand you to say that your pursuit would likely have been unsuccessful if you hadn't known your opponent?"

"No one can say what the outcome might have been under different circumstances. But once I realized who I was following, I could anticipate where she would go. With her being on foot and me on a snowsled, it was a simple matter to get ahead of her."

I appreciated him saying that. It made me feel less like a loser. Even though I was one.

Another sip of crim eased more of the sting, and I mellowed further as I listened to the rest of their conversation. I might have fallen asleep in the warm room if not for the frequent sharp glance of Colonel Redruff's disapproving eye. He sure was upset about that Groundeater.

So here's the upshot of the whole thing: Colonel Hammer was organizing a new IA team to be deployed in Arktentak, and he wanted Riah and me to be on it. "You two work well together," he told us. "And this assignment will require just that sort of connection."

And so we went off for further IA training, leaving Colonel Redruff to oversee his precious base at Memtic with no further interference from people named Freeman.

And it was no concern to this particular Freeman how much trouble he had getting the Groundeater out of the gully.

ARKENTAK WAS SMOLDERING in those days, and it was Colonel Hammer's task to prevent its bursting into flame.

When the IA Division is successful, nobody hears about it. Subversive elements are pinpointed and removed, problems are dealt with and the tension diffused, ruffled feathers are smoothed, order is restored, all without a ripple touching the rest of the world.

As history records, our efforts at Arkentak were famously ineffective, but that was through no fault of the Hammer. The mess he had to deal with was more than any mortal could handle.

He did everything wisely, followed protocol. Handpicked the teams. Made us nail down the Arkentakian dialects, culture, and traditions so we could pass for natives and gather information however we could. Recommended a plan to Centre City for gaining the locals' confidence. Removed the most intractable instigators and replaced them with City-groomed imposters to preach reason.

But he had forces working against him none of us could see.

JERIAH AND I posed as brother and sister—not hard to pull off—studying at the university in Dabamal. For the first couple of months we shared a small apartment. Then Seena came to join him, and the three of us rented a small house.

As a civilian, she had no part to play in our work other than to lend legitimacy to our cover. And, of course, to keep Jeriah happy. The Division doesn't like to separate a man from his wife for too long at a stretch, particularly when they're newlyweds.

They did give her some training, though, so she didn't stick out as a foreigner. Her job was to work for campus food services and be a traditional Arkentakian wife.

I was none too comfortable living with the two of them. Part of me wanted my brother all to myself. Not in an incestuous way, of course—I had no feelings of that sort for anyone. Another part of me saw how they loved each other, and I wanted to be happy for him.

But seeing them together made both parts of me lonely.

Other than that, I enjoyed that year—the academic experience as well as the undercover work. But at the end of the term, the Division saw fit to move us to Yarapit on Arkentak's eastern border.

Riah and Seena lived in one apartment and I lived in another down the hall in the same building. Though smelly and noisy, it was one of the nicest buildings in that part of the city. Yarapit was like two towns. The monied few had about an eighth of the whole—the part that was high and dry and well maintained—and everyone else got the rest.

Most people would consider Lower Yarapit to be low indeed, but we didn't mind living there. Having canals for streets reminded us of living in stacks along the stillwater, and the dampness and the stink had a homey, familiar feel.

I had a clerical job in a law office. Jeriah worked for the local newspaper—the perfect cover for someone acquiring information—and Seena helped with the neighborhood childcare service.

When I say we didn't mind living in those conditions, I meant Jeriah and me. Turns out Seena was less than content.

I wasn't aware of this at first, as she always kept her thoughts to herself. Also, once we moved into separate apartments, I didn't spend much time with her. But it all came to a head the morning she started to make biscuits for breakfast and a rat nipped at her from inside the flour bin.

I heard her screams from down the hall and came running.

She wasn't screaming at the rat. She killed it quickly and cut it into bits, giving the carcass a new slash with every shriek at Jeriah. "I'm through! If I wanted to live this way, I'd have stayed in Freemansland! Why do you think I left? You can keep your stinking canal, and your vermin, and all those slotty women's filthy brats. I don't care if you come with me, or if you stay here in this reeking hole. But I will not stay here one more night, do you hear me? I'm through!"

I'd burst through the door in the middle of that rant and stood in amazement as she turned the rat to mincemeat, eyes bulging wide in a face splattered with rat blood.

Jeriah kept his distance until the knife clattered to the floor, then he caught her when her knees gave way.

I slipped out, embarrassed to have witnessed the scene.

She left that very day.

He didn't.

Until she sent him word she was pregnant, saying, "I thought you might want to know." Then he put in for a transfer and was sent to Saltcreek Point, where she joined him.

And I was alone again.

Several months later, Riah sent me pictures of my brand-new niece, Kyee Jem Freeman. In the shot of him holding her, the joy on his face lit the whole photo.

And cut me clear through to my own infertile core.

Thanks to infection due to rough handling by Ibro, the doctors told me I'd die childless.

It was just as well, I'd long comforted myself. I never had a mother, so I didn't know how to be one. I'd ruin the life of any child unfortunate enough to be born to me.

Until Jeriah became a father. Then I couldn't help but wonder...

But all that was a moot point, wasn't it? I was alone.

I would always be alone.

❧ Chapter 17 ❧

FAR APART

B UT LET ME back up a bit.

Before Jeriah's transfer went through, the Division shut down our operation in Yarapit and sent us to IA's Arkentak headquarters at Yimisilit for further instruction.

Riah was gloomy over his wife leaving him. I guess I couldn't blame him, but I took his anger personally. As if he thought it was my fault. Not that she left, but because I didn't feel as badly about it as he did. Why should I, though? If she was that miserable, why shouldn't she leave?

I wasn't upset she was gone, but I did mind that he was leaving me to go after her. She's the one who left, so let her have the baby alone. It was her choice.

I never said that in so many words, but he was Jeriah. He knew I was thinking it.

That's why, though we sat in adjoining seats on the train, we were far apart the whole trip.

The Yimisilit I knew bore little resemblance to the pictures you've seen of the ancient place by that name. Those classic images are imbedded in the world's memory: centuries-old buildings carved out of the mountains. Narrow, trough-like streets slashing between ancient walls in steep, uneven zigzags. Glittering pagodas and the conical dwellings of the priestesses. The king's fabulous palace and grounds covering 500 hectares. All that is gone. When the City invaded two centuries ago, they destroyed every brick of it.

In its place stood a clean reproduction, gleaming in the sun by day and well lit by night. Though the architecture was inspired by the old, the similarity was superficial. Like all City projects, modern Yimisilit was intelligently planned, designed for both beauty and utility, and built to an exacting standard.

To the native Yimisils, it was a sacrilege.

FROM THE TRAIN station, we took a tram to the Division office in the military complex at Arkent Exalted, the old palace grounds. Despite the change in ownership, the name remained the same.

Our first task was to meet with a Situation Review committee assembled by Colonel Hammer. Representatives from all twelve investigative units in Arkentak were there, with Jeriah and me reporting for our team. All reported similar findings. Everywhere, the veneer of peace that lay across the region concealed a deep discontent.

"When you were at the university," one of the committee members asked Jeriah and me, "you reported on a quiet religious resurgence, including clandestine meetings of students rediscovering the old traditions."

I let Jeriah answer. "That's correct. The temple on campus and at least two others in town hosted student groups that were ostensibly mainstream. But their rituals and beliefs were more in line with practices outlawed by the City."

The questioning continued. "The other teams have observed similar clandestine meetings in other towns. You say several temples host these groups in Yarapit?"

"That's correct. We found three for sure, and we have reason to believe there are at least two others."

Another officer asked, "Did you ever have the opportunity to attend one of these underground ceremonies?"

Jeriah shook his head. "No, but my sister did."

He turned to me, so I had to answer. "I did, yes. I sneaked into a meeting on campus in Dabamal and observed from a distance. No one knew I was there, and I didn't participate in any ritual. You should find the details in one of my reports. I believe that was in Trimoon. The sixteen of Trimoon, as I recall."

The questioner flipped through screens on his tablet, frowning. "I see that, yes. Your report is quite detailed, but I see no recordings attached."

"I made no recordings. The opportunity presented itself unexpectedly, and I didn't have access to a recording device. Other than my phone, of course, but the battery was low. If I used it up making a video, I would have been out of touch the rest of the night. I thought it better to memorize the ceremony instead."

He lifted his head, brows high. "This is all from memory?"

"That's correct. I transcribed it while it was fresh in my mind, and it is accurate. As far as it goes. I didn't get every word."

Each of the teams' reports were similarly discussed, and the information was sent back to Analysis. It all seemed routine to me, and I had no reason to think anything big was brewing. The City was fully in charge.

Because of differences in the cultures and customs of the various peoples of the world, a few bumps in the road were inevitable. But the City always dealt with whatever came up, maintaining the worldwide peace they'd established generations ago.

Freemansland was one of the last of the independent nations to fall, and even there, the Land of Many Mysteries, the City maintained control. I had no reason to think they wouldn't manage the same here, where they'd ruled well for centuries.

After ten days at Arkentak Exalted, Jeriah shipped off to Saltcreek Point and fatherhood, and I went back to Dabamal to continue my education at the university—and conduct other information acquisition as well.

I returned at the beginning of a new school term and to a new commander, a man who doubled as a professor of Comparative Religions. His name was Ashgrey Standtall, and I disliked him at first meeting.

Well, no, I disliked him before that.

Standtall was an old City Fathers name. He was most likely a direct descendant of the early founders of the City who had rudely, if effectively, taken it upon themselves to conquer the world.

For the world's own good, of course. As we were taught in school, it wasn't mere ambition on the part of the Fathers, but a genuine desire to bring peace and harmony to the planet, to improve the welfare of everyone. They invaded with the purpose of restoration. They hurt in order to heal. The fact that all this made them personally wealthy and powerful was an unintended consequence, or so we were to believe.

Only the descendants of City Fathers were citizens from birth, claiming the status of Citizen First Class, CFC. Other people could earn citizen status through serving in the military for a minimum of ten years, as was my plan. These were made Citizens by Merit, or CM. Citizenship could also be purchased, as business owners were required to do in order to become incorporated. These were Citizens by Commerce, or CC.

So even before seeing him, I knew Professor Ashgrey Standtall, CFC, was the slimiest of all I'd always called Cityslime. Though I could no longer speak that profanity in public, I did still think it. And prior to my first meeting with the learned professor, I allowed my prejudice to color my thinking. Based on his name alone, I considered his CFC status to stand for Cityslime First Class, and I didn't think my opinion of him could sink any lower than that.

It did, though. Once I met him, I saw he was not only a CFC, but a pigeonhead first class. His brow ridge was as pronounced as any I'd ever seen.

As his name suggested, he was tall—five or six centimeters higher than Jeriah—and not one fiber of that broad, powerful back looked like it had ever seen a slouch. His dark brown hair was closely cropped, but not enough to keep a curl from falling onto his forehead. He kept his beard short and neat, and between mustache and beard, his lips were full. Above them, the heavy-lidded eyes were dark as glaffcrim, with little color variation between pupil and iris.

Everything about him gave me the creeps. I'd have rather dealt with the real Dr. Pigeon, a known entity, than have this new doctor pigeonhead standing tall over me, overseeing my actions from under that awning of a forehead.

Oh, but I was a soldier, was I not? As disciplined as the professor's hair wasn't. A wild thing of Freemansland no more, I followed orders. I acquired the information I was sent after and reported on it through the proper channels, all to the best of my considerable ability. And I looked that hated face in the canopied eye as often as it came into view.

Nevertheless, I was wary. Always watching. If he ever ogled me or invited me to flirt as so many others did—the first time he sent me to perform a task that could be considered the least bit inappropriate—the instant he gave me a reason, I'd make a harassment claim. I didn't care how big the brow ridge, how revered the name, I'd press for action against him. Not enough to ruin him. Just enough to get him out of my life.

But he thwarted me at every turn. My commander was a true gentleman. A real-life caricature, modeling the virtues of the Fathers that the history books taught but no one believed.

I didn't know how to respond.

Fortunately, his position was high enough above me that I didn't have many dealings with him—most of my interactions were with my fellow Specialists, or the Information Officer who was my immediate superior.

When I did see him, though, I may have baited him a little. Without really intending to, of course. I might have, unconsciously, hoped to encourage him to slip up.

But that straight backbone of his never bent. His manner toward me was never anything but respectful and professional.

And it drove me nuts.

⁂

A SHORT TIME after the image of Jeriah and Baby Kyee became emblazoned forever in my mind, I enrolled in Professor Standtall's Introduction to World Religions.

It was a required course, or I wouldn't have taken it. I'd tried to sign up for another instructor, but all her classes were full. Or so they said. I was sure someone was manipulating things to force me into his class, but it would have been unwise to make an issue out of it.

Gradually, the picture of Jeriah and Baby Kyee took a back seat to another impression that haunted me when I least expected it. The imposing form of Ashgrey Standtall at the front of the classroom, long arms gesturing. The cut of his vest across his powerful torso. The white of his eye as he looked to the side, the movement of his lips, the husky music of his voice.

When that image came to mind, a strange flush would come over me, and I'd try to think of something else. Like, Jeriah and Baby Kyee.

When that didn't help, I'd close my eyes and think of something awful, like what would happen when my stelli awoke, or... or Ibro.

But that only made it worse. My mouth would go dry, my head would feel light, and my belly would tighten.

Was this the beginning of my madness? I had no headache, and to my knowledge, I wasn't experiencing any blackouts. No, it had nothing to do with being a stellasede. This was something else.

Something I had no experience with.

I couldn't tell Jeriah about it. He was happy, and I didn't want to worry him. And besides, it was too personal. I was embarrassed to bring it up.

❧ Chapter 18 ❧

FURTHER

THOUGH JERIAH WAS on the other side of the world, we kept in touch. During his first few weeks at Saltcreek Point, we communicated every day. Then, especially after the initial excitement of the baby's arrival faded, we backed off a bit. With his job, marriage, and the responsibilities of fatherhood, he didn't always get around to calling me.

His new responsibilities put a distance between us beyond the geographical. If he didn't get a chance to call or message me, I wasn't in a hurry to pick up the slack. What was there to talk about, anyway? Apart from things I couldn't discuss except on a secure connection, I had little of interest to relate. The weather? Sports? Films? Music? I didn't care about any of it.

Late one night, I lay on my bed while we talked, growing sleepy and running out of things to say. For lack of anything else, I brought up my Intro to World Religions class. I didn't mention the professor, only that I was surprised that Sonmanism, the religion of Freemansland, was covered in the course.

"Why does that surprise you?" he asked. "Sonmanism is a world religion, isn't it?"

I yawned. "I suppose, but Freemansland's a pretty small part of the world. And I never realized anyone followed Sonmanism except on Freemansland. Did you know there are pockets of it all over?"

"Never thought about it."

"Neither did I." Glancing at my toes, I noticed the polish chipped on a couple of my nails. My fingernails weren't too bad, but I should get them redone too. "Gran used to do that hand- and head-washing thing before eating, but I never knew what the religion was all about, or what the name Sonmanism refers to."

"I don't either. What does it mean?"

"Some god who's supposed to be more powerful than all the rest—"

Riah snorted. "Aren't they all?"

"According to what I'm learning, not necessarily. But anyway, this one god had a son who became a man. That's what the name is all about. Son, man."

"Never knew that. But hey, did you hear about Mayne?"

I knew why Jeriah's thoughts had made that leap. We were probably both thinking of the blickweed that sometimes stuck in Mayne's hair after performing the traditional pre-meal washing ritual in the stillwater.

"Why would I hear? He's dead to me."

An exasperated sound came through the phone. "He did nothing wrong, you know. He's a good friend. You need to get over it."

"Yeah, well, whatever. What about him?" Truth was, I was a little curious.

"He's a LAST."

I yawned again. "A last what? He lose some sort of a contest?"

"No, dummy, LAST. You know, Land-Air—"

Of course. I finished with him. "— Sea-Tactical. Really? No, I hadn't heard."

I was impressed. Only the best of the best got into that division. I might have been jealous on Jeriah's behalf, except I didn't want to think of my brother undergoing the brutal training. If half the rumors were true, the things those guys went through were inhuman.

For half a second, I felt a twinge of horror for Mayne. But then I frowned, dispelling the thought. "That's all volunteer, right?"

"Right. I don't know why he went out for it."

"Crazy, I guess. Like he always was."

I wasn't sure why I said that. When we were kids, Mayne was the sensible one of our trio. "He's in? I mean, he's not just trying out, but he made it?"

"Survived training, you mean? Yeah. He made it. He's been in for a few months."

"That's good." It might not have been good, but I didn't know what else to say. "You still keep in touch with him?"

"Of course I do. He always asks about you, you know."

"How would I know that?" I yawned again, loudly—not because I needed to, but to let him know I was tired of the conversation. "But it's the middle of the night here, and I need some sleep."

"Yeah, and I'll be sure to give him your regards next time we talk. He still considers you and him promised."

"He can think whatever he wants, but it don't make it true. G'night, Riah." I disconnected the call. *That would be one loveless marriage.*

WITH THE SCHOOL TERM nearing its end, a visit to the day spa was in order.

Much like going to the hairdresser in Tresseiital, where it's scandalous for a decent woman to wash her own hair, regular trips to the spa are nearly obligatory for a woman of Arkentak.

In other words, my life there wasn't all bad.

I timed my visit to conclude just before a meeting scheduled with Commander Standtall at the Division office. We couldn't discuss our real business in a public place, of course, so the team met at a safe location in the catacombs of an Old Arkent wine cellar beneath the city. Male team members accessed the location through one of the men's clubs, and we women gained entrance through a nearby spa. The personnel who worked at the Division daily came through a third passage, beneath an office building.

The pigeonheaded-but-somehow-attractive commander had asked me to arrive for the team meeting early, as he had a special assignment to discuss with me. And so, fresh, relaxed, and immaculately groomed, I stepped into the elevator in the hallway behind the spa.

I selected P for Penthouse then entered a code on the fingerprint-sensitive panel. Instead of taking me up, the elevator descended to the lowest level, where I scanned my iris to enter the passage on the other side of the door.

Though converted from a wine cellar, the Division office was as bright and modern looking as an actual penthouse suite. Perhaps in deference to its history, though, there was always wine sitting around for anyone to drink.

As I said, life in Arkentak wasn't all bad.

As I poured myself a glass in the meeting room, the commander strode in. The men's club bouquet of incense and booze wafted in with him.

He nodded an expressionless greeting. "Specialist Freeman."

In the Division, we didn't salute in casual situations such as this, so I merely nodded back. "Commander."

"I hope you have no plans with your family over the holidays." He gestured toward a chair then pulled out one for himself. "Have a seat."

I put down my wineglass and sat. "I have no family."

"Your brother and his wife might be insulted to hear you say that."

I felt myself flush, though I didn't know why. Was it because he knew about my family? Or because what he said might be true? "They'd know what I meant."

He sat at an angle, one arm over the back of his chair. "That Freemanslanders don't celebrate New Day, you mean?"

My flush deepened. Again, for no reason. "Yes."

"That's nothing to be ashamed of." He paused. "Or embarrassed about. Though New Day is the City's biggest holiday, celebrating it has never been mandatory."

Was he watching my reaction? Because I tried not to show my feelings—which I didn't quite understand myself—but wasn't sure what my expression was doing. For some reason, his full attention was on my face.

He continued. "But however you celebrate New Day, or even if you don't, you get two weeks off from class, so it's a good thing, right? Except in this case. Because neither of us gets a holiday this year."

Lost as to what he was getting at, I took a sip of wine. "Oh?"

"Your family might not care, but mine will. My mother, especially. She puts great stock in New Day." As if to signal that he was bringing the conversation to the point, he straightened in his chair and clasped his hands on the table. "Are you familiar with the Kenta tribe in the south of Arkentak?"

"I've heard of them, of course, but I don't know a great deal about them."

"In that case, you must learn all you can in the next week or so, because we're going to Kenta City for the holiday."

That made no sense. "I didn't think they celebrate New Day."

"They don't."

"So why are we going?" Did I see amusement in those sparking eyes? Then I had another thought. "And who's *we*?"

"*We* is you and I." His big paw gestured from me to him. "*Why* is because the Division believes something is brewing there. And *we*—" He repeated the gesture "—are the two who are to find out what's going on." His gaze sucked mine into its deep glaffcrim pools. "Apparently, Colonel Hammer thinks we'd make a good team."

I felt as articulate as I'd been as a child. "Oh."

"I agree. That we can be a good team, that is."

"Oh?"

"Yes. So. It's good you had no plans for the holiday. Because now you have nothing to cancel."

"And what are we doing, exactly?"

He spent the next several minutes filling me in, concluding with, "You can get with Specialist Exaba after the team meeting. She has the clothes you'll need, the traditional Kentan koorma, and she'll show you how to wrap it properly. I hear there's a trick to it. Everything else you'll need to know, I'll send to your tablet."

Voices in the hall signaled the arrival of Den Spen, whom I'd worked with in Walpin, and Nyna Fleur.

Spen paused in the entrance. "What, are we late?"

Nyna strode past him. "No, we're early. They're just earlier." She zeroed in on me. "You've been to the spa? I didn't get a chance yet."

I admired my fresh manicure. "My favorite stylist had an opening, so I snagged her while I could."

Nyna squealed. "Oh, look, the little triangles she put under your eyes match what's on your nails. That's brilliant!"

"You should see if you can get Yace when you go. She's the best."

Make-up, manicures, personal stylists. The proper wrapping of a Kentan koorma. How far I'd come from Freemansland.

Oh, but I had further yet to go.

⁂

JUMPING OUT OF an airplane has never been my favorite thing to do.

My first time, in training, I convinced myself it wouldn't be so bad. Gritted my teeth and jumped.

But it *was* that bad. Worse than I'd expected. I hated every aspect of it.

Nevertheless, I was required to do it again. There was no way to know if I'd ever have to do it in the field, but if the time came that I had to jump for a mission, I'd already have the training out of the way.

It was almost enough to make me join a religion of some sort, so I'd have a god to pray to, to beg that he or she would keep me from ever jumping out of an airplane again.

But I had no god. There was no one to pray to when, on New Day's Eve in the south of Arkentak, I was required to jump out of an airplane.

In the dark.

With the big pigeonhead tumbling out behind me.

❧ Chapter 19 ❧

REHEARSING A NEW ROLE

'M HAVING TROUBLE telling these events in order, probably because... well, let's not worry about that for now. But if you're to make sense of the story, we'll have to go back to three days before New Day, when the commander and I entered the Third Street Pagoda for worship.

The rich royal blue and gold fabric of my koorma draped in soft, graceful folds. Below the hem, my perfectly pedicured feet breathed free in flat sandals bejeweled with colored glass. I felt like royalty.

And my arm—the Kentan term for a woman's man—would have been a suitable escort for a queen. Taller than anyone there, his manly form in the mid-thigh-length brocade jacket over silky, balloon-legged trousers drew every admiring eye in the pagoda.

That had been the plan.

It was unusual for me to deliberately be the center of attention. I was a natural at going unnoticed, and invisibility was my favorite garment. It surprised me how easily I slipped into this new role.

The Kentan culture provides fertile soil for rumors. A seed of gossip casually dropped to the ground will germinate almost the moment it lands. Unless the first shoot is squashed and the seedling uprooted, a rumor can multiply and carpet the region with blooms in just a few days.

The Division had planted just such a seed two weeks before. A man mentioned that his friend's cousin was coming to town. This woman's allure was so powerful that she'd ensnared a member of the City's ruling class. He wanted to marry her, but she would only agree on the condition he convert to Stridenism. Such was her power that he'd recently done just that. Her stipulation now met, their engagement needed only her mother's approval to be made official.

The mother was in a convalescent center in Kenta City recovering from a horrible accident that had nearly ended her life. There was a good story about that floating around as well, but I won't go into detail. The gist was, because of the mother's injuries, the couple must visit her rather than she them. And while they were in Kenta City, they wanted to worship in the renowned Third Street Pagoda.

Rumor had it that the woman was highborn, tracing her lineage through an unbroken maternal line straight from the Ishi sisters, revered by all the tribe for delivering the true faith from the goddess Striden. For one of such pedigree to have captured a son of the enemy was unprecedented. Such a coup held untold potential.

This plump nut was planted in a men's club in the city of Rikma, but the rumor's tendrils spread so quickly that no one was sure where it originated. People only knew a woman of noble birth might show up at the Third Street Pagoda on the arm of a tall Citizen First Class one day soon.

And so she did. Except for the part about her being of noble birth. That dubious distinction belonged solely to Commander Ashgrey Standtall, CFC.

But since everyone wanted to think I was regal too, I rode the wave. Just doing my job, right? By the time they learned the truth, we'd be long gone.

And yes, I did say we jumped out of an airplane on New Day's Eve. But some other things happened first.

THE EVENING BEFORE we were to make our grand entrance at the pagoda, we checked into a suite in Kent Gardens Hotel. Although we had separate bedrooms, I would have been uncomfortable with the arrangement except that the suite was huge, and the commander was such a gentleman.

Even so, I kept my bedroom door locked.

The worship service didn't begin until noon, so we had a leisurely breakfast. After sweeping the whole suite to check for listening devices, we went over the details of our plan. Everything hinged on what we learned at the worship service, so he made sure I understood what to expect, how to respond, what was required on my part to make people believe I was who they'd heard I was.

He leaned forward in his chair at the breakfast table, hands clasped in earnestness. "You can't hang back and just watch this time. You have to participate. With enthusiasm. As a daughter of the Ishi, you're going to have to throw yourself into it."

I nodded, pretending the thought didn't throw my stomach into revolt. "I can do that."

From the way those dark eyes narrowed beneath the jutting brow ridge, he didn't seem convinced. "Can you?" He shook his head. "No, I know you can. The question is, do *you* know it?"

Images and memories I'd rather remained hidden writhed across my mind, and a knot in my gut tightened. "I guess we'll find out."

⁂

OUR CAR PULLED up near the pagoda's entrance shortly before noon. The commander exited, the gold buttons on his chocolate-brown jacket catching the sun and tossing flecks of it every which-way.

Once he'd unfurled to his full height, he took the hand I extended toward him, and out I stepped. All part of the Kentan mating dance.

The car door closed. He bowed, then offered his arm. I laid my hand on it, and together we turned toward the building's entrance.

The pagoda was as fabulous as its reputation indicated, but I kept myself from gawking like a tourist. The solid, reassuring arm under my hand helped.

Music played softly, and a subtle fragrance tickled my nostrils. The elaborate visuals and the feeling of grandeur the structure induced, combined with the gentle prodding of the other senses, made it a moving experience merely to pass through the doors.

Most of the men we met gave us furtive glances as if afraid to stare. The women exhibited no such shame. They beamed at us. Gave my "arm" a good once-over and looked me up and down with a critical eye—apparently approving, because the examination always concluded with a sly smile.

One woman, in a koorma with similar colors to mine but not as extravagant, was bold enough to feel the commander's sleeve as we passed, as if wondering what it would be like to have his arm. The little fellow accompanying her was careful to avoid my eye. "Excuse me," I said to her. "May I help you with something?"

Part of the female Kentan mating challenge.

Her gaze flew to my glare, then quickly away. Addressing my collarbone, she gave a forced smile, a peace offering. "No, ma'am. I've never seen you here before, is all. Are you new in town?"

As a gracious dignitary, I accepted her offering. "Just visiting. I'm here to introduce him to my mother and wished to see the pagoda while I'm in the area." I took the opportunity to admire the vast rotunda in which we stood. "And it's certainly worth seeing. Do you come here regularly?"

Her delight seemed genuine. "I do, yes. It is a beautiful building, isn't it? And the services are powerful. As you'll soon see, Our Lady Striden's spirit flows strongly here."

She tossed a glance up at my arm, who appeared to be ignoring the conversation as he ogled the ornate artwork on the arched ceiling high above us. Then she returned her attention to me, meeting my eye this time. Meaningfully. "Would you like to be my guest in the service?"

I shook my head, forcing a smile to hide my repugnance. "Thank you for your hospitality, but no. I shall find my own way."

"As you like it." She winked, then spoke to her escort. "Come, Tenton."

As I like it? I didn't like it at all, whether at someone else's hand or my own. But I think I managed to conceal my distaste.

After the other couple had turned away, the commander bent to my ear. "You're very good at this."

By an instinct I didn't know I had, I put my finger to his lips, frowning.

His arm stiffened beneath my hand and his brows flew upward. In the next instant, an expression of humble deference erased the look of surprise. He lowered his head. "My apologies."

Something told me I'd hear about this later—but I was playing a role, wasn't I? And in this scene, the woman ruled with a firm, manicured hand. A man could only speak in public if his queen permitted it.

He understood that, though, and played his role. His character was an outsider to this culture, and still learning. The scenario between us would appear plausible and proper to any observer.

With my errant arm accepting his correction with subservience, I allowed my expression to soften. "You're still learning. But you're doing well."

The way he beamed at the false praise unsettled me. I almost believed he truly did crave my approval. To distract myself from the uncomfortable feeling his fawning created, I turned toward an image of the goddess in an alcove not far from where we stood.

"What a lovely statue." I led him forward for a closer look. "She's exquisite, isn't she?"

"She is, my dear. And so are you. Would it be too bold to say you do her honor?"

This was getting out of control.

On the other hand, there were people in hearing range, and from their posture, it appeared several were observing us. He was wise to stay in character, and I should do the same.

I managed to find words to answer. "It would be too bold, yes. I do not succeed yet, but honoring the goddess is my goal."

Now that we were near the statue, I found it more disconcerting than the conversation. The goddess Striden reclined on a couch in a position that clearly depicted her pleasuring herself.

This was the deity I was supposed to worship? It shouldn't have come as a shock, for I already knew this, in theory. But the reality of what I was getting myself in for turned my breakfast to acid.

The commander must have felt my grip on his arm tighten, for he laid his big paw on my hand and gave it a gentle squeeze. "The sculptor was very skilled, wasn't she?"

I swallowed hard. "Very. *She* does honor to the goddess. Far more than I ever shall."

For the next few minutes, we admired the artwork and mingled with the other couples. Once, when a family came in with young children, two women near the entrance escorted them through a door to another part of the building.

"There is another entrance for families?" I asked the woman I'd been speaking with.

Tiana, in a rust-colored koorma too small for her girth, nodded. "Oh, yes. What goes on here is a little intense for the youngsters."

Netine, so small she barely came to my shoulder, lifted her face to speak to me. "But of course, we instruct them properly with age-appropriate doctrinal lessons. It's important to keep the faith alive through the generations."

Tiana patted her belly. "That's right." Oh, so that's why her koorma didn't drape as it should. "After generations of neglect, we're now determined to pass it down to our daughters as our foremothers did for theirs."

The subject of babies had always unsettled me, but the thought of raising children in an environment such as this made me half sick. I tried to think of something to say. "And who does the teaching in the children's area?"

Netine seemed surprised at the question. "The grandmothers, of course. How is it done where you come from?"

I'd already rehearsed the answer to that. "The congregations there tend to be more, shall we say, restrained." I smiled. "They stick with the regulations the City has imposed concerning what should go on in a worship service."

Tiana made a knowing nod. "No reason to keep the children separate then. But of course, um—" She tossed a glance up at my escort, then back to me. "You're free to worship Our Lady however you wish in the privacy of your own homes, right?"

"Of course." I gave a somewhat lascivious smile. "The City gives us that, at least."

Chimes sounded then, and two women appeared, wearing thin, filmy hooded cloaks and little else, and stood at separate doorways while a sultry voice came over the loudspeaker. "Daughters of Our Lady, the Goddess Striden. Come, let us worship together." The woman standing in the wider doorway raised her arms.

Another voice, a bit higher in pitch, invited, "Sons of the Mother, we invite you to worship." The woman at the narrower passage made a summoning motion.

A feminine hum of delight vibrated across the lobby as the ladies separated from their arms and made for the wider doorway, while the men headed for the other.

The commander gave me a searching look.

"See ya," I murmured, then turned and joined the flow of women into the passage to the sanctuary.

❧ Chapter 20 ☙

THE PLOT

AFTER THE SERVICE at the pagoda, we took a cab to Our Lady's Healing Hands, an old mansion on the outskirts of Kenta City that had recently been converted to a convalescent center.

Part of it was, in fact, a care facility, but the upper level quietly housed secret City offices. Our actual purpose there was a meeting with the Division brass, not with a mother who didn't exist.

When I entered the cab, I was met with the lingering fragrance of a recent passenger. Whoever he was, he wore too much Vintage Seas. "Taxi, please aerate." The hum of the fan came on as the commander folded his large frame enough to get in beside me.

He gave me a meaningful look and put his finger to his lips, indicating he wasn't sure if our conversation might be overheard. Wishing I didn't remember the feeling of those lips under my finger two hours earlier, I gave a quick nod.

That wasn't all I wished. Nor all I wanted to forget. I didn't want to be in the same car with the heavy-browed commander. How had I once found him attractive? He repulsed me now. Everything repulsed me, including my own company. For the first time in years, I longed to jump into the water—not that there was any around, but it would have been good to wash away the filthy feeling—and swim away from the world.

The car started moving, and the commander pulled out his phone and activated the application that checked for listening devices. "I got a text from my mother. I should answer it."

"That's true. Mother gets first priority." *I should say something else pertinent, in case someone was listening.* "Until I do, of course."

"Of course, my queen." He studied the screen, then lifted the phone toward me. "Look at this. She's always sending me pictures of her cat."

There was no cat. He was scanning my vicinity for hidden cameras. Apparently finding none, he made another, more thorough scan, no longer disguising his actions. "We're clear. No electronic signals except from the navigational computer and the satellite radio." He pocketed the phone. "So what did you think of the Third Street Pagoda?"

I leaned back and closed my eyes. "Not sure. I need to process it."

"Understood."

His presence beside me seemed unusually large, warm, and real. And unwanted.

After a brief silence, he spoke again. "Did you win anyone's confidence? Learn anything useful?"

I opened one eye and directed it his way. "Yes, I think. And I'm not sure." I shifted in my seat. "I feel dirty. Can we stop at the hotel first? I'd like to change."

"No." His manner took on a new firmness. "In this traffic, we'll be lucky to make our appointment even without the detour. And I despise tardiness."

A sound of exasperation escaped me, unbidden. "I need to change."

"I heard you the first time, Specialist. But the playacting is over. You're not the queen."

I'd never heard that tone from him before. It reminded me of the original Pigeonhead, and I was tempted to glare at him as I did at the doctor when he irritated me. But, as he reminded me, I was a mere specialist and he was the commander. Besides, I didn't want to have to look at that hated brow ridge any more than necessary. So I stared out the window instead.

The sight there gave me no pleasure either. The roads were bloated with vehicles, and our slow progress allowed me to contemplate the shocking contrast between the shabby buildings we passed and the magnificent one we'd just left. The few people about didn't appear very lively, either. Stooped and shuffling. Almost as if they saw nothing to live for.

"If it's any comfort, you look good."

I turned toward him, feeling my eyes widening.

"I mean—" Did he blush? "You expressed the need to change. But you don't look like you need to. Your clothes—all of you—you look good."

I was trying to decide how to respond when he reached into his breast pocket, pulled out a paper, and unfolded it. He frowned as he studied it.

"What's that?"

He tossed me a sideways glance then returned the paper to his pocket. "Not sure. I need to process it." He raised his voice to speak to the car. "Taxi. Play something a bit livelier, please. And turn up the volume."

The car complied.

In the resultant din, we processed our thoughts without speaking for the rest of the trip.

⁂

WE HAD ONLY a minute and half to spare as we entered the reception room at Our Lady's Healing Hands. Though the lovely villa nestled in a striking valley, its medical reek brought back unpleasant memories of the hospital on Coldclime. Between that and the Cityslime beside me, not to mention the unsettling experience I'd had at the pagoda, my skin prickled with a sense of wrongness. As if the world I was walking through was tainted.

The desire to escape nearly overtook me as we approached the front desk.

The receptionist was absent, it being a worship day, so the commander pressed the buzzer marked *Security*. A few moments later, a burly woman approached the window. "May I help you?"

I got the impression I wasn't through with my role-playing yet and stepped in front of the commander. "We're here to see my mother, Ama Noreyal."

The woman nodded. "Yes, I understand she's expecting you."

A loud hum signaled the unlocking of the door, which the woman then opened. "Your mother is on the third floor. This way, please."

We followed her down a hallway where the smells of disinfectant and bodily effluent mingled. We passed a corridor from which drifted a mixture of music, video shows, religious chanting, and someone moaning.

Our guide didn't speak, and neither did we. I can't say what my escort was doing as he lumbered behind me, but I had to concentrate on keeping my churning stomach under control.

It seemed a long walk with numerous turns before we stopped in front of a single elevator door. The woman pressed the button. "Here you go. I trust you'll be able to find your way from here."

I forced a smile. "I'm sure we will. Thank you."

I didn't feel sure of anything, other than I didn't like being here.

The woman strode away, the elevator door opened, and we stepped in.

The commander took charge again, first selecting the third floor, then stooping for an iris scan when prompted after the door closed. I expected the car to take us into the basement like at the headquarters in Dabamal, but instead it went up.

As we rose, the commander took out a handkerchief and blew his nose. "Excuse me. That smell was getting to me."

"It bothered me too." For some reason it comforted me that he shared my distress.

The car stopped, and the door opened. My breath caught at the mountain vista beyond the glass wall. The scenery was marvelous, but I also appreciated that this part of the villa didn't smell.

"Commander Standtall, Specialist Freeman. You're right on time."

The beautiful view had distracted me from seeing the man standing there. I recognized him as Mentin, Colonel Hammer's aid.

The commander obviously knew him too. "Ah, Mentin. We must be at the right place, though you are too polite to speak of our tardiness."

Mentin shook his head. "You're at the right place *and* the right time. This way, please." He headed down the hall to the left, then stopped at a doorway and gestured for us to enter. "Everyone's assembled in the briefing room."

The four men and one woman seated at the table looked up as we entered. Colonel Hammer waved us to empty seats opposite each other. "Commander Standtall, good to see you. And Specialist Freeman. Your costume suits you well."

"Thank you, sir."

A bottle and four glasses sat on a tray in the middle of the table. Was that whisky? I eyed it, trying not to look too interested. I apparently failed, because the colonel asked, "Would you two like some refreshment?"

The commander shook his head. "No, but thank you."

I took a breath before answering so as not to sound to eager. "I would. Thank you, colonel." I reached for the bottle, but the man to my left, Specialist Eagal, beat me to it.

He poured a shot into a glass and handed it to me, then put another slosh in his own. "You're a whisky drinker?" He glanced at me sideways, not quite smiling.

"On occasion."

"I think you'll like this." He turned to me and raised his glass. "Arkentak's best, in my opinion."

I took a sniff. "Five Blue?"

He grinned. "You know your whisky."

I downed it. Oh, yes. I needed that. "I agree. Arkentak's best." If he offered to give me a refill, I wouldn't turn him down. But he didn't, and I thought it best to wait until the debriefing was over before helping myself to more.

Out of the corner of my eye I caught the commander watching me, but he looked away as soon as I glanced his direction.

The colonel was speaking, so I put both the commander and the emptiness of my whisky glass out of my mind and focus on the matter at hand.

That matter being the growing resentment against the City among the Kenta tribe in the south of Arkentak. It seemed the Kentans thought it of little consequence that the City ruled well and fairly, that the law provided more freedoms and afforded more widespread prosperity than they were willing to take advantage of. For reasons the City couldn't fathom, the people wanted to return to their old ways of life. Ways that had been romanticized through the telling, but in truth were better left to the past.

But ways to which the people were determined to return, through whatever measures proved necessary—aided, in their opinion, by the holy goddess Striden and her avenging angels.

Three of the men at the table were specialists like me, tasked with acquiring and reporting information. I listened in silence at first, absorbing the things they reported, fitting it into what I already knew, and trying to make sense out of it. When called upon, the commander gave some insights into the Stridenian religion and how it affected the tribe's values, customs, and culture.

The woman who sat beside him, an analyst, took copious notes. She frequently interrupted the other men to ask questions, but when the commander spoke, she merely listened and nodded. She looked as if she were Kentan herself, so she'd already be well acquainted with the religion. The fact that she never interrupted to make a correction told me he knew what he was talking about.

But then, I'd never had any doubt of that.

The realization surprised me. I'd been so put off by his pigeonhead brow and family name that I'd never acknowledged he was as capable as he was pedigreed. He knew a lot about everything and a great deal about his specialty. He was well spoken and gracious without a hint of arrogance or condescension. As he spoke, his smooth, cultured voice lapped against my mind like gentle ripples against a canoe, and part of me longed to slip over the side and swim in them.

I gave my head a quick jerk and shifted in my chair. Had I been falling asleep? No, I hadn't missed a word. But what had I been thinking?

That whisky must have been more potent than I thought.

Or perhaps not potent enough. Because when it was my turn to make my report, I froze for a moment. Then I sat up straighter, gave myself a mental shake, and opened my mouth, wondering what would come out.

Fortunately, I quickly slipped into report mode, and while staring blankly at a spot on the table in front of me, gave an overview of my experiences at the pagoda.

I could have gone into more depth, but a description of every detail and a recitation of every word spoken would have been tedious. But mostly, I was too embarrassed to speak of my every action in participating in the rituals.

Though I left out the personal aspects, I could tell two of the men—especially Eagal—were curious to know them. I didn't look up, but I sensed their interest. It was a subtle scent, perhaps, or some other cue that barely registered on the senses, but something exuded from them that reminded me of Ibro.

I felt more dirty than ever.

Without lifting my gaze, I continued my recitation as if unaware of their curiosity. And made certain to satisfy none of it.

The analyst interrupted me. "Did you say *another* flogging? The one scheduled for Midweek next is not the first?"

"From what I gather, the religious leaders have long worked with the local constabulary. For the past several decades, it's been common for a person guilty of a religious crime—that is, something that's forbidden by the religion but not by City law—to be arrested and prosecuted on false civil charges. But now, the entire court system has apparently been cooperating with the Order of Our Lady. The magistrates are giving the priestesses access to the prisons to administer judgment in their own way. It wasn't until a few months ago, however, that a prisoner was taken to the pagoda for a public flogging, with all the accompanying ceremony."

Colonel Hammer frowned. "That's preposterous. This official corruption has been going on for decades, and we've never been aware of it?" I wasn't sure if it was the situation he was upset with, or me, for saying it.

Before I could reply, the analyst scowled even deeper. "This is serious. We've known things were escalating, but if it's reached this point, we're in danger of losing control altogether."

The colonel addressed her. "You believe this report to be true, then?"

"Yes, sir. We've heard rumors, but they keep their business sealed up watertight. Routine audits and inspections have always shown everything to be in meticulous order, and none of the rumors have ever been substantiated."

The oldest of the specialists, whose name was Nibrik, nodded. "Too meticulous. I've participated in court file inspections in a number of provinces around the world. None are so clean and above-board as what I've seen here in Kenta. No file is incomplete, there's nothing out of place or unaccounted for, and every T is crossed with a perfect, straight line. It's so flawless you can't help but think they're hiding something, though we've never been able to put a finger on what's wrong."

Specialist Termo—the one who, like Eagal, had shown more interest than I liked in what went on in the worship service—spoke up. "And no whistle-blower has ever come forth. My team has been feeling around everywhere, but all we can find is a scent of things brewing. No cracks big enough to get our fingers in to pry the wall open."

The commander reached into his pocket. "Until now. Perhaps."

Everyone swiveled toward him, and the colonel's brows raised. "What's that, Standtall? Did you meet the man who supposedly had something for us?"

"I may have. A man handed me this in the restroom after the service." He passed the paper across the table to Colonel Hammer. "Probably the man we came to find."

Hammer smoothed out the note and read it silently while the rest of us watched. His face revealed nothing, but the pulse in his neck quickened.

He appeared to read it twice, then handed it to the analyst. "Tell us about this possible informant, Standtall."

The commander explained how the man had attracted his attention early on because it appeared he was being shunned. No one spoke to him and he met no one's eye. The man had gone through the motions of worship, mouthing the right words at the right times, but showed no passion for it. Whereas the others enjoyed some aspects with ribald pleasure, when this man smiled in response to a suggestive statement, it seemed forced. And he was fidgety, as if he couldn't wait to get out of the building.

The man also seemed to surreptitiously watch the commander. He entered the restroom as the commander was leaving and slipped him the note without a word. The commander pocketed it and didn't take it out again until we were in the car.

"Earlier," the commander said, "when I thought he was watching me, I asked one of the friendlier guys, 'What's with that weird fella sitting there by himself?' The man I asked made a face, shook his head, and said, 'He displeased the Lady. We don't associate with his kind.' I asked about something else then, so as not to seem interested in him. But between what the man said, and the way the strange guy seemed about to be sick when the upcoming flogging ceremony was discussed, I wonder if he might not have been the victim last time."

Eagal asked, "So why was he there? I'd think he'd stay clear of the place after that."

Before the commander could answer, the analyst spoke up. "Most likely he has no choice. I expect part of his sentence is that he must attend worship services faithfully from now on or endure further punishment."

Nibrik gasped. "They can flog people for not going to worship service?"

"They punish disobedience. If a man is commanded to attend worship—"

Colonel Hammer interrupted. "Do you think the note is legitimate, Miss Zakad? Do you believe the information is reliable?"

She pursed her lips. "I'm inclined to think it might be. But I'd need more verification before I could recommend acting on it."

"With all due respect," said the commander, "we don't have the luxury of time."

All three of the other specialists asked at once, "What does it say?"

The colonel nodded to the analyst. "Read it to us."

She did. "Plot to bomb City admin building in Kenta City. Finalizing plans at noon on New Day, Obicon Timbers, Bowl Rock. No joke, proof 2nite."

Everyone had questions but no answers. It was unthinkable that anyone would have the gall to bomb a City building, anywhere. But too many rumors in gossip-rich Kenta had to do with that very thing to dismiss the idea.

Obicon Timbers was a forest along Arkentak's southwestern border. But what was Bowl Rock? What sort of proof did the strange man speak of? What would happen tonight to demonstrate his reliability?

We carried the discussion into the next room where a meal had been set up for us. When the sun sank in the sky, window shades closed to keep our meeting private from anyone in the valley below.

Finally the colonel brought things to a close, concluding with a nod in my direction. "Specialist Freeman. You've made your case to your mother, but she can't come to a decision as yet. She'll have to think about it overnight and will give you and Commander Standtall an answer tomorrow. Be here at ten hundred, and she'll tell you what she's decided."

I frowned in confusion at the beginning of that statement, but by the time he'd finished, I understood. "Very well, Colonel. Or should I say, Mother?"

He smiled as he rose, and we all stood as well. But he didn't answer my question. He merely said, "I'll see the two of you tomorrow and will send the rest of you further instructions. Good evening, all."

He left the room, and a kitchen crew came in to clean up.

Eagal, who'd been eager during the meal to keep my wine glass from running dry, eyed me from my elegantly coiffed head to my bejeweled feet and everything in between. More the between parts, actually. "How about a nightcap? I know a good place not far from here."

Eagal wasn't the only one with eyes—the commander's were locked on my admirer, and something in the glint of them was unsettling.

"Thanks," I said, not certain how I'd have answered if the commander weren't there. "Sounds good, but no. Not tonight."

Eagal glanced the commander's way, then back to me. "Oh, really? Is that how it is?"

"What? It isn't anything. I just have things to do."

Eagal snorted. "Sure. But there are rules against those things, you know."

The commander frowned. "I don't know what you're referring to, Eagal, but whatever Freeman's doing tonight concerns neither you nor me."

Eagal made a show of saluting. "Of course, sir. Whatever you say." He clicked his heels together and strode out.

I followed, not to be with him, but to get out of there. Part of me wanted to tell both those sparring roosters to back off, while another part—regal in my flowing, royal blue koorma—enjoyed the attention.

But no part of me liked feeling confused. And that, I certainly was. The events of the day had turned me inside-out.

❧ Chapter 21 ❧

BABUNJA TEA

SAID NOTHING as we passed through the villa on the way to the car. Eagal walked on ahead, and the commander trailed behind me like an obedient Kentan arm.

My head felt a little dizzy. I'd drunk all that wine at dinner hoping to steady myself, but it seemed to have the opposite effect. It was good I'd turned down Eagal's offer.

But of course, he was looking for more than just drinks. Men had only one thing in mind.

That's one thing that confused me about the religion of the Kentans. With them, it was the women who had that one thing in mind, and they weren't choosy as to where they got it. Though they considered men useful for procreation, they enjoyed a variety of options when seeking pleasure. Or what they called worship, which seemed to me a Stridenian synonym for lust. A sour pool of revulsion formed in my gut.

Eagal, on his way toward a different exit, turned and called back to me. "Last chance, Freeman. Sure you won't change your mind?"

I gave a wave. "Maybe next time."

"Is that a promise?"

"I said *maybe*."

Termo's voice rang out from somewhere behind me. "Eagal! Share a cab with me?"

Eagal shrugged. "I s'pose. But you're not good-lookin' enough to share a drink with."

"Neither are you, bud."

They went their way, and the commander and I went ours.

We exited the building through the front doors. Security lights provided an island of day in the sea of dark night, where a car awaited. I headed for it, the commander's clunking footfalls echoing the rat-a-tat of my sandals across the pavement.

In three heavy strides, he was abreast of me, reaching ahead with his long, brocade-clad arm to open the car door.

I paused and looked up at him. "I could'a got that, sir."

"Yes. But if you were to write that in a paper, I would have to correct your grammar."

I ducked into the car. "As my professor, you'd 'a been within your rights."

He closed the door, went around to the other side, and climbed in. "As you would have been within your rights to accept Eagal's invitation. Specialists are allowed to fraternize with one another, you know."

I waited until he'd finished instructing the car where to take us before I replied. "I also have the right to refuse. And I can't say I care for this conversation."

He tipped his head in acquiescence. "I apologize. I didn't intend to make you uncomfortable."

"I'm plenty uncomfortable, but it's not your doing. It's the day's experiences."

He tried to cross his legs, but there wasn't room. "Speaking of uncomfortable, this cab is smaller than the last one."

I glanced around. "I think it is."

He instructed the car to turn up the music.

After less than two minutes of head-thumping bass, I'd had as much as I could take. "Taxi, change the music to a Borgeen concerto, please. As low as the volume will go."

The commander/professor arched those prominent brows at me—which in the small confines of the car came across as more than a little intimidating.

"I didn't wish to contradict you, sir, but I endured your choice of music on the way here— "

"And now it's my turn to suffer?"

I turned my face to the blank window. "Yeah, that sums it up nicely." Was it the wine or my weariness that made me so foolish? I was insubordinate, but I didn't back down. My daily ration of endurance was used up. If he wanted to bring disciplinary action, so be it.

"You should have said something."

My gaze flew to his face.

"We're on an assignment, and part of my job is making sure you're equipped to perform it. Torturing you with loud music would be counterproductive."

"Oh." My mind searched for something to say. "Thank you."

He grunted again, and neither of us found any words the rest of the trip.

IN THE HOTEL room, I slipped off my sandals. I didn't pay any attention to what the commander did but wasted no time pouring myself a drink.

What he did, I realized, was watch me.

"What?" I held up the bottle. "Want a shot?"

"No." He came toward me. "And please don't take this wrong, but you shouldn't—"

I glared at him, and he stopped in mid-sentence, then started over. "I'll rephrase. You've had enough, Specialist. Neither of us knows what duties you'll be required to perform tomorrow, but any more drinking tonight is likely to hinder you."

He took the glass from my hand.

I was too stunned to object. Something was twisted here, but my mind couldn't straighten it out.

It wasn't until he poured the contents of the glass into the sink that I came to my senses. "What are you doing? You can't do that!"

"I believe I can. In fact, I'm obligated to, as I just explained." He waved me out of the way. "Go sit down. I'll clean up here."

Clean up? There was one glass. And how was I supposed to sit in a room with him and his attitude?

When I didn't move, he frowned. "Was my instruction not clear?" He pointed to the sitting area. "You, out there. Go."

Certain there must be a regulation against a Specialist having to share a suite with an officer, I moved into the sitting area and then toward my room. "Maybe I'll just hit the sack."

"At 20:30?" He turned on the water and washed the glass in a ham-handed, too-tall-for-the-sink sort of way.

The sight almost made me smile. *I must be drunk if I find that amusing.* "Well, I'm going to shower, anyway."

"Come back out here when you're done. I'm making babunja tea." He filled the tea maker with water.

"Babunja?"

"It's very calming. My mother swears by it."

"I don't know about babunja, but calming sounds good. Very well, then. I'll be back." On the way to my room, I snatched up my sandals.

※

I'VE NEVER BEEN a tea drinker, but babunja turned out to be not terrible.

I sat on the divan, legs tucked under me, and took the cup he offered. "I hope you don't mind that I didn't dry my hair."

"Why should I mind?" He took a seat across the room.

I ran my fingers through the wet strands. "I'd never go out in public looking like this."

"We're not in public."

You wouldn't know it from the way he was dressed. He'd changed clothes when I was showering and looked like the professor again—vest, ruffled cravat, and all. But despite his perfect appearance, something about him made me squeamish. To avoid looking his way, I stared at the area rug in front of me.

Interesting design. Very Arkentakian. Whatever else might be said about these people, I did like their use of color. I closed my eyes, trying to forget the sensations I'd experienced at the pagoda. But shutting off the actual only made the memory clearer.

"You have questions."

My eyes flew open at his voice. It was a nice voice. Pleasantly raspy.

The shower hadn't cleared my brain any, that much was for sure. I took another sip of tea but didn't lift my gaze. "I do?"

"You've been disturbed since we came from the pagoda."

I took a sideways peek at him. His expression was what he wore when standing in front of the classroom. Non-threatening. There to impart knowledge.

Careful not to spill the tea, I rearranged myself on the divan. "Okay, Professor, it's true, I have questions. And they disturb me."

He waited for me to continue.

"I don't get it. Religion, that is. Where does all that come from, anyway?"

He almost frowned. "I thought we covered that in class."

"We did, and it made sense, at the time. The ancients created myths about deities to explain things they didn't understand." On my fingers, I ticked off the various points. "Once the thought is planted, spiritual entities and powers can be imagined in everything, thus appearing to confirm their existence. People offered sacrifices in a desperate attempt to persuade the unseen powers to manipulate conditions to favor them. Mankind developed the idea of an afterlife to ease their fear of death. Wanting to maintain connection with deceased loved ones, they devised traditions about their ancestors watching over and guiding them. Religion gave structure to society, serving as a framework for behavioral expectations and social responsibility."

He nodded. "Ah. You *were* paying attention."

"Yeah. So, I get all that, as far as it goes. But what I don't get is how sex fits into the picture. And violence. Blood. Pain. Why are those so integral to religious practice?"

He crossed his legs. "Perhaps because they are integral to life. Sex is for procreation, of course, but as vital as that function is, it might be considered peripheral. Reproduction is a byproduct, but the motivation may always have been pleasure—an intense and powerful pleasure. A craving that must be satisfied. Sex has also traditionally been associated with conquest, which of course intermingles with the violence aspect you mentioned. Violence and sex are powerful forces, and they're frequently linked."

No doubt about it, but why? I didn't want to ask.

"Religion is formed and fueled by the most acutely real, the most potent of human experiences. It helps people deal with the highest extremes of love and hate, fear and safety, terror and salvation. A deity that doesn't speak to these elements would be irrelevant. For religion to motivate, to reward, to offer comfort, explanation, or useful instruction, it must touch the realities of people's lives."

He uncrossed his legs. "And I can't begin to understand it."

A snort escaped me. "But you teach it?"

"I teach the theory of it, but I don't truly understand religion." Hands clasped, he leaned forward and rested his forearms on his legs in an almost imploring posture. "Religion in general is nearly universal. But the various beliefs are confusing and contradictory. It's a puzzle."

"It sure is." One I didn't care to work out.

"But underlying it all—" He leaned back in his chair. "I don't know. I have to wonder if there isn't something behind it."

I picked up my cup and found it empty. To my surprise, that disappointed me.

"As if, maybe—that is, what if there *is* a God of some sort? And all these religions are our way of searching for him?"

I dangled my empty cup from one finger. "Or for her. Did you learn nothing at the worship service today? God is a woman and woman is a god."

His smile had no mirth in it. "Do we even know God *has* a sex?"

"I think I know more about god than I care to. Enough to know she's a sick slotter."

He rose. "More tea?"

"Thank you." It seemed wrong having him wait on me. But, hey, we were in a region where men served women, right?

He must have brought a big supply of the stuff, because we each had several cups as we talked long into the night.

Toward morning, my consciousness was rudely aroused by an unfamiliar sound.

Though I hadn't been aware of falling asleep, I awoke on the divan in the sitting room, with the lights still on.

The sound that disturbed me was snoring, and it came from the professor asleep in the chair.

That babunja tea must be good stuff.

❧ **Chapter 22** ❧

THE NIGHT I DIDN'T DIE

THE COMMANDER AND I reported to the colonel at the villa the next day. The analyst was there, along with Major Wool, introduced as a man who "knows the lay of the Arkentakian land as well as anyone." He'd just returned from Center City, which was why he hadn't met with us the day before.

After the brief introduction, the colonel asked, "Standtall, have you seen the news?"

"About the multi-murder suicide? Yes, sir. But I don't think the newsfeed is providing complete information."

"It's not. And it won't. Sit down, and we'll fill you in."

We sat, and the colonel continued. "Turns out your surmise was correct. The man who passed you that note was, in fact, the victim of the last flogging."

What did that have to do with the latest news? I figured he'd get to that, but instead, he nodded to the major. "Wool will explain."

The major wasted no time. "His name was Berzan. About six months ago, he approached security at the local City administrative office. Said he had some information, but he was reluctant to say more. They tried to arrange for him to speak with someone, but he took off. He never showed up again, but next thing we knew, the local constabulary had him in custody. The priestesses apparently put them up to it."

"What did they have him arrested for?" the commander asked.

Wool shrugged. "He hadn't done anything but walk into a City office. He'd never even succeeded in making contact with anyone there. But the priestesses had him arrested on suspicion of treason. According to the official record, the constabulary couldn't find sufficient evidence for a case, so they released him. But we've recently learned that unofficially, he was taken to the Third Street pagoda for a so-called celebration and was later released with a shredded back."

I did my best not to visualize what that involved, and Wool continued. "The latest accused, the one who was to be the focus of their New Day celebration tomorrow, turned out to be his brother. As far as we can tell, his crime was refusing to shun Berzan, a charge the constabulary is calling suspicion of complicity."

Did those priestesses really have that kind of power?

"Berzan wouldn't stand by and let his brother go through a flogging on his behalf. Or at least, we guess that was his motive. For whatever reason, sometime in the night, he stabbed his own family to death in their sleep. Wife and two kids, both girls. Not sure why he did that. Then he went to the station house where his brother was being held and killed two constables while gaining access to his brother's cell. Looks like he stabbed them with the same knife he'd used to dispatch his family. With a gun he took from one of the constables, he killed first his brother and then himself. Seven dead, altogether."

The commander's brow furrowed. "I wouldn't expect the average man to be able to pull off something like that."

Wool's expression was grieved. "He wasn't average. Was one of ours once. Not in IA, but in the Land Forces. Served in Kisanland for three years, helping us bring the situation there under control back in the eighties."

The commander nodded. "That makes sense."

"He didn't complete his ten years, though," Wool continued. "He resigned after five to help with the family business. Which was furniture sales, by the way. Not exactly the stuff emergencies are made of. His record also says he showed signs of traumatic stress."

"That was a decade ago," the colonel said. "But even after all this time, his loyalties were divided."

A sharp blade of sympathy sliced through my heart. Once my ten years were up, what sort of person would I be when I returned to Freemansland?

The analyst shook her head. "Sounds like the New Day celebration is spoiled for everyone."

"Not everyone." The colonel was still speaking. "The cryptic message he passed Commander Standtall spoke of something yet brewing for the holiday. In view of all that's transpired, I believe we can trust his intel."

The commander nodded. "His note spoke of 'Proof tonight'. He must have put an end to the flogging to prove his allegiance was not to the Sisterhood."

His face grave, the colonel nodded. "I'm afraid you're right. I hate to think he'd slaughter his whole family and two constables to prove a point for us, but it seems that's what he did."

Though I doubted that was his sole purpose for the bloodbath, I didn't offer my opinion.

The whole room fell silent for a moment, but then the colonel roused himself. "We should not let their sacrifice go to waste." He picked up a controller. The lights dimmed, and a map projected on the wall. "Major, you have the floor."

Wool rose. "Thank you, sir." He adjusted his jacket then picked up a pointer. "The intel in question indicates that tomorrow, a group of insurgents will finalize plans for a bombing attack. They'll meet in Obicon Timbers." He circled the area with the pointer. "More specifically, Bowl Rock, here." He tapped a lump in the lower center of the forest. "So called because of its shape, like a bowl resting on its side."

Probably not by coincidence, a small dish lay nearby, and he tipped it sidewise on the table. "The natural feature forms a somewhat deeper bowl than this, but you get the idea. Open on one end, closed everywhere else." Like a sales person demonstrating a product, he indicated the parts as he spoke. "It's somewhat like a natural amphitheater, but the entrance is restricted by a rockslide, making it easy to guard. No windows, no back doors, no way in but a narrow entrance. And the whole thing in the middle of a wooded wilderness. The perfect place to meet and not be overheard."

He set the bowl down. "We have a pretty good idea who some of these conspirators might be, but we need names and faces. And, of course, their intended target and when they plan to strike. So—" He went back to the map with the pointer. "Tonight, you'll be dropped here, a little over five klicks west of Bowl Rock. We figure the participants will be coming from the east and north, so that will give you the best cover. We don't know what time they'll convene, nor how near the rock they'll spend the night. But you'll have to be in position at first light in case they get an early start. On the chance they're camping at the rock, your approach shouldn't arouse their suspicions if you're dropped off several kilometers away."

Drop? As in, air drop? Who's going to be air dropped?

"There's no moon, but the forecast is for clear skies. With the help of night vision equipment, you'll travel through the woods and be at the rock by morning, then climb up to where you can observe and record the proceedings. And you'll have to be very subtle about it in case they're there before you."

My mouth went dry.

"You're an experienced climber, Specialist Freeman, and you have a perfect memory. Being a woman means if you're seen, you'll have a better chance of not being killed on sight. Commander, you will contribute your own skills, including the technical expertise to deal with the necessary surveillance equipment. All in all, the two of you are a good fit for this mission."

I swallowed. A good fit? So why did I feel like throwing up?

IN JUMPING GEAR and parachute packs, the commander and I stood in the windy doorway ready to jump out into the night.

"Nervous?" he shouted.

I shrugged. "I've jumped before."

"How many times?"

I'd taken the plunge three times in training. But as I contemplated stepping out of that opening into the blackness, I wasn't sure I could do it. "Too many."

Since this isn't the sort of thing we did every day, we'd spent the afternoon in refresher training and doing dry runs. He knew all this, and that I was scared spitless. So why ask?

Probably because he was scared too and needed the distraction.

I didn't want conversation, though. All I could hear was the roar of the wind. I only understood his words from reading his lips.

Major Wool hung onto a strap nearby. He'd spent most of the flight drilling into my head a review of the mission—assuming I survived the jump. Twice, he'd gone through a checklist to verify that I had everything. Made me recite my instructions, which of course I was able to do verbatim. *I'm the one with the memory, remember? Isn't that why you chose me? So why do you think I'm going to forget?*

But even before that, I'd been in a foul mood. Shortly before we boarded the plane, I'd gotten a call from Jeriah, and he'd sent pictures. Seena had another baby—a boy this time. Named him Jeo, after our father. The kid was born yesterday, and Riah had just now gotten around to telling me. As if I were an afterthought.

It made me sick. He was safe in Saltcreek Point making babies with his adoring wife, while I jumped out of airplanes and spied on homicidal fanatics who might, if I were lucky, not kill me on sight because I resembled their goddess of womanly malice and self-gratification.

And if by some stroke of fortune I got back safely, who cared? No beaming husband. No puffy-faced little brat in a blanket. No one to welcome me home. Slime, I didn't even have a goldfish. The only pets I had were my brain worms.

I stared at the red light by the door, willing it to turn to the yellow one-minute signal—and then it did. Just like that. If I were the superstitious type, I'd think I had supernatural powers.

"One minute!" Wool explained in a shout, as if I couldn't see the light for myself.

If I willed the plane to crash, killing us all, would it happen? I took a deep breath and tried. Nope. Didn't work. Oh, well.

"Thirty seconds!"

The commander was saying something.

"What?" I screamed, then watched his lips as he shouted again.

"I wonder. Did your mother give us permission to marry?"

I'd have hollered, "Not funny!" right in his Cityslime face, but just as he mouthed the last word, the light turned green and Wool yelled, "Freeman! Go!"

And somehow, my annoyance at all three of them—Jeriah and Wool and the pigeonheaded commander with the sick sense of humor—was such that I was almost happy to jump out of that plane to get away from them.

Out I went, into the roaring blackness.

Worst. Feeling. Ever.

I mean, *ever*.

I'm going to die. The chute's not going to open. I'm going to die.

Terror flowed in a torrent.

The chute opened with a rush and a lurch and a wild flutter. The canopy caught the air, and the world was suddenly quiet.

Almost peaceful.

But I still had to land. There was supposed to be a clearing down there. Activate night vision. Clearing? I only see trees. I'm going to die, and no one will care.

Oh, what's that? That's supposed to be a clearing? It's the size of a shot glass. Oh, wait, it's getting bigger. Okay, it's a coffee table. Can I land on a coffee table? Where will the pigeonhead land? Who cares, let him find his own coffee table. But with those big feet, he'll need a banquet table.

I fought back hysteria as I hung in the air, floating down, down, down, the world a murky dream beneath. Coffee table growing into a tree-rimmed clearing roomy enough for both me and the pigeonhead's oversized boots.

I could see him not far off, sinking down, down, down like a worm on a hook into the stillwater.

Look where you're going, not at him. Rocks! Avoid the rocks! Am I going to miss them? Ground rushing up. Pull on the toggles, watch the horizon, bend the knees.

Agh! Breath knocked out of me. But at least I didn't crash on the rocks. *Can I move? Yes, I think so.* Deflate canopy.

Slots. I didn't die.

Not that anyone cared.

✦ Chapter 23 ✦

BOWL ROCK

THE NIGHT JUMP was awful. But even that wasn't as awkward as trying to play Stealth with Commander Standtall.

At his landing, such an assortment of grunts, groans, and shufflings came from his direction that I wondered if he'd fallen into some animal's nest. But no, it wasn't disgruntled beasts making that racket. Just a disoriented pigeonhead.

I came near to where he struggled to untangle himself from his chute. "Commander? Are you all right?"

He yelped and spun toward me. "Freeman! Don't sneak up on me like that."

No sneaking was necessary with the noise he made. "I thought you might need some help."

He continued with his contortions. "I got it."

If I hadn't been so rattled from my own jump, I might have been tempted to laugh at him.

He finally extricated himself. "Oh, good. Sorry I snapped at you, by the way."

"I hadn't noticed that you did, sir."

He didn't reply as he gathered the billowing, stringy mess into his arms.

"I hid mine over there."

I showed him a rock pile, and he crammed the wadded bundle into a gap. It didn't all fit, so we rearranged the rocks to cover it.

He straightened, forming a tall shadow in the eerie, night-vision-enhanced gloom. "I hear you're good at this sort of thing, but I'm not. So I hope you know where we're going."

"I've got a pretty good idea."

"Then lead on."

I'd gotten my bearings by then, so I wasted no time taking off in a northwesterly direction.

Even with night vision, it's not easy traversing unknown terrain on a moonless night. I picked my way out of the clearing and into the woods, where I knew a variety of dangers lay in wait to trip me, poke and tear me, and bog me down. But there was no denying I was good at this. Despite moving with caution, I made good progress.

Behind me, the commander was *not* good at this. Every footfall made a thud. Except when he tripped and went down like a tree—then it was a thud and a crash. If there was a dry branch anywhere near, he snapped it. In puddles, he splashed. If there was mud, he found it, his foot making a sucking schlup when he pulled it out. Branches lashed him with whip-like thwacks. And of course there was the occasional grunt and stifled yelp. We might as well have publicized our travels with flashing lights and sirens.

If not for the fact that he was my commander, I'd have had plenty to say about the situation. Since I couldn't complain, my jaw grew sore from clamping down on my frustration.

An hour into it, I stopped and took out my water bottle. I'll give him credit for not complaining, but his body language made it apparent he was glad for the break.

His stage-whispered, "What do you think?" almost made me laugh. A normal speaking voice would have been no more disruptive than his walking had been.

I mouthed a barely audible reply, eyebrows raised high to help him understand. "About what?"

"How much farther?"

The fact that he didn't ask his real questions—such as, *How lost are we? Do you have even the slightest idea where we're going?* and *Are tigers nocturnal? Because I'm pretty sure something's stalking us*—showed admirable restraint.

I pointed to the ridge we were about to climb. I made a walking motion with two fingers going up a hill. Then I shaded my eyes with my hand and turned my head one way and the other as if surveying the landscape.

He translated. "We climb that hill and take a look from there. Then what?"

Why do I bother using sign language if he's going to talk?

I made the shading-eyes-and-surveying motion again, then opened my eyes and mouth wide in a silent *Ah-ha!* and pointed, nodding vigorously.

"You'll confirm that we're going in the right direction."

I nodded.

"What if we're not? And how can you tell?"

I tapped at my eye, then my temple, as if to say *Trust me. I know.*

He sighed. "I sure hope you know what you're doing."

I nodded then held up a *wait a minute* finger.

"Oh, oh. What does that mean? Is that a *but*? But what?"

Shaking my head, I pointed to him, then put my finger to my lips.

"Oh." He put his hand to his mouth.

I nodded. Then pointed to him again, made a walking motion with my fingers, and put my finger to my lips again.

He bobbed his head and repeated the gesture, indicating he understood he must be quiet.

I gave a nod then started up the hill.

He followed. And about three steps later, tripped and fell.

The oath I uttered under my breath was quieter than his audible one, but no less heartfelt.

～⁂～

CONCLUDING THE MOST frustrating hike of my life, we came in sight of Bowl Rock.

When I pointed to its towering bulk ahead of us, he asked in a husky whisper, "Is that it? Are you sure?"

I'd long since given up the idea of keeping quiet, so I replied verbally as well. "Looks like a bowl on its side, and the coordinates are right."

He nodded. "I wonder if anyone's here yet."

Good question. And we shouldn't be making noise until we found out. "Would you like me to take a look?" I removed my pack and set it down.

My whisper must have been too low to hear, because he bent close. "What?"

I repeated my question in his ear.

"Can you?"

I nodded. "Back in a few."

I took off, and he must have stood perfectly still while I was gone, because to my surprise, I never heard him.

I didn't hear anything else, either. If there was wildlife around, the creatures heard us coming and were laying low. Skirting heavy brush required me to take a meandering route to get to the opening of the bowl, but once I reached it, I saw it was just as Wool had described. The wide entrance was blocked by a tumble of rock that had apparently fallen from above, leaving an opening barely wide enough for a man to pass through sideways.

I studied the vicinity, looking and listening with all my being, but detected no human activity nearby. Dare I go in? I stood at the opening and strained to hear inside. I heard nothing. One small, careful step brought me within the rocks but not into the bowl itself.

I still heard nothing, but some instinct warned me to go no farther. Perhaps there was a trip line or something unseen. I moved back out and surveyed the area further.

When I returned, the commander was right where I'd left him, but leaning back against the rock. His eyes must have been closed—perhaps he was sleeping on his feet—because he gave no indication he knew I was back.

After standing beside him for a second or two, I stood on tiptoe to whisper in his ear, "All clear."

He jumped away from the rock like it had bitten him. "Crying cornballs, Freeman. I didn't hear you."

"That's the idea," I whispered back.

He took a deep breath, apparently composing himself. "Let's get set up then. Do you have a feel for the place? Know what you need to do?"

I nodded. "It's a good lay-out. Shouldn't be a problem." I resisted adding, *As long as you can manage to keep quiet.*

Then he suggested, and I agreed, that we should eat a bite first.

With the Compact Foodsources we carried, a bite is pretty much what we got. CFs come in a small bar divided in three sections. You break off a section and chew it down, drinking plenty of water, and it swells in your stomach, giving a feeling of fullness. It's supposed to be a balanced meal, so brimming with good stuff you won't get hungry for several hours.

All that's true, to a point—it tastes so bad you lose your appetite and don't want to eat anymore. But, though it's a far cry from tasty, it does keep you from getting weak and shaky. So we each chewed a plug, swigged some water, and were good to go.

Next, we unloaded the equipment I'd take with me into the cave, the items that would stay with him, and the spool of thin wire that would connect us.

For fear of our transmission being detected, we couldn't risk sending a wireless signal from inside or anywhere near the entrance. But scanners inside wouldn't pick up a transmission sent from behind the rock.

The plan was for me to gain access to the interior of the bowl through an opening above the fallen rocks at the entrance. I would record the meeting on a device wired to a receiver/transmitter held by the commander in the nearby shrubbery. If his readings showed he was not being scanned behind the rock, he would transmit the data to Wool in real time. If that wasn't feasible, it would be recorded on my equipment, on the commander's, and in my mind, in hopes that at least one of those recordings could be retrieved.

The best plans can have hitches, of course. We both knew that, and expected complications. What surprised me was how easy it all seemed once we got started.

With the commander no longer stumbling around behind me, I looked forward to moving as quietly and quickly as I liked. There was something comforting about the familiarity of playing Stealth on the rocks, and the danger-fed adrenaline made me feel like a kid again.

Of course on Freedom, I'd have been climbing barefoot. I considered removing my boots, as bare toes cling better. But my foot pads were no longer hard as leather, and I didn't relish the thought of a hike back to the extraction point with bleeding feet. I kept my boots on.

By the time I was ready to climb to the bowl's opening, dawn bleached the black world to gray. Time to remove my night vision glasses. I stood at the bottom of the bowl, plotting my climb and allowing my eyes to adjust to the new conditions.

The commander bent and whispered, "Can you climb that?"

What a silly question. "With my eyes closed."

"You'd better keep them open anyway."

"Eye eye, sir."

I think he got the pun, but I didn't look at him to be sure. I had other things to think about. With my recording equipment safely zipped in a jacket pocket and the spool of wire clipped to my belt, I began the climb.

It was no worse than some parts of the sharpfall I'd scaled from the time I could walk. It was only a little challenging because I hadn't done it in years.

I never looked down, so I can't say what the commander was doing while I spidered my way to the top. Probably making sure the wire remained covered where it lay along the ground between the rock and the burrow he'd made for himself in the brush. There wasn't much he could do to disguise it where it ran up behind me, but I doubted it mattered, as it was thin and not easily seen against the rock.

The wire might be almost invisible, but it was live. When I was at the highest point of the bowl, his voice came softly through my earwig. "How are you faring?"

It struck me as an exceptionally Citified thing to say. An ordinary person would have said, *How ya doin' up there?*

I spoke as softly as I could. "A-Okay."

"I'm in place."

"Acknowledged."

The view up here would be great once it was light enough to see better. The poor visibility made me cautious that someone might be in the shadows, so I kept my communication to a minimum. "Hang on, let me check something."

Upon investigating, I decided the situation couldn't have been more perfect. A flat shelf on top of the rock fall that nearly sealed the entrance was accessible from above by a sort of natural stairway. From there, I had a clear view of the rock bowl's interior.

It was dark in there, but my night vision goggles helped me survey the area below.

Though rocks and other natural objects littered the floor, not everything I saw was mineral. The lump against the far wall was a blanket with something under it, and beside it stood a battery lantern.

My heart pounded at the thought of what might have happened if I'd gone farther through that narrow doorway.

Careful to make no sound, I set up my equipment, arranging the cameras so they would cover the whole room but couldn't be seen. Then, making sure I didn't tug on the wire and disconnect my equipment from the commander's, I crept off the shelf and back to the top of the bowl.

Some fifteen meters below, I could see the shrubbery where the commander would be hiding, but nothing should alert anyone that we were there. He'd covered our tracks as well as I would have. I whispered into my mic. "Commander?"

"Here."

"I don't see you."

"You're not supposed to."

True, but I hadn't thought he could pull it off. "We're not alone. Someone's sleeping inside."

"That means we're in the right place."

Had he doubted it? "So it would appear, sir."

"What do you see from up there?"

I turned and peered toward the direction we expected the others to come. "Nothing yet. I have good visibility, though."

"Good. We should do a check on the equipment before the rest get here."

We did tests of all microphones and cameras and ran into some trouble at first. But the commander had the technical expertise to know how to make the proper adjustments. Good thing, because I didn't have the first idea what to do. Before long, everything was working smoothly.

I took a position near the opening where I could hear if the person inside stirred and waited. Watched. And waited some more.

By full daylight, I'd heard and seen nothing moving, apart from birds and the occasional animal. Now and then I glanced down toward the shrubbery where the commander was hidden, and all was quiet there too.

The stillness and the warming sun reminded me I'd slept only six hours of the past forty-eight.

After another careful look through my field glasses revealed no one coming, I stood to stretch my legs and remove my jacket. I laid it on the ground to cushion the floor of the shelf where I'd be watching the proceedings once they finally started. The jacket wasn't very thick, but it would be better than sitting on bare rock.

I froze at the sound of a throat clearing across the room. A shaft of sunlight through the narrow opening cast enough light to see that the body under the blanket was stirring.

The deep grunts and complaints told me the person was male, and it didn't sound like he'd found the rocky bed very comfortable. While he yawned and stretched, I slipped soundlessly outside and spoke quietly into my mic. "Commander."

"Still here."

I was surprised his voice was so alert. As quiet as he'd been, I figured he must have been sleeping.

"The man is waking up."

"Roger." Brush crackled, as if he shifted his weight.

I stepped down to my shelf again as the man inside picked up his phone. I couldn't see his face in the shadows, but perhaps the techs would be able to enhance the visual. I turned on the recorder.

"Hey." His nasal Kentan dialect filled the room. "Where are you?" He threw off the blanket and rose, standing with his back to me. He wasn't wearing anything. "Trembi? And Vintak? They're on their way too?"

He bent and picked up a garment from the floor. "Good. An hour, then." He made a small bow. "The lady be with thee." He disconnected the call, dropped the phone to the blanket then pulled on a long shirt. After slipping into his boots but not tying them, he shuffled outside.

I exited too and watched from above. He ran his fingers through his hair, yawned, and ambled around the side of the rock toward where the commander hid. I climbed higher so I could see where he went.

The way he shuffled in the untied boots, he'd uncover the wire if he crossed it. I tensed. I wasn't sure where the wire was, but I had a pretty good idea, and he was nearing it.

Then he stopped and approached the patch of shrubs where the commander lay. Had he seen the wire? Was he following it to where it entered the bushes? I didn't think so, because he moved like he was still half asleep. If he'd spotted something suspicious, he'd be more animated.

Near the shrubs and with his back to me, he planted his feet, lifted the front of his shirt, and urinated. I gaped. No way was that not getting on the commander.

But there was no sound or movement from the bushes. I held my breath. The man finished, then ambled back toward the entrance. I wanted to contact the commander but couldn't risk one of us being overheard, so I hoped for the best and followed the man with my eyes.

When he entered the cave, so did I. He finished dressing, pulled something from a bag and ate it, washed it down with water from a bottle, then went and sat outside.

He waited.

I waited.

The commander never made a peep, and neither did I.

❧ Chapter 24 ❧

—❦—

FLIES ON THE WALL

—❦—

THE ROCK BENEATH, the sky above, the warm, humid air, and the earthy smell reminded me of my cave back on Freedom.

Had anyone ever found the near-empty whisky bottle in its niche in the wall? The stolen mat I slept on would be rotten by now, mildewed and mouse-eaten. Apart from the usual little critters, who'd been there since I was gone?

Freedom was far, far away.

Keeping half my mind on the man waiting beneath me, I allowed the other half to roam.

I had always been alone. Foraging for food on the sharpfall and in the water. Sneaking into the school to be near Jeriah. Lurking near the house, wishing someone would love me.

Mayne's easy smile.

I shook my head to erase the image, and a mental slideshow of Riah's most recent photos took its place. Jeriah and Seena had each other. Two children. A real family.

But I wasn't in any of those pictures. An achy lump formed in my chest.

The kids at school thought I was married to Mayne. Good thing I wasn't, since I hated him.

He'd surely found someone else anyway. A nice guy, good-looking, smart—and now he's a hunky LAST? Oh, my, but a mature, muscly Mayne Dabo would be enough to make the coldest girl go into heat.

It couldn't be true that he was waiting for me. No, he was working his way through a whole harem of women even as I sat here. I was the farthest thing from his mind.

The man below mumbled morning prayers, bowing and genuflecting. Remembering what was involved in worship at the pagoda, I was almost afraid to see what would come next. But maybe it was just the women who behaved that way.

Keeping an eye on his activities, I thought about my conversation with the commander the night before—no, two nights ago. He seemed to think there might be a god of some sort, but I had my doubts. And even if there was, why should I care? I had no intention of letting some sick deity interfere with my life. This goddess Striden was certainly nothing I cared to worship.

What did "worship" mean, anyway? What was the point? If you want to dominate your husband, or play with yourself, or have sex with other women, just do it. Don't call it religion. Did indulging yourself seem less dirty if you dedicated it all to a mythical being?

On Freemansland there was a name for women like that. And it wasn't *holy*.

The man below me finished his prayers—and, thankfully, praying was all he did—then took a walk around the rock. He went in the opposite direction from the commander's bush this time and was soon out of sight. I tried to climb to where I could see him, but there was too much loose rubble for me to get there without knocking stones down and drawing his attention.

Instead, I covered my mouth with my hand and spoke softly into the mic. "Commander?"

"Yes, Specialist."

"You still out of sight? Because Cave Man's on the far side of the rock. I can't see him, but he might be coming your way."

"Thanks for the warning."

I watched until the man made it around to the south side of the rock, apparently scouting to see if anything was amiss. He shouldn't find anything, but I held my breath.

Cave Man kept walking. He seemed to be doing a sweep, checking for transmissions. Wool's precaution of having us use an old-school wired device had been wise. The man was thorough, scanning the woods, the ground, the rock, the shrubs. But he never paused. Apparently nothing caught his attention, because he continued back to the doorway.

He shaded his eyes with a hand and gazed off toward the east. I lifted my field glasses and searched the same direction.

Wondering, in the back of my mind, what Mayne Dabo was doing at that moment.

BEFORE LONG, THREE more men appeared. Cave Man welcomed them inside.

They each produced a battery lantern from their packs and turned them on, lighting the room. They also pulled out insulated bottles from which they poured cups of glaffcrim. It smelled like an inferior brand that had been kept hot too long in the bottles. Nevertheless, the stale fragrance made my mouth water for the real thing.

I made sure the recorder was on and the cameras hidden but unobstructed, then I stepped outside. "Commander?"

"Yes. It's coming through. I'm recording it."

I hurried back inside where the men were talking.

It was gratifying to learn that our information had been correct. They were, in fact, finalizing plans for an attack on a City installation just as the unfortunate Berzan had said.

The hatred for the City revealed in their conversation was chilling. It had been years since I'd heard talk like that, and though I'd grown up with the sentiment—and once even shared it—it struck me as irrational. Did they really think the City was that bad? The poorest areas of Arkentak, the local governments most riddled with corruption, the highest incidents of violence and disrupted families, were those farthest removed from the City's power and most under the influence of the pagoda. Yet these men didn't rage against the injustices committed against them by their own people. No, they spoke of breaking out from under the City's control and evicting every citizen from all of Arkentak.

Their effort would never succeed. Didn't they realize how powerful the City was? Didn't they see no rebellion could be organized against us for long?

Against *us*. Yes, those were the terms I thought in.

I watched, listened, and absorbed. If anything happened to either my recording or the commander's, my memory would serve just as well.

If they didn't catch me. Which they wouldn't. Because no one beat me at Stealth.

Except Jeriah that once.

And Mayne, when he cheated and waited for me in the canoe.

It was as if I listened in my sleep, drifting in and out between memory and present tense, but remembering every bit of both.

And both were disturbing.

I won't bore you with the details of the meeting, for none of that matters now. We were able to identify the conspirators and apprehend them as they tried to carry out their plot. Between being caught on camera conspiring, and caught in the act of committing, their conviction was swift.

But all that, and more, came later. For now, I listened, half-sick, as they plotted the destruction of an untold number of lives, all for a cause they couldn't win and no rational person could believe in.

(But if I still lived on Freedom, and if there were freedom fighters there, wouldn't I have been the first to volunteer?)

I watched as they concluded the meeting in a loud and fervent prayer, then packed up and left, tramping off singly to the east and to the south.

The commander's voice whispered in my earwig, "All clear?"

"Let's give them a few more minutes." I scanned the area through the field glasses. I spotted them, a flash through the trees here, a figure trudging through a clearing there, all four of them heading away.

Out of earshot. Out of sight.

The world they'd left lay strangely quiet that New Day. As if the whole land stood poised, waiting, holding its breath.

I spoke into the mic. "I think we're clear."

THE COMMANDER AND I rolled up the wire and packed our gear, then headed for a sandbar on the river two klicks away where a chopper would pick us up.

We didn't say much. Both of us were disturbed by what we'd heard. Besides that, we'd been without sleep since night before last, and were stiff from crouching in our hiding places.

The commander didn't smell very good, either.

But at least he'd sent Major Wool the recording, so no matter what happened now, our job was done.

So why didn't I feel good about it?

We reached the riverbank in half an hour, during which time neither of us tried to be stealthy.

The commander spoke into the radio. "We're here."

"Five minutes out," came the reply. "Sit tight, we're on our way."

I watched the river, yearning to wade out and let it carry me away.

The commander watched a bird soaring high overhead. "You know what the worst thing is?"

"We didn't get any crim this morning?"

He made a huff of amusement. "Even worse, if that's possible."

I picked up a flat rock and tried to skip it across the water, but it only bounced once before sinking into oblivion. "Okay, so what's the worst thing?"

"We don't know what else is being planned."

I turned to him. "We heard every word. They never mentioned anything else in the works."

"I don't mean them. The whole thing sounds well organized as if there's someone higher up coordinating things. How do we know there aren't little groups like that all over Arkentak plotting other attacks?"

That CF I'd had for breakfast suddenly ceased to sustain me. My stomach plummeted and my legs went weak. "You're right. That's way worse than missing my morning cup of crim."

We both looked up then at the sound of an approaching chopper. Relief flooded his heavy-browed face, and I felt the same. I was ready to go home.

My breath caught. Go where? The tiny apartment where I kept my clothes? Only a cockroach could call that home.

Our ride landed on the sand bar, and we ducked and hurried toward it. If this helicopter could take me anywhere in the world, where would I choose to go?

I had no idea.

I'd felt alone before, but never so much as when I climbed into the tiny cabin and crammed myself in beside the big commander. Couldn't they have found a smaller bird to pick us up in?

I was tired, hungry, and my temples throbbed as I put on the headset. I needed a cup of crim—if not something stronger. Once I had a rest, a good meal, and a good drink, I wouldn't feel this way.

The pilot sniffed, glanced back at the commander, and wrinkled his nose.

The commander must have seen it, but he said nothing. What the slime, the pilot was going to think the worst of him. I tapped the pilot on the arm.

He half-turned his head and spoke into the microphone on his headset. "What can I do for you, Specialist?"

"I just wanted you to know the commander didn't wet himself."

The commander made a face as if to say, *Shut up!*, and the back of the pilot's neck turned red. "I didn't—"

"His camouflage was so good, a kyukur mistook him for a fire plug."

The pilot nodded, grimaced, gave a thumbs-up, and faced forward again, then informed the base that he'd retrieved us and was bringing us home. (Home. There was that word again.) And up we went.

The commander sat stiffly, as if trying to take up as little space as possible. I appreciated that it wouldn't be proper for him to get cozy with me, but there wasn't much we could do to distance ourselves in such a small area.

There wasn't much I could do about the smell of him, either. But the poor guy had been wearing Cave Man's mark all day in the sun, so I couldn't very well complain about smelling it on a short helicopter flight.

At least, I hoped it would be short.

On the other hand, who cared how long it took? I had no place to go and no one to see when I got there.

❧ Chapter 25 ❧

YOU'D LIKE TO WHAT?

S THE COMMANDER suspected, the rebels' plans included more than the one attack he and I were able to help thwart. Fortunately, he wasn't the only one who foresaw the possibility, and all the City's installations were on high alert. As a result of the increased diligence, two other bombings were averted as well, and the men caught trying to perpetrate them were arrested.

Tensions ran high and suspicions higher throughout all of Arkentak, including the University. For now, my job was to keep a low profile, continue playing the part of a student faithful to her Kentan goddess, and keep my eyes and ears open.

Feigning renewed zeal for the faith after the City's heavy-handed crackdowns, I attended the local pagoda more frequently than ever before. Religiously, in fact.

Fortunately, the experience was never as distressing as what I'd gone through at Third Street in Kenta City. The Dabamal version of worship was, shall we say, less hands-on.

I had no contact with the commander. And why should I? I didn't ordinarily report to him directly. I wasn't in any of his classes that term, and he certainly wasn't someone I'd want to see socially. My list of social contacts extended only to people I thought might help me gain information. Beyond that, I kept to myself.

Several weeks after New Day, however, I received a message from Professor Standtall asking me to see him at his office. Most unusual. My grade from last term's class was long since finalized and recorded, and I didn't plan for any more studies in religion or philosophy. What could he want?

Considering the tense climate at the time, he seemed unusually lighthearted when I knocked on his door at the scheduled time. "You wanted to see me, professor?"

He bounced up from his chair, his face aglow. "I did indeed."

Inwardly, I frowned at his perplexing demeanor, but I kept my face expressionless.

He stepped toward me. "I need to—well, you can tell me, I don't need to look. Is there anyone out there? Who might overhear us?"

I shook my head. "No..."

"Excuse me, I should check anyway."

I stepped out of the way and he strode past into the outer office, then opened the door and stood in the corridor beyond.

He greeted a couple of students passing by, waited for them to leave, then came back in to where I waited. "It's not that I don't trust you to assess your environment. Quite the contrary. But I had to look for my own peace of mind."

He left the inner door open. So as to not arouse suspicion, as he said. But I was already plenty suspicious.

Then he went to his desk, opened a drawer, pulled out a small box and handed it to me. "Congratulations, Information Officer Three."

Here's the story on that: on our return after the New Day mission, the commander suggested I register for the test for promotion to Information Officer. "I'd be happy to put in a recommendation for you."

This took me aback, as I'd never considered becoming an officer. Was he suggesting I make the military a career instead of leaving after ten years?

Something in the back of my mind said, *Why not? What do you have to look forward to afterward?* Another part of me said, *I'm going back to Freedom just as soon as I possibly can.*

The first part argued back. *Could you adjust to that life again? You're a different person now.*

Yes, maybe I could make a career of this. I was good at it, after all. So I said, "If you think I'm qualified, I'll give it a try."

"Qualified? There's no question about it."

So I applied, took the test, the commander and the Information Officer directly above me wrote recommendations, and I settled back to wait, as these things take time.

Months, as a rule. And it had only been weeks. So why was he congratulating me now?

I opened the box and looked inside. It contained IO3 insignia.

The commander beamed. "Your new uniform will be waiting for you at headquarters next time you're there, but I wanted to give you this personally."

I looked up at him, searching for words. "Thank you," was all I could get out.

He seemed no less agitated for having gotten that off his chest. "Perhaps you'd better put that away before someone comes in and sees it."

"Yes. Of course." I closed the box then zipped it into an inner pocket of my satchel. This would bump me up into a new pay scale. Give me new responsibilities.

Crying cornballs, as the professor/commander would say (and why was *I* saying it?), I was an officer. How had this happened? "I'm surprised I passed the exam first time. But especially that the promotion came through so quickly."

He smiled—and even his smile was somehow different today. "I don't know what your test scores were, but I'm sure they were brilliant. Your experience qualifies you to do more than the Specialist rank allows. And with the way things are heating up, we're going to need more officers with your knowledge and skill."

"Well, sir, I hardly know what to say. I feel I should thank you, because I never would have thought to apply if you hadn't suggested it."

Why did he act like a kid getting ready to open a gift? "No need to thank me. You deserved it. But you look like you're about to fall over. Perhaps you should sit down till your head clears."

I took his suggestion.

In his strange eagerness, he didn't wait for me to be settled before continuing. "You're fully deserving of the promotion, yes. But that's not the only reason I encouraged you to put in for it. My primary motive, I'm embarrassed to admit—" His flush confirmed his point— "was purely selfish."

He paused, but I didn't know what to say. I was so confounded I couldn't even form a question.

But perhaps his pause wasn't to allow me to speak, for it seemed he was searching for words himself. "This is difficult. I don't want you to get the wrong impression."

"Sir, the only impression I'm getting is confusion. What are you trying to say?"

He took a deep breath. His face seemed to be wrestling with a smile, and once he found his words, they came out rapid-fire. "Now that you're no longer enlisted, I'd like to marry you."

If he was flushed before, he now turned crimson. "That came out wrong. I mean, I would like to—That is, do you like the theater? Because I have tickets for *The Backward Traveler* at the Kazalis in Alosmtak. I know a good restaurant near the Kazalis where we can have dinner and then see the show." Eyes wide, he gulped air like a drowning man. "If you would like. I would like that. Very much, in fact." His speech had become ridiculously formal and First Class Citizen-like. "But if you are not interested, well—I would be very disappointed, but I know. This is too sudden. For that, I apologize. I—"

"Commander?"

"I am very sorry. I have put you in a bad position. I am not handling this well at all. I do not know what has come over me. But the fact is—"

"Commander, I don't mean to interrupt, but—"

"Oh, please do interrupt! Because I am in quite over my head. But I need not tell you that."

He finally stopped. And looked like an overgrown boy wishing he could run off and hide.

Seeing he was even more uncomfortable than I, was the only thing that kept *me* from running from the room. "You're right, this is very sudden." I felt my face twitch like it had to do something but couldn't decide what. "But I didn't hear anything after that first thing you said. Now that I'm no longer enlisted, you'd like to—to do what? I'm pretty sure I didn't hear you right."

Which wasn't true, of course. I heard every word. I just couldn't figure out why he would joke about something like this. If this was supposed to be a prank, he was playing it very badly. And humiliating someone like this was out of character.

He rubbed his face with both hands. "Might we begin again?"

I grabbed the suggestion like a life raft. "I think we should."

He took a deep breath. "Good. Well. Now that you're no longer enlisted, Information Officer Freeman, there is no rule against social fraternization between us. I have tickets to a play this evening. Would you like to accompany me?"

His newfound calm did nothing to slow my heart rate. I still couldn't figure this out. "I'm afraid—no. If we're beginning this conversation again, I'm going to need you to start at the top. What you said before."

Never was a face redder than his. "I didn't mean to say that. Not so soon, anyway. But the truth is, I did mean it. I've meant it for months now, and I'm glad to finally get it out in the open."

"Commander—"

"When it's just us, I wish you would call me Ash."

That caught me off-guard—but the reply I blurted shocked me even more. "Not Grey?" Had I somehow, subconsciously, secretly thought about this before?

He looked surprised as well. "Would you like that better?"

"I think I would. Ash speaks of destruction, something burned up into nothing. But Grey is a soft color, like a sky lightening at dawn, or the fur of a rock otter. Is Ashgrey a family name?"

"Sort of." Some of the tension slipped from his face.

"I see." It was as if I were listening to the conversation, not participating in it. I heard myself say, "I think I like Grey."

"I would be pleased if you'd call me that, then. When it's just us."

Just us. My stomach did flip-flops all the way up my throat. "Okay. If that's what you want." Really? Why would I say that? "But you can't be serious about, you know, marriage. I mean, that's so beyond crazy I don't know the word for it."

Though a smile played with his lips—perfectly formed ones, pleasantly full—his heavy brows feigned a hurt expression. "Why is that?"

It shouldn't need an explanation, but he sat waiting, so I searched for the words. "I can't begin to count the reasons. For starters, you don't know the first thing about me."

"I know you well enough to know you're perfect for me." His speech grew less formal. "You're intelligent, resourceful, resilient. Unafraid, but not foolhardy. You're honest about who and what you are. You have no hidden agenda. And you're tall, which maybe shouldn't be important, but to me it is, because I'm so tall, and I don't want a woman who's the size of a child in comparison. I want a woman who's a woman, and you're every bit that. The most desirable woman I've ever known."

If it was a pick-up line, it was an unnecessarily complicated one. How was I supposed to respond? "You don't know me," I repeated, feeling wholly out of my realm. "But even if you did, I could never marry *you*."

He blinked. "Why not?"

"You're a pigeonhead." Oops. Did I really just say that?

No wonder he looked confused. "What, is my head too small? Does it bob when I walk?" His hand flew to his nose. "Oh, I have a beak? That's it, isn't it? But I never thought my nose was too big. It's not too long, is it?"

If his gesticulations were intended to make me laugh and so ease some of the tension, it worked. "No, no, your nose is just fine. Pigeonhead is a word my brother and I came up with for Citizen First Class."

He withdrew his hand from his face. "I don't understand."

I explained about Dr. Pigeon, and how whenever we saw someone with a pronounced brow like his, it reminded us of him.

"I see. But—if my class has any bearing at all, I should think it would be in my favor."

"Comman—I mean, Grey." My, but that felt strange. "You're a CFC. I'm a Freemanslander. We're not half a world apart—there's a *whole* world between us. But my origins aren't the worst part. Seriously, you don't know me."

"Then let us remedy that. We can talk tonight at dinner. We'll see the show, and—oh, I forgot to mention, my brother's in it. One of the actors. I'll introduce you to him, maybe we can—"

"You want to introduce me to your family?"

"The show's playing only an hour away. I haven't seen it yet, and I'd really like to. And I'd like to see it with you. So why shouldn't we speak to him while we're there?"

I shook my head. "I can't do this." A surge of desperation poured strength into my limbs, and I stood to go. "You're a decent guy, for a pigeonhead. I might even like you—a little, anyway—if I'd let myself. But I'd ruin your life. You don't need that."

He rose too, and reached toward me—but didn't touch me. Which I appreciated. "Wait, don't go. I don't understand. Help me. Help me understand."

I worked my mouth, but nothing came out.

"Sit down? Please?"

I shook my head. "I'll help you understand, but I'm not staying. I'll speak my peace and then leave you to think about what I'm going to say. If you still want to take me to the show tonight, call me. But you won't, once you know what I am. Because what I am is—" Oh, no, I wasn't going to cry, was I? Oh, please, Lady Striden, please don't let me cry! "What I am is damaged goods. No, not just damaged, ruined. Destroyed. When I was a girl, I was raped and torn. More than once."

I'd never told anyone that before—never thought I'd be able to. But once the stopper was pulled, the words flowed hot. "Between my injuries and infections, they had to—to remove some things. I can't have children, Grey. I'd be of no use to you and your pigeonhead family." I spat the word *pigeonhead.*

From his expression you'd think I'd slapped him—his face even jerked to the side as if from a blow. Then I word-whipped him again. "Oh, but there's more. I'm a stellasede, did you know that? One day, my brain's going to explode." I put my hands to my head and flung them outward. "Boom. All over the place. So it's best I can't have children, because I'd just end up killing and eating them."

I snatched my satchel. "So now you know. I'm sorry to burst your bubble, but I'm not marriageable. You pigeonheads think you can fix everything, but believe me, you can't. Nobody can fix me."

Thank Striden—or whatever power kept me from losing it—I made it out of his office and into the nearest restroom before the tears came.

I didn't cry long, though. I guess weeping was such an unfamiliar thing I didn't know how to do it right. I made a sob or two, then dried my eyes—and smeared my makeup. Slotter. What a pain. I cleaned my face, touched up my makeup, and peeked out the door. Seeing no one around, I took off for home. Slime my next class. I'd get the recording.

⋇

HE DIDN'T CALL me. But of course, I didn't expect him to.

He came instead. That, I didn't expect.

He buzzed my apartment a couple hours after I got home. When I saw who it was, I couldn't move. Just gaped at the image on the security screen.

Then I grabbed my satchel and rummaged in it, thinking I must have left my new IO3 insignia in his office and that's why he was here, to bring it to me. But no, there it was in an inner pocket.

I turned on the intercom. "Professor?"

"May we talk?"

Would he never let it rest? What more must I do, actually slap him? I didn't answer, but pressed the buzzer to unlatch the outer door.

A minute later he was knocking at my apartment. He must have run all the way, because it should have taken longer than that. But it was him, I recognized his voice. "Jemma?"

I stood by the door, trying to decide what to do. If I opened it, my world would never be the same. It would be so much safer to keep things the way they were. Why turn everything upside-down?

Because hope stood out there, that's why. Hope of a future. Of the sort of love Jeriah and Seena had, which I'd never dared even think about for myself.

But no, it was an illusion. If I let go of what I already had—what was real, and secure—I'd find the hope was just a brightly lit fog that would never take form. It would only clear away and reveal a life full of emptiness.

But he said he wanted to marry me. And he was an honest man. A good man. And he wanted *me*.

What should I do?

I took a deep breath and opened the door. Steeling myself for the worst, because the best never happened. Not to me.

There he stood, tall and straight, but with a face full of emotion. His voice was husky. "I listened to you. Now it's your turn."

Heart hammering, I stepped back so he could come in. "Fair enough." I tried without success to slow my pounding heart. "Have a seat."

He chose the threadbare sofa that came with the apartment. When I started to sit in the chair opposite, he said, "I'd like it if you'd sit next to me."

I wasn't sure why, but I did as he asked.

"Thank you for telling me those things. It must have been very difficult for you to say them."

I was afraid to try my voice, so I said nothing.

"And even harder to know those things, to carry them with you everywhere. A heavy burden to bear alone."

A weight I never knew I had rose up from my gut and seized me in the chest. *I shouldn't have let him in here.*

"You were right, I didn't know you. The real you. But now that I've glimpsed it, everything makes so much sense. Your—your lack of interest in men, your drinking, your self-imposed isolation." He almost smiled. "The way you hold foul language up like a shield between you and the world. You might have hoped those things would make you invisible. Or untouchable. But you were never invisible to me. From the first time I saw you walking across campus two years ago, I was drawn to you. You were a mystery. Someone I wanted to learn more about, to—" He reached a hand toward me, but again, didn't touch me. "To gently peel back the layers to find the gem inside." His hand dropped back into his lap. "The precious Jem."

I was disappointed he'd dropped his hand. What? Yes. I was hungry for his touch.

He went on. "The things you told me? You're right. They do make a difference. They make me want you all the more. I want to give you the love and protection you've never known. I want to make sure you're never hurt again."

That lump of horror that was lodged in my chest moved up into my throat.

"I want to be there when the worms wake up. I can't stand the thought of you being alone then. And who knows, maybe they won't wake up? I can't believe they always do."

I wanted to say, "But they do. They always do," but something squeezed my voice.

"And as far as fatherhood goes, well, I did look forward to having children. But I've lived thirty-one years without them, so not being a father will be no change. My brother and sister are both keeping the family line going, so that doesn't rest on me. And besides—" The corners of his eyes crinkled. "The world doesn't need any more pigeonheads." He leaned toward me. "But I need you beside me. You, Jemma. And nobody else."

In romantic scenes in films, this was the part where they kissed. Or something. But we sat there not touching. He wouldn't take my hand? Well, then... I'd take his.

There must have been a switch on it or something, because when I picked it up and held it (so big and warm and smooth), his eyes lit up.

I marveled. "I'm the one who's got worms in her head, but you're the one who's insane. If you're so all-fired certain about this, I'll go to that show with you tonight."

He looked like he was about to jump up and shout, so I kept hold of him, kept talking. "I won't promise anything more, so don't go introducing me to your brother as anything other than your date."

A grin the size of Arkentak split his face. "But you'll think about marriage?"

"Are you kidding?" I caught a touch of his contagious grin, and it manifested itself as a half-smile. "I doubt I'll be able to think of anything else."

❧ Chapter 26 ❧

UPSIDE-DOWN AND INSIDE-OUT

AT GREY'S SUGGESTION, I wore the blue koorma from our undercover visit to Kenta City.

I wondered if wearing it was a wise idea, but he wasn't concerned. "It doesn't matter if someone recognizes us, because that part of our cover is true now."

I knew what he meant, but I wasn't ready to accept it. "What part?"

"Our engagement. I believe your mother agreed to it."

Standing in front of my open closet, I glared at him. "But did yours?"

I glared, because I resented his pushing his way into my life like this, into my personal space. Wanting to choose what I wore to the play, seeing my pathetic wardrobe on display. The small, half empty closet contained nothing but everyday clothes. And that koorma. So of course he'd suggest it, for I had nothing else even vaguely appropriate.

"I can buy something," I'd said.

"No time for that. We have to leave in a little over an hour." He fingered the silky garment. "We have reservations at the restaurant for six o'clock."

I narrowed my eyes. "You made reservations before you knew I'd go with you?"

He held the koorma in front of me as if to see how it fit. "I could have eaten alone."

Of course he could. I did it all the time. "Okay, I'll wear it. But—" I snatched the hanger from him and put on my fiercest frown. "We're not engaged."

He merely smiled.

"We're not. Get out of here. I need to get ready."

His smile widened. "So do I." Then he sobered a little, though the smile still played at the corners of his perfect lips and deep, dark eyes. "And I apologize for barging into your boudoir. It won't happen again." He took my hand. "At least, not until—"

I pulled away. "Get out before I change my mind."

Yeah, sure. As if that would happen.

From the way he chuckled when he turned and walked out, he knew there was no danger of it.

I'D ALWAYS ASSUMED the life of a CFC was different from anything in my experience. But that night I learned the disparity was wider than I could have imagined.

Take dining, for instance. When we arrived at the restaurant, we had no wait but were ushered into a room of our own, where we were seated on upholstered chairs at a table covered with real linens and ornate table service you could use as work-out weights. On the other side of a screen, someone quietly played a classical kitare.

Grey had ordered for us ahead of time, and servers began bringing the meal shortly after we were seated. First, a delightful wine with a fruity sweetness and a hint of spice, served with an appetizer of oysters in a rich, smoky sauce.

Grey seemed amused at my obvious enjoyment of them. "Pace yourself. There's more to come."

Indeed. Next, the servers brought a kashka fin and amarone soup, a wondrous gooey mess that I had a hard time eating slowly enough to be decorous. More than anything I'd seen since leaving Freemansland, it reminded me of home.

Though I was no longer hungry, I was sorry when they removed those bowls—Grey hadn't eaten all of his, and I looked after it with longing when the server took it away. But I knew I'd be able to find room for the entrée that came next: a baked fish fillet rolled and stuffed with rappu meat, with a side of roasted, shredded kohlheads tossed with a fiery dice of hot peppers. And, of course, a light, pale wine so white it was almost green.

I tried to eat slowly, I really did. But it was difficult, especially after I saw how they took Grey's soup before he was done with it. I didn't want them to take my plate until I'd eaten every scrap. I'd never experienced such flavors before, and it didn't seem possible I ever would again.

Grey's knowledge of the meal impressed me. Since leaving Freemansland, I never paid much attention to what I put in my mouth, but he knew the names of all the dishes, the world cuisines that inspired them, and the places the ingredients came from, not to mention the names of the wines and their vintages.

When I set down my near-empty glass of the greenish-white delight, a ten-year-old Vin Bahar from Sorona, the server stepped over to refill it, but Grey lifted a hand to stop him. "Thank you. You may take the bottle away now."

The wine was fabulous, but I was enjoying the meal too much to be upset that he'd cut me off. They'd probably bring a different wine with the next course anyway.

They did. A bity white called Ferrao Kenifir accompanied a salad of mixed greens sprinkled with tiny shrimps and a light dusting of grated sharp cheese.

I'd thought my belly would burst, but when they took my empty salad plate away and placed a stemmed glass of ice cream in front of me, I polished it off.

As we sipped a fragrant finale of glaffcrim—Gracious Hen, no less—the chef came out to inquire how we'd enjoyed the meal.

Grey rose and shook the man's hand. "Winhar, it was marvelous. You and your crew outdid yourself."

Beaming, the chef turned to me. "And the lady? Did she enjoy it?"

I remained seated, partly because I wasn't sure I'd be able to rise without belching. "*Enjoy it* doesn't come close to describing the pleasure your handiwork gave me, sir."

The chef stretched out his arms and lifted his eyes heavenward. "Who is this angel, Mr. Standtall?" He took both my hands. "This woman of exquisite and discerning tastes? I will cook for you anytime, beautiful maiden." Still holding my hands, he kissed first one and then the other, then started over.

Grey clapped him on the back. "Easy, Winhar. The lady's name is Jemma Freeman, and she's not edible."

The chef let go of my hands. "She is very sweet, though." He straightened up, still fixing me with his dancing gray-blue eyes. "You didn't think the meal too fishy? Mr. Standtall requested seafood in every course. Except the dessert, which he insisted be ice cream. I advised him you might prefer he go with some other meats, but he wouldn't change his mind."

"I could never get tired of fish." I lifted my eyes to meet Grey's. "But you knew that, didn't you? How did you know?"

"You're not the only one who's observant." He reached out his hand. "The show will be starting soon. I hope you're not too full to walk across the street?"

The chef intercepted Grey's hand to shake it again. "And I must get back to my kitchen. It's been a wonderful pleasure. When may I cook for you again?"

Grey tossed a glittering glance my way before answering the chef. "Do you do weddings?"

That gave me the energy to rise. "We're not engaged."

The chef winked at me. "You will give me a call when I can be of service?"

"As soon as we've set the date." Grey ignored my glare.

The chef gave a little bow to each of us. "I look forward to it."

We followed him out of the room, but he turned toward the kitchen and we to the exit.

The meal hadn't made me mellow enough to keep me from speaking up. "A bit presumptuous, don't you think? Talking about a wedding?"

Grey chuckled. "I wanted to check. You know, just in case."

Surprised when he headed straight for the door, I asked, "Aren't you going to pay?"

He seemed startled at the question. "Oh. Yes. I already did. In our restaurants, we pay when we order."

Our restaurants. Did he mean the pigeonhead kind? "And you order before you arrive?"

"Sometimes. Depending on what you want, you must order several days ahead to give the chef time to ship in the ingredients."

We stepped out into the street. Across the road, the lights of the Kazalis glittered a welcome. A limousine pulled up in front of the theater, and a footman hopped out to open the door for the couple who stepped from the vehicle in elegant splendor.

At the same time, a uniformed employee of the restaurant who stood a post outdoors bowed to Grey. "May I walk you and the lady across the street, sir?"

Yes, I had much to learn.

I HAD MUCH to learn about many things, not just what it was like to be a pigeonhead.

The very next day, I began a crash course on what it was like to be an Information Officer during wartime.

Except *wartime* wasn't a word we used. Officially, the City had put an end to war a generation ago. Only nations could be at war, and Centre City was the only sovereign state in the world.

Though there were no other national governments to fight with, one faction or another of the City's disparate peoples sometimes got out of line, chafing under the benevolent City Fathers' headship. That resulted in the occasional unrest here, a skirmish there, or an outright rebellion that must be firmly squelched.

The latter was the term used for the situation in Arkentak. Officially, that is. Those of us who were involved called it war.

Despite heightened security, the City's takeover of local law enforcement in three southern cities, and the apprehension and detention of several high-placed rebels, the Priestess's arms were not broken. In fact, she seemed to sprout tentacles. And they were well munitioned. Where the rebels got their weapons was a mystery yet to be solved, but they had them and were not squeamish about using them.

But I'm getting ahead of myself again, aren't I? Here's what happened:

We saw the play—in which Grey's brother, Bark, had the lead. He hadn't told me that before, only that he had a part, and I was surprised to see he was the star.

Afterward, we met Bark for drinks. He's two years younger than Grey, similar in size, build, and gentlemanly sophistication, but with less craggy features. Better looking, in other words. Not that Grey was unattractive, but Bark looked like a video star.

Which he actually was, soon after. The day I met him, he'd just signed on for a new vid series. He played a secondary role, but the audiences loved him, and it shot him to stardom. As soon as I said Grey's brother's name was Bark, I'm sure you knew who I was talking about.

We parted from Bark and went home to Dabamal. Just a few hours after Grey deposited me at my apartment—and no, he did *not* kiss me. But that's another story. For now, I'll just say he brought me home to an apartment that suddenly seemed drab.

I'd never thought about it before—never cared what my home looked like, as long as it contained all the necessities and was reasonably clean and neat. Because I'd spent my formative years in the wild, neither *clean* nor *neat* were part of my nature. But between first Aunt Lanie, then Freemansland Academy, and now the military, I had developed a taste for it.

That night, though, after having caught a glimpse of the CFC life, my humble world seemed colorless.

My feelings that evening were hard to describe and even harder to understand. I was both weary and energized. Deeply satisfied and filled with yearning. Both proud and ashamed of my simple roots. Disgusted by the CFC lifestyle, yet feeling as if it were somehow my glorious, tremulous, exquisite destiny. Fearing tomorrow while looking forward to it.

Turns out fear was the more appropriate emotion where *tomorrow* was concerned.

Less than six hours after I'd curled up on my mat—given the choice, I never slept in a bed—I sat in my first morning class. It was difficult to find value in a lecture on Walpinian Influences on

NaHoran Literature at a time like this, as the only thing that seemed relevant was Pigeonhead influences on a lonely young woman.

Professor Gannetesta spoke as if it were of vital importance, though—which it was, where my grade was concerned, so I forced myself to pay attention—as she droned, "We see a reflection of the Walpinian Mitatrin myth in the epic poem—" when a short series of deep, rumbling explosions shook the building.

The professor stopped speaking. Someone ran to look out the window. Most people exclaimed some variation of, "What the—"

My skin prickled. I had little doubt that a new rebel plan had been carried out—successfully this time. The only question was where.

And who had been caught in it.

My stomach curdled, and I remain rooted in my seat.

Sirens wailed. More people moved to the windows, but there was nothing to be seen.

Every phone in the room went off at the same time with an automated message from the university. *Remain where you are until further notice. The campus is NOT under attack. More information will be provided as soon as it's available.*

Above the sirens, conversation buzzed. Speculation ran rampant, much of it wild, some of it not far from what I assumed was the truth—and I took note of the woman whose guess sounded most knowledgeable.

And that's how, at the same time as my personal world went upside-down, my professional life went inside-out.

THE EXPLOSIONS WE heard that morning were from one of the five simultaneous attacks that shook all of Arkentak.

In my neighborhood, Stridenian radicals stormed the clock tower of Dabamal City Academy, from which they fired mobile rockets at police headquarters. True, some of their own were killed in the process, but the City had taken it over, and the rebels wanted to make a statement that the Kenta people wouldn't tolerate that sort of thing. Sixty-eight people died, including four at the school who'd tried to stop them. Dozens were injured.

In Yarapit, explosive-laden autocars plowed into a shopping plaza with an exclusive citizen clientele. Some minor injuries resulted, but the explosives failed to go off, so the damage was minimal.

An unmanned plane coming into the City airport at Yimisilit crashed into a terminal where Land Forces troops reported for maneuvers. Unlike the incident at the shopping plaza, the explosives it carried detonated, killing thirty and injuring twice as many.

A ship offshore at Eyrie launched missiles into a Sea Forces base, killing a hundred and ten, then put out to sea again before the defenders could retaliate. Hours later, a Sea Forces vessel found the ship they believed to have been the one used in the attack, but it was abandoned.

And finally, in the courthouse in Kenta City, men posing as reporters in three different courtrooms suddenly rose and emptied their automatic weapons on everyone in sight before attempting to fight their way out of the courthouse. All three died, along with the thirty-two they'd gunned down.

Until now, public reports had played down the unrest in Arkentak. Figuring there was no reason the rest of the world should know every detail, the City Fathers made sure the news reports made it sound as if the incidents were small and isolated. They suggested it was just a few troublemakers flexing their muscles, with the perpetrators swiftly and justly dealt with and the peace quickly restored.

Now, the events touched too many lives and required such a mobilization of City forces that the extent of the problem could not be concealed.

Being in the division of Information Acquisition, I was among those tasked with answering one key question: where did the radicals get their weapons? Learning this was top priority, and several teams worked around the clock to get answers.

What we learned was disquieting in the extreme.

❧ Chapter 27 ❧

WOW, THAT WAS A FIRST

CITY TROOPS POURED into Arkentak, imposing stringent curfews and travel restrictions and generally throwing their weight around.

The university closed its doors. Classes resumed after two weeks, though only virtually, to allow the students to complete the last of the term from home. The labs and other campus facilities remained off-limits.

The spa and the men's club—points of entrance to the IA Division's underground headquarters—were closed for business, making it difficult to come and go. So, except for when we worked in the field, those of us who had no families to attend to sometimes spent day and night at HQ.

We no longer tried to blend in with the general population. It was safer to go about town in uniform than risk being accosted by a patrol for being out on the streets illegally.

I didn't mind most of this as much as you might think. Don't get me wrong—it was unsettling. I hated the violence that infused the whole town—the anger that caused people to kill, and the rage with which the City retaliated. The feeling of security provided by the usual day-to-day routine was destroyed, and I missed my regular visits to the spa. But I'd had no personal or social life anyway, so nothing changed there. And between the sudden surge of work and finishing my school term, I had no trouble keeping busy.

The good thing was that I was often able to see Grey. Not "see" him in the intimate sense, but we spent a lot of time in the same building on the same sort of work, so our paths crossed frequently.

As did our glances. And the looks we exchanged held a secret promise that once we got on top of this thing, we'd make time for each other.

This was not a one-sided promise, for I'd given up pretending I wasn't interested. Life had become too short and too complicated to not be honest about the things that mattered.

And it surprised me how very much Ashgrey Standtall mattered to me.

AFTER TWO WEEKS, I was sent to the Land Forces base at Memtic in NaHora. My last visit there had been a frigid experience, so I was glad it was now late spring, when a medium weight jacket should suffice.

Nor was I going for a training exercise this time. We'd been able to trace the origins of some of the rebels' weapons, and the last known location of a few—the rocket launchers used to attack the naval base in Eyrie, in particular—was at Memtic. I was part of an investigation team sent there to learn more.

I planned to pick up some things from my apartment before I left, but first I stopped at the HQ lunchroom. Even before all this, I seldom ate at home, and when I did, it was leftovers from a previous restaurant meal. I had a taste for pelti that day, so I got the City Food Services version and carried it to a table where Grey sat frowning at a tablet while chewing a soggy egg sandwich.

And I do mean frowning. That heavy, puckered brow looming over those dark, deep-set eyes would have cast a pall over the whole room, if things hadn't been so gloomy around there anyway.

I set my tray at his table, but for propriety's sake, not too close. "Grading papers?"

He lifted his molten glaffcrim eyes, and his brow smoothed. A little. "Yes." His frown returned. "I thought it might be a welcome change from the usual frustrations, but I was mistaken." He flipped the tablet closed with almost enough force to crack the screen. "These people just don't get it. It's bad enough they don't listen in class and so haven't a clue what I'm looking for." He leaned back in his chair. "But they write like elementary students. When you took my class, was there any question in your mind what I was looking for in a paper?"

I shook my head. "You spelled it out the first day." I quoted him. "*All I want is clear, concise prose that shows comprehension of the material.* What's to not understand about that?"

"Exactly!" He slapped the table. "I make it a point to tell that to every class on the first day. I say, 'When I return my students' graded papers, I hear people crying, *I don't know what he wants from me!* So I'll tell you up front what I want.' And I proceed to do so. But what do I get?"

I swallowed my mouthful. "I'm guessing not what you're looking for?"

"Correct." He sighed. "It's frustrating. Why do people even take the class if they're not going to pay attention?"

"Same reason I took it. Because it's required."

His expression suggested that possibility had never occurred to him. But then he shifted gears. "Enough about that. When do you leave for NaHora?"

"Fifteen hundred. I have to go home and get some things first."

"Do you think the commandant there—what's his name? Redruff?"

My mouth was full, so I just nodded.

"Do you think he's actually giving arms to the rebels?"

I swallowed. "I don't suspect him of treason, no. But he's certainly guilty of lax discipline. He has no idea what's going on under his command. I expect someone's been stealing from the base and he never had a clue. Slime, I once stole a Groundeater right out from under his nose."

Grey choked on his sandwich. "You *what?*"

I didn't know if he turned so red because of his coughing or because of what I'd just said.

I chuckled. "I didn't steal it, exactly. Just borrowed it. I never took it off the base." I ate my last bite. "But I should be going."

Still coughing, he lifted a wait-a-minute finger, and I sat until he'd composed himself enough to say, "I'll go with you."

I rose, lunch tray in hand. "To NaHora?"

"To your apartment." He stood and gathered his trash.

"What, you think I need a chaperone? I know I look like a native, but the patrols don't give me any trouble as long as I'm in uniform."

He put his trash on my tray and then took it from me. "I meant so we could talk, but now that you mention it, I like the chaperone idea, too. Besides, I could use the fresh air."

"Well, then, sure." I waited while he disposed of the trash. "I could use the company."

That may have been the first time in my life I'd ever said those words. But I meant them.

Public transportation was shut down and cabs were hard to find, so we walked. It was only a few blocks, though, and the weather was delightful.

And, of course, so was the company.

As both of us were officers, there was no rule against our being together. But without discussing it, we each chose to remain discreet. Not secretive, but not obvious, either.

Which meant I felt uncomfortable bringing him into the building with me.

He answered my unvoiced concern. "I'm chaperoning you. In case anyone asks."

"Since when does an Information Officer need an escort?" Once in the building, I hurried to my flat as if to put distance between us.

Which I couldn't, of course, because his legs were longer than mine, and he answered without shortness of breath. "These are perilous times."

We reached my door, and I unlocked it. "No one would ask. They'd just jump to conclusions."

"Let them think what they want." He followed me in.

Leaving him to close the door, I went right to the bedroom, pulled my bag out of the closet, and tossed it on the bed. The bed I never slept in, but it came with the apartment. I took a uniform off a hanger and folded it.

He didn't come into the room. I wondered at that, then remembered the last time he was here, when he'd promised not to barge into my boudoir, as he'd called it, until... He'd never finished the sentence, but I knew what he meant. Until we were married.

When my bedroom was his.

The thought should have given me a chill. Fact was, it did. But not a thrill of fear so much as... as what? Gripping my last pair of clean underwear before putting it into the bag, I paused. I didn't like these feelings. I didn't understand them. They made me hot and cold and frightened and happy and all sorts of things I'd rather not deal with.

I crammed in the underwear, zipped the bag, and turned to find him leaning against the doorjamb. I jumped. How had I not heard him? It wasn't like me to let someone creep up on me like that.

"I didn't mean to startle you."

"You didn't. I mean, I don't care that you're there, I just didn't know you were there."

Feet still in the doorway, he reached into the room. "May I take that for you?"

All I could think of was my underwear in it—him reaching for my underwear. I snatched up the bag. "I've got it."

He shrugged. "Suit yourself." He moved out of the way so I could pass. "But it's hot in here. Since you don't have to leave right away, why don't you turn on the air so we can be more comfortable while we talk."

I dropped my bag on the floor by the sofa. "I am comfortable." I wasn't, but it wasn't the temperature that bothered me. "I'm from Freemansland. We like it hot. That's one thing I like about Arkentak. The climate."

He shook his head. "I'm glad somebody does. I find it miserable."

Before I sat, I turned on the ceiling fan. He was my guest, so I should probably try to make him comfortable. I'd never tried the air and didn't know if it worked. "Does that help?"

He smiled. "Yes."

He took my hands. I pulled back a little with a reflexive jerk, but I didn't pull hard, and he didn't let go.

A look of concern crossed his face. "What's wrong?"

"Just a little tense, I guess."

Still not letting go, he led me to the sofa. "We all are." His voice was soft and husky. "Sit here. I'll bet you've got some wine in your kitchen. Let me pour you a glass."

The thought of him going through my cupboards almost threw me into a panic. I shook my head and clung to his hands. "No, please don't. I don't want any. I don't need anything. Just—" Just what, I couldn't say. *I just don't want you to see my stash of booze?* "Just don't leave me."

Don't leave me? Great goat beards, where did that come from?

He sat beside me, studying my lying face. Close enough that I could tell he was right about being uncomfortably hot. His face was filmed with perspiration and he smelled overheated. Not in an unpleasant way—not like a gym locker—but close and hot and earthy.

I had to salvage this. "I just meant, don't bother getting me anything. I'm fine, really. I don't need a drink."

I don't need a drink? Another grouping of words of a wholly foreign construction. Was there no end to first-time utterances this afternoon?

But still my lips kept flipping out nonsense. "So, Commander, you said you wanted to talk." Realizing I was still grasping his hands, I let go as if they burned. Surely my face was burning. "What did you want to discuss?"

Brow wrinkled with what looked like concern, his gaze went from one of my eyes to the other, then down to my lips—which made me flush hotter—slime, that ceiling fan wasn't doing a bit of good!—then back up to my eyes. "If I'm just the commander to you, then I'm afraid we've nothing to talk about."

My heart skipped a beat, my throat seized, and the only thing that came from my mouth was a weak gasp.

His expression softened. "We're both tired and under a lot of stress, and things aren't going at all the way I'd planned. Did you have a good night when we went out? You seemed to enjoy yourself.

I know I did. But we haven't had a chance since to talk." A smile played at one corner of his lips. "You said you'd think of nothing else, but recent events have probably pushed everything about that night out of your mind."

"It's all still there."

His brows rose.

"It's all still there." I tapped my temple. "Everything we saw. And ate. And heard. Every word you said."

Amazing how that seemed to erase the strain from his face and replace it with hope.

"And I replay it daily."

"And?" He reminded me of a kyukur who'd dropped a ball at his master's feet and waited for him to throw it. "Have you thought about— I mean, have you considered, um, what we talked about... " He pursed his lips. "We both know what I mean, so let's quit wasting time. Will you marry me?"

My heart didn't just skip a beat. I'm pretty sure it actually stopped cold for several seconds.

What was the matter with me? It's not as if I hadn't thought about it, and constantly.

And it's not as if I didn't know the answer.

The problem was, I couldn't tell him the answer. I couldn't tell myself the answer. I couldn't face it. In all my thinking about it, I'd never been able to bring myself past this point, the point of telling him the answer. Of telling him...

"Yes."

The catch in his breath made my heart resume beating. Those weren't tears in his eyes, were they? Why wasn't he saying anything? Didn't he hear me?

Maybe I should clarify. "Yes. I will, if you're sure that's what you want. But if it is, I can't figure why. I'm all wrong for you, you know that, don't you?"

He cleared his throat. "We're perfect for each other. You can't see that yet, but you will. I look forward to showing you just how perfect we are together." He leaned toward me. "Have you ever been kissed? And I don't mean by your aunt."

Tears stung behind my own eyes then, but I refused them entrance. He was wrong. This would never work. "You want the honest answer?"

"Of course I do. I want nothing but honesty from you, now and forever."

In that case, ours would be a painfully short *forever*.

I took a deep breath. "Then I'll tell you." I took another breath. "I have been bitten. I have been slapped. I've been thrown down and kicked. I've been slammed against a wall, and dragged by the hair. But no. I have never been kissed."

It wasn't my imagination—those were tears in his eyes. And one of them escaped.

He let it trickle into his beard without hindrance. "I'm sorry all that happened to you. I truly am. You may... tell me about it sometime, if you want. You don't have to. But I don't want you to be afraid to tell me. Tell me that, tell me anything. I just don't want you to be afraid."

I couldn't look at him. What must he think of me?

"I would like..."

Like to what? To walk away? To put as much distance between us as possible? I couldn't blame him.

"I would like to kiss you."

I looked up. Seriously?

"But I won't." He edged back. "You're frightened. That's okay, I don't blame you. But I don't want to frighten you. I don't ever want you to be afraid of me." He reached up slowly and touched my cheek with his fingertips, barely touching me. "Are you afraid?"

If a dry mouth and racing pulse were any indication, I must be terrified. I tried to nod, but it turned into a blink and a shudder.

"I won't kiss you, then. Not until you're ready."

I wanted to cry, "I'm ready!" I wanted to throw my arms around him and never let go. But all I could do was croak, "I—"

His lips twitched. "No, I won't push you."

"I—"

He slowly rose. "You have to leave for NaHora, and I have work too. I'd better leave. When you get back, we'll talk more."

I hopped up. "What the slime, Grey! You're not going anywhere until you kiss me."

Another "first" tumbling out of my mouth. Apparently there truly *was* no end to them this afternoon.

He paused in obvious surprise for half a second then took me in his arms.

He was right—they were a perfect fit for me.

He looked down, not into my eyes, but at my lips. He was right about that, too—he didn't have to look down far, because we were the right height for each other.

"I don't know. Do you really want me to?"

I gazed up at him, wondering what that beard would feel like against my face, those lips against… "Um hmm."

"*Um hmm?* That's not very certain. You have to ask me." He flashed a quick grin as if struck by a sudden thought. "No, you have to beg me. I'll kiss you if you beg me, but not until. Make me sure there's no doubt in your mind."

I'd never put my arms around a man's neck before, but it seemed natural to do it now. Perfectly. "Kiss me? Please?"

I had one more "first" for that day. But that one was from *his* mouth.

ఌ Chapter 28 ఌ

⟳⟳

BREAKING THE NEWS

⟳⟳

WHILE JEWELRY WAS not part of our uniform, women were permitted the City's traditional engagement and marital bracelets, and men could wear the corresponding key.

Until that conversation with Grey, wearing a bracelet had never crossed my mind. Marriage was for other people, not me—particularly not marriage to a citizen. Yet here I was, wearing a delicate wrist chain of woven gold that fit snugly enough that it didn't dangle and gently enough to not constrict. Its only ornament was a small faceted *ganienne*, a popular blue gemstone, on the locking clasp. Though a thoroughly City convention, my engagement bracelet was lovely and tasteful.

It wasn't noticeable beneath my long uniform sleeve, and the tiny key Grey wore on a matching chain around his neck was hidden under his uniform as well. But it didn't matter if no one saw them. We knew they were there.

The bracelet was light, but I wasn't accustomed to jewelry, and at first, I was aware of it constantly. I found it a comforting reminder that someone loved me.

Someone loved me! That simple, intangible fact made me feel as if I could face anything.

Anything, that is, except telling Jeriah about my engagement. I dreaded the prospect so much that I didn't mention it to him for over a week—and then, only after giving myself a rousing pep talk for three days, planning how best to break the news.

He liked to do video calls from home so I could see and talk to the kids—who, of course weren't able to carry on a conversation. Usually all they'd do was make it hard for Jeriah and me to hear each other, and he'd have to go into another room to continue the call.

I might have put it off even longer except Riah wanted to arrange one last video call a couple of days before his deployment to Arkentak—an event that didn't surprise anyone, but had Seena in a dither. He said it would be my last chance to talk to the kids for a while (as if I couldn't call Seena when he wasn't there?). Mostly, though, I think he wanted her to see that I'd been in Arkentak since the beginning of the uprising and nothing bad had happened to me, so she needn't worry about him going there. Whatever his motive, I decided to tell him about my engagement during the call.

At first we chatted about the children's developmental milestones and Kyee's desire to hide rather than say hello to her Auntie Jem. Trying to squeeze behind her mama so I couldn't see her, she almost pushed Seena off the sofa where she sat beside Jeriah nursing baby Jeo, who also ignored me. Riah pulled Kyee out from behind her mother and plopped her on his lap, but she wriggled away and went off to play alone.

We talked about a few inconsequential things after that. Riah seemed to avoid the topic of his shipping out, and Seena, face taut, was almost as uncommunicative as her children. I guessed she wasn't dealing well with the impending separation.

I couldn't put it off any longer. Hoping to ease the discomfort, I slipped into the homey Freemansland dialect. "Hey, I gotta show ya somethin'." I pushed up my sleeve and held my wrist to the camera to show off the bracelet. The chain was so thin I wasn't sure Riah and Seena would be able to see it, so I spun it around to where the jewel-studded clasp was on top.

Riah's jaw dropped. "What the slot-slime is that?"

Seena scowled and put a protective hand on Jeo's exposed ear. "Jeriah, the children." Then she took a look at the screen. "Oh, my, Jem. What the glish *is* that thing!"

I almost hung up on them right then and there. Though I hadn't expected them to be overjoyed, their response seemed a bit strong.

But—no more so than mine would have been if it had been Jeriah wanting to marry a Citizen First Class.

I ignored the thought. "Can't ya see it?" I moved the clasp back and forth so it would catch the light. "It's an engagement bracelet. I'm gettin' married."

Behind Jeriah's hurt expression, anger struggled to its feet after being thrown to the ground by this revelation. Even now I could see it dusting itself off for a fight. "Married? To what? That looks like— What's he giving you a Cityslime bracelet for?"

"Jeriah!" Seena glared at him. "If you don't clean up that mouth, I'm taking the kids out of the room." She turned to me. "Really, though, Jem, I'm shocked. I can't believe you'd accept such a thing."

Riah's rising anger cracked its knuckles. "What about Mayne? He's waiting for you, you know."

I wished Riah were there in the flesh so I could punch him. "Yeah, right. He's likely got women in every district by now."

"What are you talking about? Mayne? That's about the stupidest thing I've ever heard. But it's not as stupid as what I'm seeing on your slotting wrist. A slime-chain?"

Seena rose with an angry huff and extended her hand to the off-camera Kyee. "Come with me. We're not going to listen to Daddy use bad words."

Riah ignored their exit. "Don't you know what that bracelet represents? You marry a Cityslime, you're enslaved for life. You'll never see Freemansland again. Why would you agree to such a thing? And who the slot is this guy, anyway?"

"His name is Ashgrey Standtall. We're going to be married."

For a second, it looked like that punch I'd been wanting to give him actually connected. But he recovered quickly. "Standtall. You mean he's a real CFC, not just a wannabe? You're telling me the slime is a dripping, slotting *pigeonhead*?" He rose. "Jem, what do you think you're doing? This is crazy." He put the phone close to his face so that all I could see was enraged blue eyes in a florid face. "You are NOT going to marry a CFC, do you hear me?"

I took a deep, shuddering breath. I couldn't stand it when he was mad at me. "Riah, listen. I know, it's out of character, but—"

"Out of character? It's out of the question. This is wrong. You can't get mixed up with a slithering CFC slime, you just can't." He sat back down with a plop. "City people aren't good for us, Jem. He'll hurt you. He'll—he'll be the death of you."

I couldn't be sure, but I thought his eyes welled up. The reason I couldn't be sure was because I couldn't see through my own tears. "It's not what you think. He doesn't want to conquer me, Riah. He loves me." It came out sounding choked. "I wouldn't have believed it myself, but he's a good man. He's an IA officer, a commander, and I've known him long enough to see that he really is good. And, for reasons I can't figure out, he—"

I took a deep breath. "He's crazy about me, Riah. And I feel the same about him."

Riah bit his lip and looked away.

"You've got Seena and the kids, and all I've got in this world is a cold, hard screen with your faces on it. Be happy for me, Riah." I could hardly get the words out. "Be happy for me. Please?"

He wiped his eyes. "I can't. Can't see you marrying anyone other than Mayne—"

"Forget about Mayne." I didn't mean to snap—or maybe I did. That name still riled my blood. "He's forgotten about me. Anyway, last I saw him, I promised to hate him as long as I lived, and I'm still alive. And I—I want to *live*, Riah. I'm tired of watching you have a life and me just sitting here like a rotting stump. If you love me, don't fight me on this. 'Cause I'm gonna do it, with your approval or without it."

He shook his head. "Then do it. I can't stop you." He sighed. "But that doesn't mean I have to like it."

He was softening. Relief took my voice away, and I had to swallow twice before I could speak. Even then, it was little more than a teary whisper. "Thank you." I swallowed again. "Once you're here in Arkentak, I hope you'll be able to meet him. We'll see if we can figure out how. You'll like him, I promise. You can't know him without liking him."

"I'll bet I can."

"Give him a chance."

A sudden commotion arose in the background. Both kids were crying, and Seena shrieked, "Jeriah!"

He looked away from the camera then back to me. "I gotta go. I don't like this one bit, sister dear, but, slime. If you're determined to do this—"

"I am."

"If he hurts you, I will hunt him down and cut off—"

"Your family needs you. Go see what's wrong." I disconnected the call.

His lingering bitterness made my ears ring.

THE ICE WAS BROKEN. Riah and Seena knew, and now they could learn to deal with it. For me, it was easy to deal with. At a time when many were discovering what an ugly place the world could be, I saw its beauty for the first time, now viewing it through the narrow lens of love.

The grim, wide-angle view revealed that the Kentan rebels had collaborators beyond Arkentak—like the two men who took advantage of Colonel Redruff's inattention and shipped rockets, launchers, and several crates of ammunition off the base and into the hands of the rebels. I'm happy to say I was able to help with their apprehension, though I'd rather not think about what happened to them afterward.

As for Colonel Redruff, despite his CFC status, he was charged with incompetence. There were other charges, too: dereliction of duty, conspiracy, and one charge of complicit manslaughter for each of the naval personnel who died in the attack on the base in Eyrie. All charges but one were dropped, though, and Redruff was only found guilty of incompetence. Yet that was enough to not only destroy his career but also strip him of his First Class Citizenship. He had a heart attack at the sentencing and died the next day.

Though he was the highest ranking of the security leaks we found and his fall the most spectacular, his crime was not the only one the IA uncovered. Nor was it the most serious.

The worst thing was that there were so many. It seemed people in various regions sympathized with the Kentans in their desire to throw off the City's rule, and the more we looked, the more we discovered. Like a house infested with termites, some key beams of the City structure were riddled with holes.

If not for my relationship with Grey, I might have found myself sympathizing with the rebellion myself. But thanks to him, there was no question as to my allegiance. My loyalty was to Ashgrey Standtall and whatever cause he stood tall for.

If he'd been a Kentan arm, I'd have clung to it. If he were a mass murderer, I'd have been by his side with blood on my hands. If he were a god, I'd have worshiped him.

Fact is, he was a god to me. And I did worship him. I didn't think of it in those terms, but that was the size of it.

Now, in retrospect, I thank the real God that Grey was a good man, for I'd have followed him anywhere, done anything for him.

Being a good man, he didn't lead me astray. Being a good man, he led me to God.

But I don't want to get ahead of myself. First, let me tell you how he took me to Centre City to meet his family.

❧ Chapter 29 ❧

MIMMA'S GIFT

ENTRE CITY, THE hub of the World.

Unless you understand the cultural backdrop, you can't grasp the enormity of all that those words implied. Please allow me to give you, therefore, a brief glimpse of the aura surrounding Centre City.

Surrounded by numerous satellite cities called adjuncts, the City proper encompassed almost ten thousand square kilometers in the middle of Jamahar, the world's largest continent. The behemoth was comprised of sixteen districts, each divided into a complex mesh of sections, precincts, zones, and tracts, all so carefully organized that it somehow ran smoothly.

History isn't clear on what variety of apocalypse wiped the world nearly clean of human life a millennium ago. What we do know is that afterward, pockets of survivors around the globe clustered in closely-knit tribes. Isolated at first, the tribes grew into violent nations that fought one another constantly, keeping the world in a constant state of war.

After six centuries of never-ending bloodshed, the leaders of four nations in Jamahar made peace with one another in order to channel their violent tendencies outward. As a coalition, they handily defeated the unallied peoples around them. In one short decade, the central two-thirds of the continent of Jamahar was at peace for the first time in modern history. The seat of power was Centre City.

The brains behind all this then directed the people's energies toward building rather than destruction. They and their successors spent the next century organizing and implementing procedures for the production and equitable distribution of food, quality housing and sanitation, education of children, medical care, manufacture of goods, support for the arts—whatever the people needed, the good City Fathers provided.

The rest of the world was not impressed. Rather than emulate the astonishing success of the united continent, they continued to fight among themselves.

Until the maritime nation of Omaseen attacked Alachen on Jamahar's western coast.

The City's retaliation resulted in the swift and complete subjugation of all the sixty thousand islands of Omaseen. With Centre City's authority firmly established, the islanders began to realize they'd never had it so good. Their warlord leaders had treated the populace like so many slaves, as each desired only to increase his personal wealth and the firmness of his grip on the island he ruled. In contrast, the City seemed concerned for the people's welfare.

The Omaseeni's enthusiastic embrace of City ways got the Fathers to thinking: With the rest of the world killing each other, the City possessed the power to put an end to the carnage and free the populations from the despots that held them hostage. Wouldn't it be criminal to turn a blind eye to the world's plight? Indeed, according to their highly developed sense of morality, it was their obligation to intervene.

Virtue may not have been their sole motive, of course. The minerals mined from the Omaseen Islands and the delightful variety of fruits and vegetables that had hitherto been unavailable could have brought the Fathers to the same conclusion. They may have reasoned that if they took over more nations, the City would gain more resources for manufacturing, more arable land to support their ballooning population, and a broader tax base to support the burgeoning government. All this, and bring peace to the world besides? It was a win for everyone.

Except for the ones who lost.

Which was every country the City went against.

They lost a few battles along the way, but by the time the dust settled a generation before I was born, Centre City owned the world.

SIX MONTHS AFTER our engagement, Grey and I were each granted personal leave and permission to travel to Centre City.

While making preparations for the trip, Grey practically burst out of his skin with anticipation. Among his frenzied activities was a plan for a shopping trip together. "I need to buy Mimma a birthday gift. A sixtieth birthday's a pretty big deal, you know."

He'd spoken of his mother before our engagement, but always as "my mother." Now that he and I were on familiar terms, he spoke of all his family in the familiar.

I couldn't imagine what a woman of Mrs. Standtall's social stature could possibly want or need. "I don't know a thing about it. We never celebrated birthdays when I was growing up. In fact, Jeriah and I don't even know what our birth date is. The City assigned us one when we were eleven or twelve."

His heavy brow lifted. "Seriously? No birthday torte, no baubles, no presents? Not even one little firecracker?"

"It's not something we do on Freemansland." I shrugged. "No one does." I shifted away from the subject of my childhood. "What sort of gift will you get your mother?"

"I don't know. I'm off tomorrow. Are you off tomorrow? If we're both off tomorrow, let's go to the Concourse Bazaar in Alosmtak to pick something out."

His childlike enthusiasm made me smile. "When? Tomorrow?"

"Yes, tomorrow, if you can get off."

"My morning is busy, but maybe in the afternoon. I can't go to the Concourse, though. Only citizens can shop there."

He winked. "You can if you're with me."

True. Not many doors are closed when you're with a pigeonhead.

We got to Alosmtak in mid-afternoon and arrived at the Concourse Bazaar just before fifteen hundred. The sprawling building looked nice from the outside, but once we entered, I almost stopped stock still with amazement at the grandeur. I didn't though—didn't want to embarrass Grey. I just walked beside him and tried not to gawk.

We entered an enormous lobby where well-dressed people stood talking or sat in upholstered chairs holding drinks. The ornate ceiling, glittering chandelier, thick carpet, and lush drapes created the feeling of a wealthy person's parlor, not a shopping plaza.

A few steps in, a uniformed attendant with a nametag identifying her as Tareen, Shoppers Assistant, approached. "Good afternoon, Commander Standtall." Being in uniform, we had nameplates too. "Information Officer... Freeman." She probably didn't see that name in here very often, but she didn't question it.

She did, however, direct her question to Grey. "How may we help you today?"

"Good afternoon, Tareen. Do you have a portrait photographer?"

Huh? He'd never said anything about portraits. But I smiled like I knew what he was talking about.

Though I didn't know what he was talking about, she did. "Oh, are you in the market for a betrothal commemorative?"

He put his arm around me. "Yes, we are."

"Well, congratulations to the both of you! I believe..." She consulted a hand-held device. "Yes, Mr. Stam is available, and he's the best in Arkentak. Does wonderful work. Would you like me to reserve him for you?"

Grey nodded. "That would be appreciated, yes. Please."

She tapped this and that on her handheld then showed it to Grey. "His studio is in A-3." She pointed out its location on a diagram on the screen. A thin line traced the path to it from a star-shaped *You Are Here* icon. "Would you like me to accompany you?"

Grey glanced at the diagram then gave her a polite smile. "No, thank you, Tareen. We can find it."

"Very well, sir. If you need anything at all, don't hesitate to ask any Assistant you see. We're here to help."

"Thank you." He pulled a small card from his shirt pocket and handed it to her.

She scanned it with her device and returned it with a smile. "Thank *you*, Commander."

He slipped the card back into his pocket. As we headed toward the photographer's studio and she went back to her post near the entrance, I leaned toward Grey and asked softly, "What was that?"

"What was what?"

I patted his pocket. "That."

"Huh?" He put his hand there as if to remind himself what I was talking about. "It's just a tip card."

I was embarrassed to ask, but I had to. I leaned closer and whispered, "What's a tip card?"

He laughed. "You've never seen one before?"

"No. You used it to pay her for answering your question?"

"That's right. One swipe is ten urexi. For a bigger tip, you tell the recipient to key in however many multiples of ten you want to give them."

That time, I did stop stock-still. "You gave her ten urexi for answering a simple question? Isn't that her job?"

"It's her position, yes, but it doesn't pay any wage. Bazaar employees only make what they get from customers' tips."

We started walking again. "What's this about a betrothal commemorative?"

"That's what we're giving Mimma for her birthday. A photo of us together showing off our marital jewelry. She'll love it."

"But we're in uniform. Not even dress regalia. You want a fancy photo of us looking like this?"

We neared the studio, where samples of Stam's work stood on display. None of the people in the photos were in uniform.

"Of course not. We'll pick out a costume."

Costumes. Yes, that was what everyone in the engagement pictures was wearing. Or rather, in the betrothal commemoratives. The photos were more like displays in shadow boxes than simply photos in frames.

At the bottom left of each display rested an oval miniature of a little child, probably a childhood photo of the man. A little girl's miniature sat at the bottom right.

"I see," I said. But I didn't. Couldn't fathom the need for costumes. But mostly, I wondered how he planned to pull off a proper betrothal commemorative without a baby photo of the bride-to-be. No one had ever taken a picture of little Jem Freeman, the non-person whose father wished she had never been born.

Another Shopper's Assistant met us at the studio's doorway. "Good afternoon, Commander Standtall, Information Officer..." She peered at my nameplate as if making sure she'd read it right.

"Freeman," I finished for her.

After glancing up at my face for a half-second, she flushed, pasted on a smile, and turned her attention to Grey. "How may I be of service to you?"

Though her tag identified her as Arin, he didn't call her by name, and his manner was all business. "Mr. Stam is expecting us."

She consulted her handheld. "Ah, yes, I see. You're here to pose for a commemorative. Please come in. I'll let Mr. Stam know you're here."

She touched something on the screen, and we followed her into the studio's small, comfortable foyer.

As we entered, a heavyset middle-aged man emerged from a doorway at the back. "Welcome, welcome!" He beamed a smile back and forth between us. "What a handsome couple. I can already see yours will make one of the finest betrothal pieces in my collection."

Arin spoke up. "Would you like me to help you choose costumes? Will you wish assistance for your other shopping needs?"

Grey shook his head. "No, thank you. I believe Mr. Stam will be able to see to everything for us." He didn't pull the tip card from his pocket.

The assistant paused a moment, then made a face before pasting the smile back on. "Very good, Commander. We hope you and, um, the Information Officer will have a pleasant experience shopping with us today." She strode out.

I asked quietly, "You didn't tip her?"

"I don't like her attitude." He turned to Mr. Stam. "We haven't been able to come to a decision as to what sort of setting and costumes we'd like. What do you recommend?"

Haven't come to a decision? I'd never even heard of this until now, but he made it sound as if we'd been arguing about it. Though it rankled me, I thought it best to play along. "Yes, Mr. Stam, we need you to settle this for us. And I hope you have better luck talking sense into him than I. There's simply no reasoning with this one."

The photographer's eyes widened, but Grey's laugh defused the tension. He gazed at me with genuine affection. "I love a woman who speaks her mind. I need to be kept in line." He turned to Mr. Stam. "Let's hear your ideas. What do you think suits the two of us?"

Mr. Stam led us into the staging area. "I have a personal favorite for betrothals this time of year. Of course here in Arkentak, we don't see much change in the seasons. But it's winter in the southern hemisphere. And I assume, Commander, being a Standtall, you'll be presenting one of these commemoratives to your family in Centre City?"

Grey nodded. "That's correct."

Mr. Stam turned on an electronic display of possible backdrops. "I grew up in Centre City myself, and it's especially beautiful in the winter. I recommend going with a snowy scene to commemorate your winter betrothal." He showed us three wintery settings. "We could use any one of these in a variety of ways. I could put you in a sleigh, if you like. I could give you falling snowflakes, or snow on your hats and cloaks." He pulled up a collection of costumes. "And I have a variety of vintage winter attire that would go wonderfully with any of these scenes."

Grey scrolled through the selections. "Are all these simulated effects? You surely don't have each costume in every possible size on the premises."

"That's correct, Commander. We'll put you in a neutral costume and then superimpose on it whichever of these looks you choose. Same with the setting and background. None of it will be real, but it will look lifelike enough to make your cheeks rosy with the cold."

As Stam made his presentation, my mind played with the possibilities.

I hated cold and snow, as you already know. But I'd always hated the City, too, not to mention pigeonheads, with their extravagance, privileges of birth, and snooty judgments. If I were to marry into that life, why not commemorate my entrance into it through a show of faux snow? I prided myself on the poetry of the thought and laughed. "I love it!"

Grey pulled back and stared at me, brows lifted high. "You do?"

"It's perfect. Don't you think?"

"If you like it, I like it. Let's do it."

The photographer rubbed his hands together. "You're in agreement? Wonderful!"

We spent the next hour donning the garments the photographer's magic would transform into vintage winter clothing, then posing in various arrangements before different simulated backgrounds, both standing and seated. In every shot, my sleeve was pushed back to show my bracelet. Sometimes Grey held the matching key. In other shots, the key hung on his neck by the chain but lay across the bracelet as my hand rested on his chest.

The shoot finished, we changed back into our uniforms and went to the viewing room. There, Stam showed us the preliminary proofs, still two-dimensional and with the simulated additions only roughly applied. He urged us to choose the three we liked best, which he would then perfect and mount in whatever frames we picked out.

"Oh, yes," he said, almost as an afterthought. "I'll need photo files of you both as children."

Grey pulled out his phone. "I'll send them to you, if I can have the number."

Mr. Stam handed him his card, and Grey entered the number and sent him the files. Files, plural. One for each of us? I wondered, but didn't want to ask in front of the photographer.

We readily agreed on our three favorite poses as well as the frames. In each case, the three I picked were the three he chose, so no one had to compromise.

Stam seemed genuinely pleased. "I predict you will enjoy a wonderfully happy marriage. I seldom serve a couple who's in such complete harmony during this process. There's usually a bit of bargaining between them at this point."

I glanced at Grey, and the delight on his face made me warm all over. This whole thing was crazy, but I probably looked as pleased as he did. "Thank you, Mr. Stam. I believe you're right. We will be wonderfully happy."

I wasn't sure what it was like to be happy, wonderfully or otherwise. But I truly believed I was about to find out.

❧ Chapter 30 ❧

—❧—

A BRACELET, OR A SNARE?

—❧—

MR. STAM EXPLAINED it would take a couple of hours to finish his work on our betrothal commemorative.

"I can order you some refreshments, and you may wait in the foyer, if you wish. We have a selection of films you can view." He gave me a conspiratorial smile. "Including romantic ones, which might interest a young lady in your situation." He turned to Grey. "Perhaps you'd also like to browse a catalogue of photographic services available? Or—"

I was getting ready to agree to some drinks and a mushy film, but Grey interrupted. "Thank you, Mr. Stam, but we have other shopping to do, and I don't know that we'll be able to finish in just two hours. Is it all right if we take more time?"

Shopping? For more than two hours? How could anyone shop that long?

But Stam didn't blink. "Of course, Commander. Take all the time you need. I'll be here until you get back, no matter how long it takes."

"Thank you. We should be back by twenty hundred."

Grey took my hand as we exited the shop. "I hope that Arin woman isn't still prowling the area. I didn't like her."

A different Shopper's Assistant approached. This one, Mapin, had a pleasant manner. "Good afternoon, Commander, Information Officer. How may we help you?"

I was curious to hear his answer, because I had no idea what he had in mind.

Grey put his hand on my back as if showing off a prized possession. "My betrothed would like to update her off-duty wardrobe. What clothier would you recommend? Someone who will understand how to highlight her natural beauty and style."

If I hadn't felt his warm hand on my back, I might have wondered who he was talking about.

Mapin's smiling gaze appraised me with an air of anticipation. "I'm very pleased to meet you, Information Officer Freeman." She didn't stumble over my name. "And to congratulate you on your betrothal to this fine man. He's right, you know. That Land Forces uniform does nothing for you, but I can see the potential—" She paused. "Oh, no, far more than potential. Your beauty is already realized, but it needs a more womanly wardrobe to set it off. Hmm..." She tapped her lips thoughtfully then brightened. "I know just the designer for you. Bluehawk will do you justice."

She turned to Grey. "I can take it from here. Would you like to wait in the men's club? We can let you know when we're through."

Grey's reply, "I would like to come with you," sent a wave of relief through me. I had no idea how to shop in a place like this— even with an assistant—let alone how I'd pay for purchases. I doubted I could afford a pair of socks in this bazaar.

He was right about how long it would take. We visited Bluehawk first, and then two more shops—Tigwoo, and Dresser & Draper. Four hours later, I had seven new outfits, each more beautiful than anything I'd ever seen before, let alone owned. And that's not counting the winter outerwear we purchased. I had no idea such marvelous things existed.

Let me rephrase: I was promised those things. We left the shops with nothing but pictures of the clothing and the assurance that they would be completed and delivered—some to my apartment, and the rest to Grey's parents' home. "Having them shipped there will mean less for you to pack," he explained.

Mapin provided valuable assistance. I was in awe of the depth of her fashion knowledge. Besides being current on the latest trends, she knew which styles most flattered which body type and what was most appropriate for any specific occasion.

Of course I had no idea what occasions I'd need them for, but when Grey answered her questions for me, she didn't seem to think it odd that I couldn't speak for myself. Moreover, her enthusiasm and cheerfulness never waned no matter how long I hesitated over a decision or how many times I changed my mind.

After she escorted us back to Mr. Stam's studio, Grey handed her the tip card and told her to multiply by twenty. She thanked him, but I got the impression she didn't consider the amount unusual. I supposed if our first assistant had earned ten urexi for two minutes' work, two hundred for four hours wasn't over-generous.

Even though I thought the concept of betrothal commemorative displays a bit silly, Stam's handiwork was breathtaking. No one would have known we hadn't posed in those costumes styled to look like they were 150 years old. The sleigh and the snow looked absolutely real, right down to the flake melting on my eyelashes. And whatever material he'd printed the photos on, every detail was fully dimensional.

And then there were the miniature portraits in the corners. On the left was an adorable curly-mopped boy of about two with a grin and a dimple just like Grey's. On the right was a well groomed girl of about the same age, wearing a shy smile and a bonnet that would have been stylish two decades earlier. Goosebumps skittered up my arms. She looked like she could have been me. I touched the glass covering the photo and looked up at Grey, trying to wordlessly convey my question.

The corners of his eyes crinkled with a gentle smile. "What do you think?"

I tore my gaze from the little mystery in the corner and studied the whole display. In the image, my manicured hand—the spas had opened for business again by that time—rested confidently on Grey's broad chest, my bracelet catching just the right amount of light. The small key on Grey's chain lay on the back of my hand beside the bracelet's clasp, twinkling in ownership. The pride in his eyes as he stared into mine, and the devotion in my expression as I held his gaze, needed no photographic tricks to look genuine.

I had to swallow hard before I could answer. "It's wonderful. Absolutely perfect."

Stam had been watching my reaction with apparent tension, but his face relaxed into a smile. "I'm so glad you're pleased. And the others? Are you equally pleased with the ones you've chosen for your family and for the Commander's?"

For my family? I envisioned presenting one of these to Jeriah and Seena. I almost laughed, but that didn't seem the appropriate response, so I merely smiled at Stam and said, "I love all three of them."

And I did. But I was growing weary of all this stiff pigeonhead formality and wanted to be alone with Grey. I had some things to discuss with him.

Grey's face radiated pleasure. "You do excellent work, Mr. Stam. Very impressive."

The photographer glowed. "I could scarcely fail, with such handsome subjects. And the snow scene becomes you both. I'm happy you chose it."

"As are we." Grey ran his finger around one of the frames. "Will you wrap these for us? And have them delivered?"

"Of course, Commander."

Grey chose the wrappings—plain for ours, a birthday theme for his mother, and what he called a standard betrothal design for the bride's family—and provided his home address for delivery. "You have my payment information?"

"I do, Commander. I just need you to verify that everything is correct." Stam passed a device to him, which he signed with his finger after only a cursory glance at the data.

He handed the device back. "Thank you, Mr. Stam. We'll recommend you to our friends."

"Thank you, Commander. And the lovely Information Officer. It has been a true pleasure." The photographer could light a room with that shining face of his. "Do you have other errands in the bazaar this evening? May I summon an Assistant for you?"

"You may direct us to a restaurant, but we won't need an escort."

I was glad he said that. For one thing, I was hungry. For another, I didn't care to have an assistant hovering over us.

Stam recommended a steakhouse, but, knowing I didn't care for beef, Grey assured me they'd have other entrée choices as well. "I'm pretty sure they even have one or two seafood choices."

"Then I'm in."

We found the restaurant with no trouble—though we were accosted twice along the way by Shopper's Assistants hoping to round out their day's take—and were seated promptly when we arrived. The server poured our wine then left us alone.

Grey took my hand and fingered my bracelet. "You've been amazing today."

Tingling at his touch, I lifted my not-so-prominent brows. "I've *seen* amazing today, but I don't think I've *been* it."

He chuckled. "Of all the things I've seen today, you're the best by far. No one could know how new this all is to you. Everywhere we went and everyone we dealt with, you acted with perfect grace. As if you were born to it." He squeezed my hand. "I hadn't thought it possible you could make me love you more, but you just might have pulled that off today."

I couldn't see myself, but my glow probably would have challenged Stam's. "I don't make you do anything. But—I would like you to tell me something."

"About that baby picture of you? I figured you'd wonder about that. When you told me last week you'd never had your picture taken until your aunt enrolled you at the Freemansland Academy, I swore I.O. Zhemna in Cyber to secrecy and asked if she could do a reverse age-progression of your ID photo for me."

"And add a bonnet? Nice touch."

"And give you a little smile. I like the result, don't you? I'm guessing it's a good reflection of what you looked like then."

The world dimmed for a second. "I don't remember much from those days." Only that terror and pain had been my constant companions.

I closed my eyes tightly to press away the memories, and when I opened them, Grey's dark eyes studied me. He frowned in concern. "Are you cold? You shivered."

I shook my head. "The air conditioning's a little cool, but I'm okay." I took an enthusiastic sip of wine. "I was wondering about the picture, yes. But there's something else."

"Is it too drafty? Would you like me to ask for another table?"

"No. I said I'm okay. But I'll tell you what I'm not okay with."

Was it what I said that surprised him, or my tone of voice? When I saw his expression, I realized I had sounded a little sharp.

But his reply was curious concern. "All right. What's bothering you?"

"You told me you wanted me to come with you while you picked out a birthday present for your mother. But you knew all along what you were getting her, didn't you?"

He looked a bit sheepish. "Well, yes, but—"

"We could have had a photo taken anywhere. We didn't have to come all the way to Alosmtak for that. The real reason you wanted me here was to buy me a new wardrobe, wasn't it?"

"I've never known a woman to object to shopping for new clothes. And I got the impression you enjoyed the search."

"I did. But if you wanted to buy me clothes, why didn't you just say that? Why make up a story about picking out a gift for your mother?"

He pursed his lips. "I wanted to surprise you."

"Well, you did. But mostly, I feel like I was lied to. In the future—that is, if we're even going to *have* a future—I would like you to be honest with me. Isn't that what you said you wanted from me?"

His eyes narrowed. "Whoa, back up a minute." Then he took a breath, and his frown smoothed away. "I mean—yes. I do value honesty. I hadn't intended to deceive you, but I can see why it feels like it from your position. I apologize for that. Truly, I do." Then his voice formed a bit of an edge. "But what's this bit about *if we're even going to have a future?*"

My heart raced and I felt my face flaming. "I love you, Grey, but if I can't trust what you say, I can't see a future for us together."

I didn't know what sort of response I expected. Another apology, but sweeter? A promise to never repeat his error? I'm not sure what I wanted. But what he did took me by surprise.

"Show me your bracelet."

I didn't know what he was getting at, but I extended my hand.

He took it and pinched the glittering chain between two fingers. "What do you think this means?"

My mind went blank. What was he getting at?

He tugged, not roughly, but with a disquieting insistence. "What do you think this means?"

My mouth went dry. "It... means we're engaged, of course."

"It means we're two words away from being married. There's nothing to be said now but *I do* before we're united for the rest of our lives. You agreed to allow me to put this bracelet on your wrist, and it can't be cut off. Did you know that? It can only be removed with the key."

I shook my head, speechless before his stern manner.

"There's a thread of altago woven into that chain, and no ordinary cutting tool can dent it. The clasp is an altago alloy and can't be broken. You'll wear that bracelet until I take it off—and I have no intention of doing that until I add the platinum band at our wedding."

Jeriah's face floated between Grey and me, warning, *City people aren't good for us, Jem. He'll hurt you. He'll be the death of you.* I blinked, and the image was gone. But the words echoed in my mind. *He'll hurt you. He'll be the death of you.*

"But, listen." It was Grey speaking again, and his voice was softer, his hand gently holding mine. "I have moved too quickly. It was not fair of me to press you for a promise if you didn't know what you were getting into."

My heart started beating again.

But seized up once more as he pulled the key out from under his shirt. "If you're not sure you want to do this, I'll release you. I can take off that bracelet, we'll eat our dinner, and we'll go back to our lives as they were before." A sad half smile softened his lips.

"You can even keep all the clothes I just bought you. I'll have them sent to your apartment instead of my parents' house."

Back to our lives as they were before? The thought made me feel like I was falling off a cliff. "Put that back!" The words came pinched, as if someone's hands squeezed my throat. "The key." I gestured. "Under your shirt."

He wrapped his hand around the key. "Are you sure? I won't force you to do anything you don't want to do. You know that."

"I know you've told me that. I just need to know I can believe you."

He let go of the key but left it dangling. "I'm sorry I wasn't completely honest with you about this trip. I've never deliberately kept anything from you, but sometimes I assume you're more familiar with our ways than you are. I promise that from now on, I'll be completely open about everything. You can believe what I say. Always."

I took two deep breaths, listening. Jeriah's anxious voice had been silenced. And when I spoke again, mine was steady. "Put the key away. Please. You can't release me, or I'll die."

The relief and love that flooded his face might have moved me to tears except for the server's sudden appearance. "You ordered the rappu salad, ma'am?"

❧ Chapter 31 ❧

STANDTALL

TWO WEEKS LATER, we took a commercial jet to Centre City Global airport, or CCG. From there, a private plane would fly us to the small airfield in the Standtall tract, where a limousine would be waiting to drive us to Sentinel Pines, the family estate.

Yes, the family owned a whole tract. Six hundred hectares of prime City real estate. Sentinel Pines, the Standtalls' ancestral home for eleven generations, sprawled across fifty hectares in the center of it. Though I accepted this as a fact when Grey told me, I couldn't grasp the enormity of it.

As we made the approach to CCG, Grey took my hand. "Nervous?"

Nervous? That didn't begin to describe my distress. Every fiber of my body was stretched tight, and I didn't know how I'd managed to keep my breakfast down that morning. "A little."

"I thought you might be, but you look as serene as a sunny day."

"Serene, no. I'm about ready to crawl out of my skin. I must be as good an actor as your brother."

"You're not acting. You're just a classy woman."

I snorted.

"That's what Bark told my parents. When they learned he'd already met you, they asked him what he thought."

I leaned against his shoulder, hoping his warmth and strength would soothe my anxiety. "And what did *you* tell them about me?"

"Only the truth."

No help at all. "Not all the truth, I hope."

"All they need to know, for now. That you're the most beautiful, intelligent woman I know, and that I'm confident you'll never make them ashamed."

I looked up at him. "Thank you for that."

"For what?"

He really didn't know what I was talking about, did he? But why should he? He'd never had reason to be ashamed of anything.

"Did you tell them... that I can't have children?" I hoped so, because I was absolutely terrified someone would bring up the subject.

He shifted his position so he could put his arm around me. "I did, though I didn't go into any detail. I just said you were injured when you were young, and the doctors told you the damage was permanent." He whispered, his mouth against my head, his words like tender kisses. "That as a result, you can't bear."

I couldn't speak for gratitude at his gentleness.

He turned his head so he no longer spoke into my hair. "But I have to warn you. They're going to want the family's doctors to check you out. They're willing to accept it if it's true, but they really do hope it's reversible."

I swallowed. "Do you? Hope that?"

"That would make me very happy. But I don't expect it to be the case, and I've told them as much. And however it goes, it doesn't affect my delight in you."

I pressed my face against him and took in his feel, his smell, his solidity. And in spite of the weeping of my innermost being, I smiled. "These family doctors. Are they named Pigeon?"

A chuckle rumbled in his chest. "No. But I'm pretty sure they have pigeon heads."

☀

THE PHOTOGRAPHER WAS right. Centre City is lovely in the winter. At least, when seen from the air. Once the cold hit me, I wasn't so fond of it.

The jet descended below the clouds, and the City came into view, spreading to the horizon in a neat, white-rimmed patchwork. Its very name had once caused my bile to rise, but the sight of it now almost made me feel... I'm not sure. Proud? No reason for that, as I had nothing in it. But something like pride elbowed aside my former resentment. *This is our City. Our*, as in Grey's and mine. We were part of it. And that was nothing to be ashamed of.

I shook my head, trying to settle the unfamiliar thought into a more appropriate place, but I couldn't find one for it. The concept was altogether new.

I watched in fascination as the City grew closer, the details coming into focus as the jet lowered. Grey pointed out some notable sites, things I'd heard of but had never even tried to visualize before. There they were, though, in their snow-covered splendor: the magnificent Oddany Government Complex, almost a city itself in size, boasting twenty towers and, according to urban legend, twenty acres of glass; Centre City Park, an almost rural oasis walled in by a grappleball arena, an indoor sports complex, an amphitheater, and a natural history museum; and, so far distant that it poked up from the curve of the earth, the thousand-meter-tall New Day Apogee, celebrating the City's embrace of the world's peoples within its strong, benevolent arms. All this and more amidst orderly arrays of small streets and broad avenues, buildings of all shapes and sizes, courtyards and plazas, and swarming activity.

I couldn't stop staring out the window, trying to take it all in.

AFTER DEPLANING, WE walked at a good clip for twenty minutes before exiting the terminal, then took an autocab to another runway to board a Standtall-owned plane that would take us to the family's tract. Where there was, of course, a private airfield called Standtall. Though we had baggage, we never went to claim it, as Grey told me it was taken care of.

It was a short flight to Standtall Airfield, where a limo awaited us. After the driver transferred our luggage from the plane, we took off for Sentinel Pines. The car seemed the size of a house—which explained why the long-legged Grey didn't like the tight confines of the standard autocab. It was manned by a chauffer, who didn't drive but was there to make sure everything functioned and that our every request was met.

The snow on the ground was fresh and clean, and a few flakes still fell when we approached the estate.

If the car was the size of a house, the house was the size of a town. Beyond rolling snowfields dotted with trees and white mounds of what I assumed were hedges and gardens, the mansion sprawled between the towering trees for which the estate was named. Every surface was coated with white and glittered sleepily in the hazy sun.

All this, within Centre City. For someone who'd grown up thinking of the City as nothing more than a gigantic version of Freemansland's ugly, jumbled stacks, this defied comprehension. By the time we reached the house, I was speechless with awe.

If you're thinking, *Wasn't she often speechless?* you'd be right. Under most circumstances, I kept my mouth shut. But I was now so comfortable with Grey that I'd become quite talkative around him. And, having seen so much of the world in recent years, I found the City's muscle-flexing and the efficiency of their organization less intimidating than I once had. After all, I myself was a cog in its mechanism, so why should I be impressed?

But this? This impressed me. Formerly, much of the City's mystique had been theoretical. I'd seen little snippets of the extent of their reach, a few cells on a slide under a microscope. Seeing a larger portion of the organism made me more aware of its depth and scope. The City was truly a behemoth.

And I was to be its bride.

I could hardly breathe.

The limo crept over the bridge and up the lane toward the house. The road was smooth and clear, and I wondered if the limo went slowly for dramatic effect, to give me a chance to appreciate the grandeur of the scene. If so, it worked.

Grey clasped my hand, and I hung on tight. What was going on in his mind as he watched my expression? I made every effort to maintain my veneer of calm.

The car pulled beneath an elaborate drive-through enclosure called a coach door, where we could exit the vehicle without being troubled by the weather. How I knew to wait for the footman to hurry out to open my door, I'm not sure—perhaps from seeing that done in front of the Kazalis Playhouse in Alosmtak a few months before. As the footman handed me out, the chauffeur opened the other door for Grey. Another servant ushered us into the house, and still others brought in the luggage.

Grey had told me we wouldn't be the only visitors coming to Sentinel Pines for Mimma's birthday bash. Other guests included his brother, Bark, with his wife and three little ones, and his sister,

Silver, her husband, Fenn, and two children. Also, the brothers and sisters of both of Grey's parents, with their spouses. Besides the family, the Standtalls hosted others who were there to provide entertainment at the party, and they'd brought on extra help to tend to everyone's needs.

With all those people, the house should have seemed full, but because of its size, all was quiet as Grey took me through the mansion to the room his parents had assigned me. Because Grey and I were not married, my suite was separated from his by two stories and the length of a hallway. I was glad not to share a room with him—I wasn't ready for that yet—but the distance between us seemed excessive, and I wasn't sure how to take it.

But Grey's explanation made sense. He, as well as Bark and Silver and their families, stayed in the rooms they'd used when they grew up, on the family floor. As I was not yet family, I was given a guest suite—the one, he told me as he accompanied me there, they reserved for their most honored visitors.

While we made our leisurely way through the museum-like manse with Grey playing tour guide, I tried to take it in as much as I could without going into overload. Between the tangibles to see and the concepts I wrestled with, my mind was almost numb.

When we arrived, the door was already open, with my luggage stacked just inside. I guessed that was the reason for Grey's lollygagging while we walked—to give the servants time to deliver our things before we needed them.

I was surprised when he escorted me in rather than depositing me at the door. Hadn't he promised not to enter my room until we were married? But it wasn't a bedroom we entered. It was a sitting room, with two doorways leading to other parts of the suite.

A small frown creased his pigeon-brow, and he picked up my bags. "Why did they leave these here for you to trip over?" He strode toward one of the doorways on other side of the room. "Would you like me to carry them in for you?" The opening he headed for must lead to the boudoir.

I crossed the room toward him. "No, just set them down. I'll take care of it."

He seemed to consider a moment then eased the bags to the floor. "You're right. I did make you a promise." The next moment, his hands were on my shoulders, and he kissed me.

We'd been together long enough that his touch should no longer make my skin tingle. The press of his lips on mine should no longer take my breath away. But it did. Even more than usual, the way my mind was already reeling at the very Standtall-ness of him—the sight, the smell, the aura. He stood tall. Polished. Powerful.

And he loved me. How could he? I couldn't fathom.

The kiss was brief, and his voice cut through my reverie. "I'll be back in half an hour to get you."

"Hmm?"

"I'll change for dinner then come back to get you so we can go in together. We're to meet in the family dining vestibule at half past eighteen hundred."

The family dined in a vestibule? That made no sense, but I'd figure it out when the time came.

I must have successfully concealed my confusion, because he kept on talking. "You should wear the gold one with the satin ruffles on the sleeves."

I blinked. Oh, yeah, we were changing for dinner. He was talking about one of the new outfits he'd bought me. But... "Where is it? I haven't seen it." I felt dull and stupid.

The corners of his eyes crinkled in that adorable not-quite-a-smile of his. "It should be in the closet in there." He nodded toward the room we stood before. "Along with the others we ordered. Mimma told me they arrived, and she had them hung up for you."

"Wait here while I go check."

His smile moved down and tickled his lips. "Okay, but hurry up. I have to change too."

I gave him a brief kiss to thank him for being such a gentleman before stepping into the boudoir.

I wasn't surprised at its spaciousness nor the elegant décor. But where was the closet? Not seeing a door, I wandered through the room until I passed an alcove with a doorway I hadn't been able to see when I first came in. When I went around the corner, I found myself in a room that resembled a high-end boutique, with shelves, drawers, clothing rods, multi-view mirrors, a jewelry armoire, and an upholstered sofa. But the shelves were empty, and the only things hanging were those we had recently purchased.

I grabbed the gold gown and hurried back to Grey with it. "Is this the one you had in mind?"

A smile bloomed across his face. "I love that one. Yes. It looks so much better on you than that uniform."

One more kiss, and he was gone, his parting, "I'll be back in twenty-five minutes," lingering in my ears.

❧ Chapter 32 ❧

MEET THE FAMILY

WHEN GREY LEFT ME alone in that vast, elegant suite, I was scared spitless, certain I wouldn't be able to function until I'd wet my mouth with a drink or two.

But as I removed my uniform to freshen up and change, I remembered I was trained to work undercover. Yes, that's what I'd do. I'd play the role of a woman worthy of the Standtall name. Tackling it as a professional challenge rather than a personal one made it doable.

And so, as I donned the new dress, I donned the persona I was tasked to portray. I styled my hair in a simple but graceful upsweep, fastened with a gold filigree chignon pin. I downplayed the makeup. I slipped on low-heeled sandals dripping with fine gold chains then stood tall before the mirror to survey the result.

In the reflection, my pupils widened with surprise.

Slime, but I was beautiful.

It wasn't really me, of course. Beneath all that, I was the naked, muddy little Jem, preparing to tackle a dragon to please her Pa. I'd been ready for anything that day, certain I could perform, just as I was ready for anything now. Determined to please the new man in my life, but using different tools.

Seeing the pretend me in full regalia, I had no doubt I could slay this thing.

When I heard Grey at the door, I hurried to open it, stomach fluttering. Curtain time.

He wore a suit of dark goldenrod that complimented the color of my gown. The perfectly fitted jacket was of a simple yet elegant cut, and the vest boasted a long row of ten buttons. Instead of the usual cravat, he wore a collar adorned with an oval broach of burnished metal etched with the Standtall family crest.

Very stylish. And very handsome.

Beneath the broach, the key to my bracelet hung outside the vest in a declaration of ownership. His glittering black crim eyes lit on me, and his mouth turned up at the corners. He'd shaved his mustache and much of his beard, leaving only a patch below his lower lip to meet the inch-wide brown band that traced his jaw from ear to ear.

My lips twitched as his did. I ran my forefinger and thumb along his newly trimmed beard. "I like it."

His smile broadened. "I'm glad. You look..." He seemed to search for words. "Perfect doesn't describe it. Every woman at the table will be jealous of you." He bent to give me a gentle, gentlemanly kiss. "And every man will be jealous of me."

I closed the door behind me and walked beside him down the hall. "I don't believe a bit of that, but I love hearing you say it."

His grunt made me turn my head to see him frown. "You should know me better by now."

"What do you mean?"

"I don't lie, and I don't flatter. I only speak the truth."

"I wasn't calling you a liar. I just feel out of place. This is your world, not mine."

He took my hand. "No, it's ours."

～∥～

AS WE TRAVELED the length of the house to the family dining vestibule, Grey explained that our destination was the room where the family gathered before meals. The guests who were not part of the family ate in a separate area.

His parents had asked us to come a little earlier than the others so they could be the first to meet me. The rest of the family, including Grey's nieces and nephews, would join us after fifteen minutes. Once the children greeted their grandparents, the nannies would take them to the children's dining area.

Children. There was that word again. Perhaps the doctors were wrong. Or... even if I was infertile, maybe we could adopt. If the Standtall children were raised by nannies, did it really matter that I had no idea how to be a mother?

"After dinner," Grey went on, "the children rejoin us and the nannies are dismissed for the evening."

"I see."

"Some of the City Fathers leave the raising of their children to trained professionals, but our family makes it a point to be active in the children's upbringing."

So it did matter. Adoption was out of the question.

I shuddered...

I'm very small, probably younger than two. I've been hiding in the house hoping to find some food, but somehow I catch his eye. "Who the slime let this into the house?"

He drags me out from beneath the table. I learned early on never to cry, or Papa would hear me and know I was there. But it's too late for stealth now. I let out a terrified shriek.

He grabs me by the throat, turning my scream into a gargle, and carries me across the floor. "Get out, you useless piece of slithering slime." He thrusts me through the hole in the floor, swings me through the air, and tosses me into the stillwater. I miss hitting the dock by a hairsbreadth.

"Are you cold? I can send someone to get you a wrap."

I forced my mind back to the present and rubbed my arms. "No, I'll be fine. I was remembering the day my father taught me to swim."

Grey put his arm around me. "He must have been a good teacher, because you're an excellent swimmer."

"I learned many useful things from my father."

Like how to stay out of sight and not be heard. How to cover my tracks when stealing.

How to suffer in silence.

"I'm sorry I never met him."

I'm not. "But I'm glad I'm finally meeting yours."

"Me, too. And here we are." His stride quickened as he led me toward a doorway through which the murmur of voices could be heard. Two voices. A man and a woman in relaxed conversation.

The waif from Freemansland wanted to balk at the door, but the professional Jemma stood tall and, Grey's hand warm and strong around my own, moved forward without hesitation.

His parents sat in the comfortable sitting room like a king and queen on their thrones. As well they should, for Grey's father was the City's Minister of Domestic Peace, the most powerful position in the world behind the three City Fathers.

He reigned broad-chested, long-legged, and heavy-browed in his wide-lapelled brown suit. His wavy hair, more salt than pepper, was smoothed back and stayed put with a rigid obedience Grey's curls had never learned. His dark eyes searched me with a penetrating intensity before moving to his son, the sight of whom seemed to fill him with quiet delight.

Only slightly less regal, Mimma sat in the chair beside his. She wore a knee-length jade-green jacket over culottes of the same color.

The jacket's front plunged deeply to showcase the high-necked blouse of tan lace beneath. Multiple strings of pearls hung around her neck. The jacket was trimmed with ropes of the same tan as the blouse, and her ankle boots, snugged with at least six buttons, were of the same color as well. Her smile when we entered grew wider as we approached.

I could feel Grey's excitement as we crossed the room. "Papa, Mimma."

His parents rose, and I waited while they embraced and expressed their pleasure at seeing him. The segue into introductions was so smooth I hardly noticed until Mr. Standtall was taking my hand in his and brushing my cheek with his whisker-rimmed lips. "Welcome, Miss Freeman."

I quickly came to my senses. "It's a pleasure to meet you, Minister. Call me Jemma, please."

His mother hugged me with welcoming exclamations.

"I'm delighted to meet you, ma'am. Your son has asked me to call you Mimma. Is that all right with you?"

She held both my hands and looked me over with approval. "I shall be insulted if you do not. Come, sit beside me." She drew me toward a low-backed settee, and the men took seats nearby.

"Ashgrey has told us so much about you," Mimma went on, "but his description fell short. You are a princess! Are you sure the blood of no City Fathers runs in your veins?"

"Quite sure, ma'am."

Mr. Standtall seemed unable to take his eyes off me. "I hope you feel no need to earn our approval. True, it is unusual for our family to—" He cleared his throat. "We seldom marry outside of our class. But Ashgrey has always been a good judge of character."

Mimma beamed at her son. "And we knew he would marry once he found the perfect bride."

Grey had told me all the family wasn't so sure. Just a year ago, his brother-in-law confidentially asked if the reason he didn't have a woman was because he preferred men.

Mr. Standtall nodded. "Our son knows what he is about. If he has chosen you, we are satisfied. We have no requirements beyond his happiness."

"Thank you, sir. You are very generous."

Mimma picked up my hand and admired my bracelet. "Nonsense! We are so pleased he has finally decided to marry—"

When she hesitated, I mentally finished for her, —*a woman*. But what I said was, "We all want the same thing, ma'am. To make Ashgrey Standtall the happiest man in the world."

Like Grey, his parents wore their feelings on their faces. And from their expressions, that statement was the best thing I could have said.

For the next few minutes, we chatted comfortably—seriously, I was comfortable with them—until we were interrupted by the others who trickled into the room in small groups. Mimma made the introductions all around, presenting me to the family as if I were a wonderful discovery she'd just made.

Grey's parents were right when they said he was a good judge of people. But so am I. And I could see that not everyone was ready to welcome a Freeman into the family with enthusiasm. If at all. But they were civil and polite, and I didn't care what they thought of me. I was Grey's, and he was mine, and that was all that mattered.

I was, though, more relieved than I could express that his parents were on board. He and I were determined to go through with our plans no matter what anyone else thought, but their support of his decision filled each of us with the feeling that nothing could possibly go wrong.

It would be no exaggeration to say those three days at Sentinel Pines changed my life. I saw and experienced more things in that visit than I can explain. One thing, though, was especially significant.

That first evening at dinner, Grey's father made the comment that it was time to replace the bathhouse window. As he said this, he looked back and forth between Grey and his brother. Although his manner was casual, I got the impression the words were not.

Why should Grey and Bark care about the bathhouse window? Didn't the estate have groundskeepers and maintenance people at their disposal? And why bring it up now, when preparing for a big birthday celebration?

Whatever the subtext was, the brothers plainly understood it. They exchanged glances then both said, with an air of sudden deference, "Thank you, sir. We'll see to it promptly."

Their father nodded. "Good. But it can wait until morning."

The conversation shifted without a ripple, and no one but me seemed to think it unusual. But the next morning after breakfast, Grey told me he and Bark were going outside for a while. "You're welcome to come, but I know how you feel about winter."

I shuddered. "You're right. I think I'll pass."

Nearby, Bark's wife, Pearl, laughed. "I don't blame you. I don't like the cold either. I can't figure out why the parents spend winters here when they have a house on Lake Crater in Steefren. Mimma could have her party on the beach and we wouldn't have to wade through a half meter of snow to get here."

Grey's sister, Silver, came toward us. "She loves winter, that's why. Says when the temperatures drop, she comes alive, and all this fresh snow is a birthday gift from the gods."

I made an exaggerated shiver. "What are Ashgrey and Bark going out there for?"

Silver exchanged glances with Pearl before answering. "Repairing the bathhouse window."

"Doesn't the family employ people to do that? And anyway, it's snowing. Seems an odd time to work on a window."

After a moment during which both ladies seemed unable to respond, Pearl pulled out her phone. "I understand your confusion, but I think it would be best if they explained it themselves. If you'd like to go out with them, I can ask them to wait for you."

This was uncomfortable. I was an odd shaped piece trying to fit into the wrong puzzle.

I suddenly needed to be with Grey, right now, even if I had to go out in the cold to do it. "Would you? I'd appreciate that, thank you."

As she made the call, Silver told me how I could find the exit the brothers would be using. After thanking them, I hurried to my room to get my outdoor clothing then tried to find my way out through that maze of a house, pulling on coat and hat as I went. I hated to keep them waiting.

They didn't look like they minded, though, and Grey smiled when I approached. "What made you decide to come?"

I shrugged. "Just wanted to see what you're up to."

Bark glanced at my feet. "You might want something more substantial than those shoes."

"Oh." I flushed. "Boots. I forgot."

It didn't take much rummaging in a nearby closet for Grey to find me a pair that fit well enough, and soon the three of us were outside, trudging toward the nearest outbuilding. They called it a shed, but it could have housed the population of a small town.

Slime, but it was nasty out there. I hugged myself, but it was no help against the freezing wind.

Grey glanced at me with amusement. "Cold? Already?"

"I'll survive. So what are we doing?"

"Bark and I are repairing the bathhouse window. I'm not sure what you're doing. Supervising?"

Bark opened the door of the building, and we stepped in out of the wind. When Grey pushed a button, a larger door, big enough for a tram to pass through, rolled up. The daylight that came in revealed neat rows of snow machines, motorbikes, and what seemed to be every small recreational vehicle mankind had ever invented.

Grey headed toward the snow machines. "Want to drive one of your own? Or would you rather ride with me?"

"I'll ride with you, thanks. Unless you'd rather I didn't?"

He flashed me a smile. "Have you ever known me to object to your arms around me?"

I flushed and glanced at Bark, but he didn't seem to notice us as he removed the blocks that supported one of the machines, keeping its runners off the ground.

"Can't say as I have. But this whole thing is a mystery. Why are you fixing a window?"

Grey went to a second machine. "It's a long story." He glanced up at Bark, who was crossing the room. "Getting the stuff, brudder?"

"O'course. But you'd better tell her the story, or she'll give you no rest." He opened a cabinet and reached in. "I speak from experience."

While they gathered the necessary equipment and readied the machines, they took turns explaining. Or at least, they started. But then it was time to move out, and the conversation ceased until we reached the bathhouse a few frigid, windblown minutes later. The whole story, without the interruption and leaving out the brotherly banter, goes like this:

When Grey was fourteen and Bark was twelve, they were tossing a grappleball back and forth near the bathhouse, and the ball—thrown by Grey but fumbled by Bark—went through a window. No big deal, except for two things. For one, they weren't supposed to be playing ball in that area. There was a grappleball field on the property for that purpose, and activities with balls and other missiles were forbidden in any part of the estate where things could be broken. The reason the boys had disobeyed on that occasion was because girls were swimming in the nearby lake, daughters of some visiting dignitaries and friends of the Standtalls. Grey was rather proud of his developing physique as well as his skill with the ball, and he'd hoped to impress one of the pretty visitors.

That was the first problem. The second arose from their response to the panic that filled the boys at seeing the shattered window.

First, they looked at the lake to see if the girls had seen what had happened, but the whole group was swimming the opposite direction. It was unlikely any had heard the crash. The boys sneaked into the bathhouse, retrieved the ball, and after scouting around to double-check that no one had seen them, they took off and continued their game at the grappleball field. But mostly, they didn't play. They plotted.

When the girls eventually went back to the bathhouse to change after their swim, they discovered the broken glass and reported it. Inquiry was made, and Bark and Grey casually mentioned—or rather, Bark mentioned, and Grey confirmed—that Santry, the newest groundskeepers' assistant, had been in the area that afternoon with a weed trimmer.

The groundskeeper was summoned and apprised of the situation. When he confronted Santry, the young man professed ignorance of the events, but the groundskeeper dismissed him anyway.

A short time later, their father set the day aside to relax and enjoy his family. That evening, after tossing the grappleball with his boys, he went into the sports shed to return the ball to its place when he spied another ball in the bin—a ball with a long, sharp cut along its surface. Much like a piece of glass might make if the ball were thrown through a window.

The truth came out. And the brouhaha that ensued was of unprecedented proportions.

Breaking the rules, trying to impress the girls, that sort of thing was just part of growing up. It would have been dealt with, as all juvenile infractions, with the usual equanimity. But lying? And making an innocent person take the fall? To allow someone who depended on the family for his income to lose his job, and possibly his reputation and future employability, merely to avoid the temporary discomfort of well-deserved correction? No Standtall would do such a thing. It was unconscionable.

First, the boys must try to ameliorate the damage. Papa ordered them to go to the groundskeeper and explain the situation. The groundskeeper then took them to visit the unemployed Santry at his home, to whom the boys confessed what they'd done. The groundskeeper then offered to reinstate him and pay back his missed wages.

Finally, Papa instructed the maintenance department to remove the new glass from the window they'd just repaired, and made the boys repair it themselves using a sheet of clear plastic film. He wanted the fix to be temporary so they would have to do it again and again. Each time, it would be a reminder of the seriousness of what they had done.

"And so," said Grey as he hammered the last tack into place, "we do this every year or so. Whenever Papa tells us it's torn again."

Bark closed the box of tacks. "And we'll keep doing it until Papa's gone. One of the provisions of his will is that the window be repaired properly."

"He wanted it to be a lesson we'd never forget." Grey ran his hand across the film to make sure it was taut all the way across.

Bark's voice was deep and serious. "And we never have."

"And we never will."

I'd listened to their tale, told in bits and pieces, without comment. But its import continued to well in my heart as I listened, until by now, if I'd tried to speak, I'd have melted into a puddle of tears.

The distance between their world and mine was infinitely greater than I'd imagined growing up on Freemansland, hating all Cityslime. But the vastness of the difference wasn't what overwhelmed me. It was the realization that it was they who were good and we who were vile. That's what knocked my legs out from under me.

By training and experience, I'd been taught to lie, cheat, steal, and duck the consequences any way I could. Most parents in my world would praise a child, not punish him, for deflecting the blame so neatly. Even Uncle Rhe, whom I considered the finest man on the island, wouldn't have been as upset as all that.

The pigeonheads had every reason to look down on us.

But somehow, this family didn't look down on me. Because their son loved me, they accepted me.

My second life ended that snowy day. As I stood by the bathhouse in speechless awe, I resolved to be a Freeman no more. From now on, I would be a Standtall.

If anything dragged this family down, it would not be me.

End of Book 1

Jemma's story continues in Book 2, *Citizen*.

The Four Lives of J. S. Freeman:

Stillwaters

Citizen

Free

Telling the old, old story of Jesus and his love, but in surprising new ways…

Yvonne Anderson writes
fiction that takes you out of this world

☆Fly through the **Gateway to Gannah**☆
for some serious sci-fi adventure

Book 1: *The Story in the Stars*
(Finalist, ACFW Carol Awards, 2012)
Book 2: *Words in the Wind*
Book 3: *Ransom in the Rock*
Book 4: *The Last Toqeph*

Also, check out "First Love," Anderson's novella in
Coming Home: A Tiny House Collection
Seven stories from seven authors featuring
characters who live in tiny houses.

www.YsWords.com